Dear Reader,

Home, family, community and love. These are the values we cherish most in our lives—the ideals that ground us, comfort us, move us. They certainly provide the perfect inspiration around which to build a romance collection that will touch the heart.

And so we are thrilled to have the opportunity to introduce you to the Harlequin Heartwarming collection. Each of these special stories is a wholesome, heartfelt romance imbued with the traditional values so important to you. They are books you can share proudly with friends and family. And the authors featured in this collection are some of the most talented storytellers writing today, including favorites such as Laura Abbot, Roz Denny Fox, Jillian Hart and Irene Hannon. We've selected these stories especially for you based on their overriding qualities of emotion and tenderness, and they center around your favorite themes—children, weddings, second chances, the reunion of families, the quest to find a true home and, of course, sweet romance.

So curl up in your favorite chair, relax and prepare for a heartwarming reading experience!

Sincerely,

The Editors

GINGER CHAMBERS

has been published by Harlequin Books since 1983. She has written for the Harlequin Superromance, Harlequin Everlasting Love and Harlequin American Romance lines. Before writing for Harlequin Books, she wrote for Dell Publishing in the Candlelight Romance, Candlelight Ecstasy and Candlelight Ecstasy Supreme lines. A native-born Texan, Ginger now lives in California.

HARLEQUIN HEARTWARMING

Ginger Chambers

Her Forever Texan

TORONTO NEW YORK LONDON
AMSTERDAM PARIS SYDNEY HAMBURG
STOCKHOLM ATHENS TOKYO MILAN MADRID
PRAGUE WARSAW BUDAPEST AUCKLAND

Recycling programs
for this product may
not exist in your area.

ISBN-13: 978-0-373-36421-3

HER FOREVER TEXAN

This book originally published as BORN IN TEXAS

This edition published by arrangement with Harlequin Books S.A.

For questions and comments about the quality of this book please contact us at Customer_eCare@Harlequin.ca

www.eHarlequin.com

Printed in U.S.A.

Her Forever Texan

For Steve…forever…

CHAPTER ONE

"JODIE-GIRL, is that you? Speak up! I can't understand you." Mae Parker's command traveled the distance between the ranch in West Texas and the apartment in Austin in a heartbeat.

Jodie stepped outside onto the narrow balcony. "It's me, Aunt Mae. Tate's asleep. I can't—"

"I still can't hear you!" Mae complained.

"I can't talk any louder. Tate was awake for most of last night, and I don't—"

"Another bad night?" Mae demanded.

"To go along with another bad day."

"I was callin' to see how he's doing. Not good, I take it."

"No," Jodie replied tautly.

Mae burst out, "I feel so dang helpless! If I could do anything to make things better, I would. You know that."

"I know."

"He still won't see anyone, won't talk to anyone?"

Jodie adjusted her grip on the cordless phone. "No."

"Maybe he should go back to the hospital, let the doctors—"

"That would kill him for sure, Aunt Mae." Jodie's declaration ended in a strangled gulp as the control she'd kept for so long on her emotions finally crumbled. Tears trickled down her cheeks. She was near the end of her ability to cope. At a loss about which way to turn, what to do for the best. If Mae felt helpless, it was nothing to what she felt!

"Jodie, you listen to me. You have to keep bein' strong for the pair of you. You can't let down. Tate's been through so much. I know you have, too, but he's the one we—"

"He's the only one I think about, Aunt Mae," Jodie said, swiping at the escaping tears. "I think about him all the time. What's best for him, how I can help. But he won't let—" She stopped. She'd told her great-aunt a lot but not everything. Some matters were so private, just between her and Tate, that they couldn't be put into words. Painful things that had to be borne alone.

Mae Parker, the matriarch of the Parker family, who always was so fiercely protective of the Parker name, of Parker land, of the Parker way of life, allowed a gruff tenderness to brush her words as she offered, "Would you like me to come stay for a while? Maybe Tate would—"

"No. That wouldn't work at all, Aunt Mae," Jodie cut in. "Thank you, but he wouldn't—Tate wouldn't—" She stumbled to a stop.

Mae was silent. "Then why don't the two of you come here. What better place for him to recuperate than on the ranch? It helped Shannon get well after the plane crash. Why not Tate?"

Jodie squeezed her eyes shut. Go home to the Parker Ranch. She'd thought of it before and rejected the idea. But so much had happened in the interim. Tate had dismissed himself from the intermediate-care facility—too soon, the doctors who'd wanted him to start rehabilitation had said. His homecoming—an event she'd barely allowed herself to dream about during his days in intensive care, when she feared she'd lose him forever—had turned out less than happy, with him treating her like a stranger.

"I'm not sure it would help," she said.

"Fresh air, sunshine, family all around who're willing to do anything to see him get better? Of course it would help!"

"He's not— Tate's not like he used to be, Aunt Mae. He's...changed."

"That's not surprising. It takes a lot out of a person to come so close to dying. Then he's had to fight his way back. He's a strong man, used to doing things for himself...he'll hate that he can't do what he wants when he wants." Mae paused. "Darlene and Thomas will be headin' off soon on that Australia trip they've been planning. Their house'll be empty for close to three months. No reason you two can't use it."

"I can barely get him to leave the bedroom."

"Then it's even more important that you two should get yourselves out here!"

Her great-aunt's bullying tactics had always grated on Jodie. As a teenager, she'd resented it to the point of rebellion, and had acted out first by befriending one of the ranch's less savory cowboys, then escaped by going away to college. Ultimately, she'd hidden out in Europe for a year. That she'd succeeded only in hiding from herself was something she realized later, after she'd returned to the ranch and at long last found her proper place in the family—along with rediscovering the one true love of her life, Tate Connelly. At the moment, Mae's bullying felt good, though. As if someone cared. Jodie's resistance weakened.

"Maybe—maybe you're right. Maybe we should come home. Tate would be closer to his mother and to Jack—"

"Of course I'm right!" Mae retorted. "When would you like your dad to come get you? There's more room in the Cadillac than in that little thing you call a car. Tate'll be more comfortable. My car can carry more of his things, too. I'll tell Gib to give you a call and let you know when to expect him."

Typically, her great-aunt had taken over and removed even the smallest decision from her hands. Deciding the matter herself was important to Jodie, though, even in her distracted state. "How about if I call him, instead? I—I have to see what Tate thinks."

"Tell Tate I'm expectin' you," Mae directed her firmly.

"I'll tell him," Jodie agreed, but she doubted that she would go through with it. Tate wasn't receptive to much of anything she proposed these days.

A noise came from inside the apartment.

She turned to see Tate standing in the bedroom doorway. He leaned weakly against the frame, his shoulders hunched, a protective hand to the left side of his midsection. His eyes met hers and Jodie's heart fluttered, both from guilt at what he might have overheard and because, even after these past five and a half months spent reeling from one form of hell to another, she still loved him.

"I—I have to go, Aunt Mae. Tate's awake. He—"

"Don't let me interrupt," he murmured flatly, and headed back the way he'd come.

Mae started to protest, but Jodie's quick "Bye, Aunt Mae" shut her off.

Jodie's hand trembled as she set down the phone and went to join her husband. Because Tate's movements were labored, he'd managed to cover only a few feet. Perspiration glistened on his forehead and around his lips. She wanted to reach out to him. She even instinctively lifted a hand, but stopped herself. He would reject any assistance.

She stood by and watched as, with considerable effort, he made it to the bed, then lowered himself onto the mattress, a succession of quick shallow breaths following. He was so weak. In the months since the shooting, he'd lost more weight than he had to spare. The bones in his face had become more prominent. His pajamas hung loosely on him.

Fear, these days an unwelcome but familiar companion, knotted in Jodie's stomach.

"I— That was Aunt Mae," she explained.

"I heard."

"She said to tell you hello."

He stretched back cautiously to rest against the double set of pillows and made no comment.

"She—she wants us to come stay at the ranch. Aunt Darlene and Uncle Thomas are going on another trip and she says we can—"

"I've told you what I want," he interrupted her tightly.

A muscle ticked along Jodie's jawline. "She thinks it might help you get well faster."

"I'll get well here. As well as I'll ever be."

"I want to go," Jodie said, and braced herself for what would follow.

"Then go."

"I want *us* to go…together. Tate, we—"

He broke in again. "Why don't you listen to what I say?"

Jodie rushed over to the side of the bed and

fell to her knees. She tried to capture his hand, but he evaded her.

"Aunt Mae said we can use their house while they're gone. It's bigger than here, Tate, and you won't have to negotiate any stairs. Your mother can visit easier…so can Jack. I know Jack wants to see you more often, but he can't get away. If we're closer, he can!"

"You've got it all worked out, don't you?"

"No… I— It just makes sense. There's nothing to keep us in Austin. You won't see Drew for more than a few seconds when he stops by." She named the head of the elite anticrime investigative task force that a little over a year and a half before, had brought them to Austin. "You won't see the other investigators or our friends. You refuse physical therapy. I've quit my job at the gallery, so that won't interfere."

"I knew you'd get bored."

"I'm not bored. I'm worried…about you!"

He turned his face to the wall. "I want you to file for divorce."

The knot in Jodie's stomach twisted tighter. "I'm not going to do that."

"Like I said…you don't listen."

"I want *us* to go to the ranch," she repeated unsteadily, a lone tear escaping.

There was a short pause, then he said, "If I agree...will you?"

She frowned, taken aback. "You mean... will I agree to a divor—" she choked on the word "—if you—"

"That's exactly what I mean," he said, turning back.

Jodie wanted desperately to kiss him, to hold him, to whisper so many words of love that she would smother the stubborn idea that had taken root in his mind over the past few weeks. Up to this moment she'd been able to deflect it—to pretend it hadn't been said. Now she could no longer use that ploy. "I'll have to think about it," she said.

He continued to watch her steadily, and for one hopeful second Jodie thought she saw an answering spark of love, but it disappeared so quickly she couldn't be sure.

"You do that," he said quietly, dispassionately, putting the lie to any fantasy she might harbor.

When he said nothing more, Jodie's only option was to leave him in his lonely room.

Emotion overwhelmed her as she stumbled back out onto the balcony. If crying would help, if it would change anything, make Tate better, she would cry forever!

Her fingers curled round the decorative railing and held tightly. They'd been so happy! From the first day they'd moved into this apartment, they'd loved the view. It was so different from the near-desert region of West Texas where they'd both grown up. Green trees, green grass, a profusion of water. They'd stand on the porch each evening to gaze at the lake formed by the Colorado River and hold each other, drinking in the beauty made all the more beautiful by their love.

They'd married in haste, some had cautioned; without really thinking it through. Jodie's aunt Mae, her cousins, Tate's mother—all had had misgivings. Their love had only grown stronger, though. By the end of their first year together they were on solid enough ground to start thinking about the future, to talk about the family that they might one day—

Jodie moaned. *The future.* Did they have a future? They wouldn't if Tate had his way.

It was shortly after their first anniversary that the terrible event had occurred. She'd been working at a tiny up-and-coming art gallery, where she seemed to have found a niche for herself, while Tate had been on the job—that day in nearby Hays County, where he and another investigator were assisting the local sheriff's department.

Like any new spouse of a law-enforcement officer, she'd been doing her best not to worry about him all the time. It helped that he had so much experience and training. Four years with the Dallas Police Department as a patrol officer, six years in Briggs County—their home county—as a deputy sheriff, then close to two years heading the Briggs County Sheriff's Department himself before being handpicked by his old Dallas supervisor, Drew Winslow, for the special statewide task force. Tate had every faith in his abilities and so did she. The commendation he received a few months after joining the task force had only underscored his accomplishments.

Then it happened. Tate and his fellow investigator had walked into an ambush set up for the man they were on their way to question. Automatic weapons' fire had caught them from both sides. The other investigator had been able to dive for cover and protect himself. Tate had been hit right away. A spray of bullets had ripped through his body.

Jodie would never forget the call from Drew Winslow. Unable to speak at first, he'd finally told her that Tate had been shot and was being life-flighted by helicopter to the trauma center in Austin…and that she'd better get there quickly herself. His tone informed her that it was bad.

Once she'd managed to shake free of her frozen state, she'd dropped the phone and run out of the gallery. City traffic patrols must have been looking the other way, because she raced to the hospital without them stopping her. She arrived just in time to see Tate being wheeled into a treatment room. He was ghostly pale, already intubated, with portable medical equipment all around him. Blood soaked the tattered remains of his shirt and smeared the gloved hands of the emergency medical technicians who'd flown with him from the scene and were now busy transferring information to the hospital trauma specialists trotting briskly alongside the gurney.

"Tate!" Jodie cried, and rushed to catch up to them.

Drew Winslow had taken hold of her at that point, preventing her from following the gurney into the treatment room. "Let 'em do what they do best, Jodie," he'd advised, his words raw with emotion.

"Tate!" Jodie had cried again, straining

against the strong arms that held her back. "I love you, Tate. *Don't die!*"

The fervid admonition still echoed in her mind, a symbol of all the hours of agony and uncertainty that followed. Tate had hovered for days between life and death. For days she'd kept vigil, unwilling to leave the hospital for even one second.

From somewhere deep inside himself Tate had found the wherewithal to step away from the abyss. To step away several times. He had clung to life, and she had clung to him. Only...had she gotten him back to lose him again? This time, not from an outside force but because it was what *he* wanted?

Jodie released her grip on the railing and crossed her arms. It all seemed like some kind of bad dream. Maybe, if she waited long enough, she'd awaken and the entire experience would vanish. She'd open her eyes and Tate would slip behind her, wrap his arms around her and draw her against him the way he used to, his body a refuge—warm, strong, comforting, loving. She ached to have him close to her again, to have him smile at her the way he used to.

What was she to do? If they remained here, the situation would only disintegrate further. For all intents and purposes, Tate had cut himself off from the world. It was as if, glimpsing the kind of life that might lie ahead of him—one where he would never recover adequately or be able to return to active law enforcement—he'd decided he'd done the wrong thing in surviving and was intent on correcting the oversight.

She *had* to get him away from here! If she didn't—

Her left hand dropped to cover her stomach.

Whatever it took she would do! If he wanted a promise that she would break free of him, she would give it.

As long as that got them to the ranch.

CHAPTER TWO

THE NEAR TEN-HOUR JOURNEY was exhausting. Tate barely said a word, preferring to sleep—or pretend to sleep—in the wide backseat of Mae's favored old black Cadillac.

In fact, he'd said very little since receiving Jodie's assurance that if he went with her to the ranch she would seek a divorce. When she told him, he'd gazed at her, she'd gazed at him, then he'd turned away, seemingly satisfied. It was all Jodie had been able to do to get herself out of the bedroom without breaking down. Afterward, she'd called her father and arranged for him to come to Austin to pick them up.

Jodie could sense her father was startled by the changes in Tate. Weakness, weight loss, halting movement were only to be expected for someone who'd suffered the physical devastation he had—the blood loss, the bone, tissue and organ damage, the system shock and infection. It was the rest—the uncaring attitude, the occasional surliness, the indifference to her—that was so completely unlike him.

Gib did his best to keep a conversation going as they traveled along the highway, chatting about this person and that from the ranch or the county, as he filled her in on the latest goings-on. Jodie knew he was trying to distract her, to cheer her, but nothing could keep her from comparing this trip with the other return trips she and Tate had made together during the first year of their marriage. They'd enjoyed every moment of the long drive, lowering the top of their little coupe, welcoming the wind and the sun in their faces. They'd been so completely carefree then.

She glanced at Tate, who was stretched out on the backseat, his eyes closed. Her heart ached to make him remember.

"He still sleepin'?" her father asked.

"Seems to be," Jodie replied, turning back.

"Not much longer now," Gib said, smiling.

They'd left the interstate an hour or so before and a short time ago had passed into Briggs County. They were almost to the point of turning off the narrow blacktopped highway onto the even narrower private road that led to Parker Ranch headquarters.

"A lot of people are gonna be glad to see you," Gib said. "Every time I go into Del Norte, one person or another stops me to ask about Tate. I wonder if he realizes just how highly the people of this county think of him. As soon as he feels up to it, you two should take a little drive into town. He'd find out then, for sure. Might perk him up. And Jack...Jack's been like a bear with a sore paw, wishin' he could get away but not being able to. If anyone should understand what that's like, though, it's Tate, seein' as how he was sheriff here himself once an' all."

Jodie nodded. The closer they got to the ranch, the stronger her emotional response. She'd never felt this kind of *need* to be there before. She was like a lost child at last sensing home.

As they made the turn onto the private road, her throat tightened. Not all that long ago she'd rejected everything to do with the Parker name. She hadn't wanted it; she hadn't wanted what went with it. She hadn't understood the value of family. Not until almost too late did she recognize that being a member of such a strong unit could be a positive thing. And now, here she was, risking everything on the hope that her family could somehow make things right for Tate…and for her.

"You think maybe you should start wakin' him up?" Gib asked. "He might like a few minutes before everyone descends on you."

"I'm awake," Tate murmured, and grimaced as he struggled to sit up.

Jodie watched him run a hand through his thick brown hair—hair that was far longer than it had ever been. All his life, through all his jobs in law enforcement, he'd worn it clipped short. Now it curled onto his neck and down across his forehead…which, for her, did nothing to dampen his appeal.

Her gaze slid back to the safety of her father. "Everyone will be here?" she asked.

"Almost everyone," Gib said. "I'm not sure about the Hugheses. They might wait till later to pay a call." For years Dub Hughes had been a fixture of the Parker Ranch, working as foreman—a job his son Morgan had inherited. They were closer than that, though. The Hugheses had always been considered family, and now they truly were, because of the union between Morgan and Christine, a Parker heir.

Jodie was thinking about them—looking forward to seeing them, too—when the car turned into the long U-shaped drive. She had to choke back tears as they passed first the house where she'd grown up, then the house belonging to her cousin Rafe, which he shared with his wife, Shannon, and their two young sons, then Mae's two-story stone structure at the head of the compound, before rolling to a stop in front of her aunt Darlene and uncle Thomas's house. Completing the compound was the house next door which belonged to her cousin LeRoy Dunn, his wife, Harriet, and their three children.

Relatives converged from all directions as her father cut the Cadillac's engine. Children squealed with excitement; a dog barked. Gib stepped out onto the hard-packed gravel drive, and after a short conference, the children and the dog were sent off to play on the far side of the courtyard. The noise level diminished immediately.

Jodie smiled as best she could as she, too, stepped out of the car. She planned to see directly to Tate but was prevented from doing so by a series of enveloping hugs.

"So good to have you home, Jodie!" Shannon said warmly, her pretty heart-shaped face alight with welcome. Her blond hair and blue eyes were a marked contrast with the dark hair and dark eyes of the majority of the others.

"Oh, yes," Harriet agreed, gripping Jodie enthusiastically to her chest.

"Good to have you both back," Rafe said.

"Things'll be right as rain before you know it!" LeRoy chimed in, grinning widely.

Jodie glanced around in time to see Rafe reach out to help steady Tate, who'd taken it on himself to emerge from the car. One look at the taut lines of his face revealed what a strain the feat had been.

"Here," Rafe offered, motioning for Gib to join him. "Put your arms across our shoulders, and we'll have you inside in no time flat."

"I can do it myself," Tate muttered shortly, gritting his teeth.

Mae arrived on the scene unnoticed. "Don't be a fool, son," she said, scolding him. "Anybody can see you need help."

Tate shot her a sullen look. "When I need help, Mae, I'll let you know. Until then, keep your nose out of it."

The family was stunned by Tate's uncharacteristic rudeness and waited for Mae's response. Though she was nearing ninety, she wasn't accustomed to having her authority challenged. Her hawklike eyes snapped, her strong features tightened, but Jodie's palpable distress must have reached her, because she tempered her response. "All right," she said shortly, "if it means that much to you...do it!"

Tate straightened as best he could, and ignoring the looks of compassion, he moved haltingly around the car, steadying himself against the vehicle when the hard-packed gravel underfoot caused difficulty. He didn't stop until he arrived at the spot opposite the walkway. From that point to the narrow porch he would have nothing to rely on but himself.

Shannon squeezed Jodie's hand in encouragement, and Harriet, on Jodie's other side, gently placed an arm along her shoulders.

Jodie didn't want Tate to feel humiliated, but she could foresee no other eventuality. For weeks he'd gone no farther than the few feet to the bathroom or occasionally to the bedroom window, to stand for a moment and gaze out. He wouldn't be able to complete the distance to the porch, not without a crutch or a cane, both of which he rejected. Her heart bled for him, but she didn't know how to change anything. If she intervened, it would only make the situation worse, because then the family would witness his rejection of her. That was something she wasn't ready for them to see—at least, not so soon after their arrival. They would learn about it eventually, of course, if he held to his stubborn determination. A goal his present behavior all but guaranteed.

The tense moment stretched out as everyone waited, each person held prisoner by a genuine affection and admiration for the Tate each used to know.

Shannon nudged Rafe's arm, urging him to intercede. He responded with an almost imperceptible shake of his head, denying her request. The current manager of the ranch, Rafe had worked all his life among men who stood fast to a certain code of conduct. Cowboys had been known to summarily quit because their judgment was questioned. On the job they were told *what* to do, not *how* to do it. A man had a right to work things his own way. So did Tate.

Tate took a tentative step forward, wavered and fell back against the car. Perspiration dampened his shirt. "Guess…I'm gonna hav'ta accept your offer, Rafe," he said tightly. "That is, if you're still willing."

Rafe moved quickly, as did Gib, and with their support Tate moved slowly into the house.

The children laughed as they played across the courtyard. Jodie saw them through a haze of tears. She hadn't been able to watch the trio of men the entire way. She knew Tate wouldn't have wanted her to. Maybe they shouldn't have come back here. Maybe they should have stayed in Austin and she could have found another way. Maybe—

"It's just a little bump in the road," Mae decreed. "It's not the first one he's faced and it sure won't be the last. Stop lookin' so glum, Missy," she ordered. "Things could be a whole lot worse and you know it!"

Jodie nodded, wiping her tears while trying once again to smile. "You're right," she said. "I know it."

"Tate's very brave," Harriet proclaimed staunchly. "He should get a medal or somethin'." Her gaze moved to her husband, who was emptying luggage and other gear from the trunk of the Cadillac. It lingered on him, as though she was wondering how LeRoy would react if he were suddenly thrust into Tate's position. She gave a little shiver.

"He looks—" Shannon started, then stopped.

Her frown remained in place when, prodded by the curiosity of the others, she continued, "He looks a lot like I felt when I first came here. I didn't care about much of anything then, not even myself." She turned to Jodie. "I didn't realize the situation had deteriorated so badly. You never hinted in your letters or when we talked on the phone."

Mae harrumphed. "Girl never was much good at communicatin' things. Remember when she spent that year in Europe? We hardly ever knew what was going on."

"That's all in the past now, Mae," Shannon murmured.

Rafe and Gib emerged from the house and came down the path, passing LeRoy, who, loaded down with luggage, was on his way inside. Gib went to collect the few remaining things, while Rafe rejoined the women.

"He's settlin' in," he reported to Jodie. "Seems pretty tuckered out. I asked if he needed anything—a drink of water, whatever—but he just shook his head."

Jodie murmured, "I'll go right in."

Rafe, in his own way, could be just as intimidating as Mae. He had the classic dark Parker looks and the same commanding will. But instead of pinning Jodie down with a probing question as Mae would have done, he merely nodded.

"Thank you. All of you," Jodie began, including LeRoy and her father in her gratitude when they rejoined the group. "I'm sure coming back here will make—" She stumbled to a stop.

"Just give it a little time, Jodie," Shannon advised quietly.

"Emma knows you're back, doesn't she?" Mae demanded. "You did tell her you were coming?" Emma, Tate's mother, lived in Del Norte, Briggs County's largest town.

"I promised I'd call when we got in."

"Don't forget."

Jodie nodded and forced another all-inclusive smile, before starting down the walkway to Darlene and Thomas's house.

Her father caught up with her on the porch. "I know you're tired," he said. "Both of you are. I'm feelin' a little beat-up myself, but if you want some company later on, I'm available. I'll be glad to come visit. Or, if Tate's restin' and you're in need of a little outing, I'll either be at the house or in the shed, painting."

Jodie reached out for her father's embrace. It felt so good to be in his arms that she didn't want to let go. Letting go meant she'd have to face reality once again, meant she'd have to deal with Tate's seemingly unyielding decision to set her free.

"I love you, Daddy," she whispered, then she slipped inside her temporary home.

TATE LAY in the unfamiliar room, an arm crooked over his face, hiding his eyes from the light. In effect, hiding himself. He couldn't possibly have looked more of an idiot than he had moments earlier. Returning to the ranch a shell of the man he used to be had been difficult enough. Now he'd gone and created a spectacle by insisting that he could do what he knew he couldn't, and in the end having to ask for help.

The front door opened and closed and he heard Jodie's footsteps. Moments later, he sensed her presence in the room. As always, when she came near him the air between them seemed to vibrate.

"Tate?" she said softly, hesitantly.

It tore him up inside that she approached him with trepidation, as if she was afraid he might yell at her or strike out.

She slid something onto the bedside table,

and from the slight scraping sound he knew it was a tray.

"I've brought you some cold water," she said. "Aunt Darlene left the nicest note, telling us to make ourselves at home. She—she sends her love. Uncle Thomas, too."

A little laugh followed her false words of cheer. He moved his arm and looked at her, and it was everything he could do not to pull her down beside him, to kiss her and run his fingers through the long red-gold strands of her sweet-scented hair. Memories were all he had left now, and they sometimes gave him as much pain as his slowly mending wounds. He turned away again, unable to gaze at her any longer. "I'll get it later," he said tightly.

"Are you in much pain?" she murmured.

"I'm all right."

"If the ride was too much—"

"I said...I'm fine!" He hadn't meant for his reply to come out so harshly. When she recoiled, he hated himself. But the kindest cut was the one made in a single stroke. He had to stick to his course. He couldn't waver.

She was still for a moment, unwilling even after that to abandon him. He shut his eyes, blotting out the busy decor of the master bedroom. Darlene, it appeared, liked to combine stripes with bright, flowery wallpaper and elaborately ruffled curtains.

Eventually, when Jodie finally did leave, Tate curled his hands into fists at his side. Why hadn't he just gone ahead and died when he'd had the opportunity and saved them all this trouble? Saved Jodie the trouble.

BEING IN THE HOUSE without Darlene or Thomas felt strange to Jodie. She'd known the place since childhood, yet she had never stayed overnight. She might have been an intruder as she walked through it. The rooms were neat and tidy, but the decor was too fussy for Jodie's taste. Every room but the living room had ruffles and print flowers and walls covered with knickknacks. The living room boasted several tall floor lamps, blond veneer tables and chests, a couch, a black leather easy chair and a late-model wide-screen TV. The kitchen was accented in avocado—countertops, stove, refrigerator.

The telephone was difficult to locate at first, surrounded by a plethora of wall ornamentation. Jodie took a deep breath and punched in Emma Connelly's number in Del Norte. She would try her mother-in-law at home first, before ringing the sheriff's office, where Emma had worked for many years as a dispatcher.

The call was answered on the second ring.

“Hello, Emma? This is Jodie. We’re back at the ranch. We just got in.” She paused. “I’m not sure it would be a good idea for you to come out this evening—it’s so late and Tate’s resting.” It was already past seven o’clock, and would take Emma at least an hour to drive out from town. “So if you’d rather— You’re welcome, of course. You’re always welcome.”

Jodie and Emma had entered their mother-in-law/daughter-in-law relationship on a sense of strain. Jodie had always felt that Emma disapproved of her, that she didn’t think her the right person for her only child. But something had shifted while the two women had waited together at the hospital in Austin, Emma having rushed there the instant she’d received word about Tate. Jodie sensed that her mother-in-law might have begun to see her in a new light, although she wasn’t sure.

“He’s resting,” Emma repeated. “Comfortably?”

“I don’t think so. The trip— It was hard for him.”

Emma was silent. “I think you’re right. I

won't come out tonight. I'll let you both rest. Tell Tate…tell him I'm thinking of him. And Jodie, you take care of yourself, too."

"I will."

"No, I mean it. What you're tryin' to deal with is a hard thing. Tate told me what he wants you to do. I tried to talk him out of it, but he's pretty intent."

An icy hand closed around Jodie's heart. Tate had already told his mother? "I can't think about that right now, Emma. I have to—" She searched desperately for something she had to do. "I have to make us something to eat. Some soup, I think. Something light."

"I'm sure all he needs is to get his feet back under him. Regain some of his strength and stop hurtin' all the time. People can't think straight when they're hurtin'. That's what I told him."

"I hope so," Jodie whispered.

The silence between them drew out. Emma didn't know what else to say and neither did Jodie.

Finally, Jodie managed to get out, "I—I have to go. The soup."

Emma sighed. "You hang in there, Jodie. Don't you give up on my son. Not for one second, do you hear?"

"Yes, ma'am," Jodie breathed, and, swallowing tightly, replaced the receiver.

Someone knocked lightly on the front door a short time later. When Jodie went to answer it she found Axel, the husband of her aunt Mae's housekeeper, Marie, on the porch. Axel was a big, powerfully built man, with a round face and a smooth bald head. His size might have made him an alarming presence, but Jodie had known him all her life. He was nowhere near as fierce as he looked.

Axel extended a covered pot like an offering. "Marie made this special for ya," he said in a surprisingly high, thin voice. "It's one of her stews. The kind Tate liked so much when y'all'd come to visit. She didn't think you'd feel up to cookin' this evenin'."

No stranger to cooking himself, Axel was the camp cook during the ranch's twice-yearly cattle roundups. He also prepared daily meals for the single cowboys who called the bunkhouse home. When it came to grub, cowboys far and wide swore by Axel's abilities.

Jodie invited him in and he headed straight for the kitchen. "Stew's still pretty hot," he said as he placed the pot on a burner. He glanced around. "Tate in bed already? I shoulda brought this over sooner."

"He's resting—he's not asleep. Axel, this is so sweet. Tell Marie thank-you...please. I know Tate will appreciate it."

A friendly grin split Axel's broad cheeks. "She thought he might," he said, then he sobered. "You know, Miss Jodie, we were right sorry to hear what happened to 'im. It's always the good'uns, ain't it? The no-accounts always seem to slip around trouble." He shook his head. "It just don't seem fair."

He headed back down the hall and Jodie accompanied him. She was just about to thank him yet again, when he paused at the front door.

"You know?" he said. "All the time Tate was here nothin' happened to 'im. Then he goes off to that new job and gets hurt. Makes you wonder if he should'na stayed home. But then, that didn't help his daddy before 'im, did it? He was close by, and he ended up bein' shot dead on the highway by those escaped robbers. I guess if misery's s'posed to find ya, it's gonna do it, no matter what. You can't run away from it."

Jodie didn't move after Axel left. He hadn't meant to upset her, but he had...by putting into words things she tried very hard not to think about. It *wasn't* fair that Tate had been shot. He *was* one of the good guys! He shouldn't have been made to suffer this way.

She should've taken better care of him. She should've had some kind of intuition. Known in some way what was about to take place. Then she could have prevented it. She could have pretended to be sick so he wouldn't have gone to Hays County that day to question the man who had such vicious enemies. The interview would've been postponed, and Tate and his fellow investigator wouldn't have walked into the ambush. He'd have been at home with her, *safe*. None of this would have happened. If only she'd—

She'd gone through the counseling the state provided. She knew with the more rational portion of her mind that there was nothing she could have done. Still…

Had Emma Connelly experienced similar feelings when Tate's father had been killed? Wasn't it only human nature to wonder that if you'd done this or if you'd done that, the terrible thing—whatever it was—wouldn't have occurred?

Jodie had never fully appreciated what Emma Connelly must have gone through all those years before. What it must have been like for her to talk with her mortally wounded husband over the police radio as the life force drained slowly from his body. Trying to offer him comfort, trying to bring him hope…telling him, for the last time, that she loved him and hearing him breathe weakly back that he loved her, too. Everyone in the county knew the story, because Jack Denton, Dan Connelly's best friend and sheriff at the time, had arrived on the scene to cradle Dan in his arms during his final moments.

Tate had been only eleven years old at the time. He'd also had to deal with his father's sudden death. Some would say that because of this, he knew what he was letting himself in for when he chose a career in law enforcement. That what had happened in September should've come as no surprise. Enforcing the law was in Tate's blood, just as caring for this land and protecting what was on it was in Parker blood. Who better than a Parker to understand?

Jodie did understand. She just couldn't do anything. Like Emma before her, she felt that she was witnessing the life force drain slowly from the man she loved.

What was it Emma had said to her? *Don't*

you give up on my son. Not for one second, do you hear?

The problem was…Tate had given up on himself.

CHAPTER THREE

JODIE AWAKENED the next morning with a start, confused about where she was. The room had a closed feel, as if it was rarely used. Boxes stood stacked in one corner, clothes sat folded on a chair and were draped across its back and arms. A conglomeration of items, from a boy's toy airplane to an empty hat box from Neiman Marcus, littered the top of a desk.

She was in Darlene and Thomas's house… on the ranch…in the spare bedroom. She had no idea what time it was, but bright sunlight streamed in through a crack in the curtain.

A noise from the kitchen made her leap out of bed on a rush of guilt. *Tate!* After discovering last night that he was asleep when she went to ask if he would like some of Marie's stew, she'd stored the stew in the refrigerator and fallen into an exhausted sleep herself. Tate had barely eaten yesterday, nothing more than a few bites of his usual slice of morning toast. Hunger must have driven him to scavenge for himself.

She dug around in her suitcase for her robe, then hurried down the short hall past the master bedroom Tate was using to the kitchen. Only it wasn't Tate who stood at the counter. It was Harriet.

Surprised by Jodie's sudden appearance, Harriet swiveled and her hand flew to her mouth. "Oh! I woke you!" she exclaimed. "I thought I could drop this off without making a sound." *This* was a plate of homemade muffins. "I snuck in by the back door and was plannin' to sneak out the same way." She paused to grin. "I should know better than to think I could 'sneak' anywhere. Maybe a few pounds ago I could, but not now."

Harriet had always been full figured—as well as tall and strong and radiant with good health, from the top of her chestnut hair to her solidly planted size-nine feet. A little extra weight may have accumulated over the past year, but she looked comfortable with it.

"You didn't have to do that," Jodie murmured.

"Yes, I did." Harriet's gray eyes grew serious. "I know it's been a hard time for you,

Jodie. I wish you'd've told us, so one of us could've come to help."

"There's nothing anyone could have done."

"Shannon feels the same way. At the very least we could've taken turns bein' there with you."

"Our apartment is very small."

"I still fit on a couch. And Shannon's such a slender little thing you could put two of her on it." She motioned toward the master bedroom. "How'd he pass the night? How does he pass most nights? Is he able to sleep?"

"Not very well. He has some pain pills, but he won't take them."

"He's probably afraid to start relying on 'em. But in his position—" She gave Jodie a considering look. "I have to tell you, he's worse than I expected. He's lost so much weight! He seems...breakable somehow. Not at all like the Tate we used to—"

"I can hardly believe how fast the kids are growing," Jodie interjected. She couldn't bear to hear a litany of Tate's physical deficiencies. She knew them all by heart, and each terrified her. "Anna's what now? Seven? Is she going to start school this fall? Or did she start last year? I can't remember."

Harriet sympathetically accepted the change of subject. "She started last fall. I thought she'd hate the idea of being reined in all day. She's such a little tomboy. But she surprised me by enjoying it. We made sure she had the same teacher as Gwen and Wes when they started school, so I guess that paved the way."

"And how are they?"

"They're fine. Both of 'em are at that age where they think they know everything. Particularly Wesley. He's moved into high school this year."

"That barely seems possible," Jodie murmured. She'd picked up an undertone of concern in Harriet's voice, but before she could question her, Tate came into the room from the hallway. He walked stiffly, slightly hunched, one hand trailing the wall to brace himself, the other at his midsection.

His eyes were hollowed as he caught Jodie's gaze and held it for a second, before switching to Harriet.

"'Morning," he said gruffly.

"Now I've managed to disturb you both!" Harriet returned wryly.

"I was awake."

"Yes, well—" Harriet's glance included the

two of them. "You might as well sit yourselves down and I'll serve breakfast. I've brought along some of my extra special carrot-apple-and-cinnamon muffins, Tate, but if you'd rather have somethin' else, just say the word. You, too, Jodie. The fridge is full—so's the pantry."

Jodie watched as Tate debated whether to stay or leave, then took the few remaining steps to the nearest chair, where he lowered himself gingerly.

"Coffee'll be ready in a minute," Harriet said, taking the old-fashioned percolator to the sink for water.

"Don't you need to see to your family's breakfast?" Jodie said.

"LeRoy's home. He'll take care of it. He can also get the kids on the bus." She glanced at Tate. "You drove the school bus for a while, didn't you, Tate? Before you went off to college? The district's finally bought a new one. Not before time, I say. I betcha Rafe and LeRoy rode that old one when they were kids. Anyway, this new one's real nice—better seats, more comfortable. All this is according to Gwen. Wesley doesn't seem to care." She noticed that Jodie was still hovering. "Sit down, girl. Let someone take care of you for a change!"

Immediately, Tate scraped back his chair. "I'll pass on breakfast," he said tightly.

"But—" Harriet faltered as she reached for cups.

"Tate!" Jodie reproached him.

Tate didn't answer. He made his way painfully back across the room, then turned into the hall without another word.

Harriet gestured her confusion. Only when the door to the master bedroom closed did she ask with hushed anxiousness, "What did I say? What did I do? The bus— I don't understand why talking about a new bus would—"

Jodie collapsed into the chair Tate had just vacated. "I don't think it was that," she said tiredly. "He's just— That's the way he is lately."

"But...what did I say?" Harriet persisted. "I told you to sit down...that you should let someone take care of you for a— Oh, my heaven! I made it sound like Tate's been *forcin'* you to take care of him. That wasn't what I meant at all! I was just—"

"I know what you meant. He does, too. He's just...a little touchy right now."

"I'll go apologize," Harriet said, and started to move away.

"No, let him get settled first. He wouldn't want you to see him…struggling."

Harriet slipped into a chair opposite Jodie. "I truly had no idea it was this bad," she said sadly.

Jodie ached to pour out everything to this woman who had always been there for her, ready to lend a compassionate ear. Especially when she and Mae had clashed, which was frequently. Jodie's problem today, though, went much deeper than anything from the past. It couldn't be solved merely by listening.

"No wonder you seem so…strained." Harriet's observation caused Jodie to start. "I thought when Tate left the care facility it meant he was getting back to normal, even if he did check himself out early. I remember when you told us, I thought—well, I thought it was because he was chompin' at the bit to get back to you. But just now, and yesterday evening…he didn't seem any too—"

"He won't listen to anyone about taking therapy. Or about—"

"I was going to say…" Harriet paused, as if searching for the right approach. In the end she settled on her usual directness. "Has somethin' gone wrong between the two of you?"

Jodie rubbed at the furrows etched in her brow. Pressure was building to the bursting point. Moisture trembled just behind her lashes. "Oh, you could say that, I think," she admitted.

Harriet caught Jodie's free hand and waited. When Jodie failed to continue, she said, "Tell you what. There's no need to rush this, is there? I'll fix Tate a muffin and some coffee and go have a little talk with him. I don't want him thinkin' I think he's been taking advantage of you. Then, later on, if you feel like it, you can come over and we'll have a nice long talk."

Jodie knew she would have to open up soon to the family. She'd brought Tate to the ranch so they could help, and they couldn't help without having some idea of what was going on. Yet she couldn't discuss the situation with Tate lying in the next room.

Harriet stood up. "Oh, and before I forget, Mae's sent word that she wants to see you this mornin'. So you'd better get yourself prepared. You know what her command performances are like."

Jodie smiled wanly. "Oh, yes. I remember."

"She'll want to talk about...everything," Harriet jerked a thumb toward Tate in the other room.

"I'm sure she will."

"She'll have a plan."

"I hope she does."

Harriet eyed her consideringly. "You really have grown up, haven't you? I guess with everything that's happened, you couldn't *not* have."

"What time does Aunt Mae want to see me?"

"Sometime before noon."

Jodie looked around for a clock and, like the phone, found it mounted on the wall among various bric-a-brac. It was a little after eight. She breathed a sigh.

"Have you talked to Emma yet?" Harriet asked.

"I phoned her last night and told her we'd arrived. She'll visit later today."

"Jack'll want to come visit right away, too. He stops by every time he's out this way to see if we've heard anything."

"I should call him."

"Emma's probably already done it."

Jodie wished she could relax, but she couldn't. All she could think about was Tate. How he—

"—who else has come back?"

Jodie had caught only a part of what Harriet said. At her confusion, Harriet repeated herself.

"Do you know who else has come back? Jennifer...Jennifer Cleary. Or whatever her married name is now. She showed up a couple of weeks ago. I haven't seen her myself yet. Or her baby."

"She's come for a visit, you mean?"

Harriet pursed her lips. "I get the feelin' it's more than that."

Jennifer Cleary was the daughter of Jim Cleary, a longtime friend and the closest neighbor to the Parkers. Jennifer and Jodie had been childhood buddies, playing together every minute they could when Jennifer and her father flew in from their home in Dallas to vacation and spend holidays at their ranch. The friendship had grown strained in their late teenage years after Jennifer had broken a confidence Jodie had entrusted to her. The divulgence had resulted in Jodie's run-away cowboy friend, Rio Walsh, being found when Jodie had been trying to help him hide after he'd been falsely accused of murder. Then Jennifer had chosen to go to college in Massachusetts and finally settled there. The last Jodie had heard of her was shortly before her own marriage to Tate, when Jim had told her that Jennifer and her husband were happily awaiting the birth of their first child.

"Did you hear why?" she asked.

"Mae talked to Jim last week and he's not sayin' a thing."

Jodie nodded, unable at the moment to comment further. Her priority was her own marriage. "I—I'll go get showered," she said. "Then I'll deal with Aunt Mae."

"If you want me to come along when you see her, I will," Harriet offered.

Jodie was already shaking her head. "No," she said quietly. "This is for me to do."

HARRIET HAD GONE HOME by the time Jodie finished her shower. On the table she'd left behind a muffin, a cup and an early rose freshly clipped from her garden. Jodie sniffed the rose but turned away from the rest. She couldn't eat or drink anything. Not before facing Mae.

As she passed the master bedroom on her way to dress, she heard Tate give a muffled curse. She hesitated only a second before tapping on the door. When she opened it she found Tate attempting to deal with a coffee spill. Most of the liquid had splashed on his shirt, but some had spread to the sheets.

Jodie hurried over. "Here, let me," she murmured, relieving him of the cup. Then she grabbed the large linen napkin Harriet had provided with his breakfast and blotted up the excess liquid.

Tate remained complacent throughout. It was only when she straightened that he said flatly, "I coulda done that. I'm not totally helpless."

"I know," she breathed. Her objective hadn't been to underscore his disability but to help. Still— "Did you get burned?" she asked. Not long ago—not even two years—she'd suffered a painful burn from hot coffee, and Tate had taken her to his house to administer first aid. This was around the time they were first starting to admit their strong mutual attraction. He'd taken such gentle care of her at the time….

Her eyelids fluttered shut on the sweet memories, then she forced herself to forget them. Motioning jerkily to the soiled sheets, she said, "Tate, you have to let—"

"You do everything," he completed.

"That's not what I—"

"Oh, but it is," he contradicted flatly. "Whether we like it or not, *this* is our reality."

"Tate—"

"Oh, go ahead," he said finally, jerking away his gaze. "Do what you want. I can manage to change my own shirt, though, if you'll find me one."

LeRoy had left the suitcases next to the closet. Jodie opened the first one she came to and extracted a clean pair of pajamas. For a man who never used to wear them, Tate had gained an extensive collection since September.

She turned to find his gaze back on her, and again, for a second, she thought she saw a spark. But it was gone as quickly as it had arrived. She ignored the disappointment that threatened to overwhelm her.

They'd made love only once since he'd been shot, and that was at her behest. She'd needed so badly to be close to him, to gain some kind of reassurance that their lives would return to normal. But afterward, the darkness of the anger he'd directed against himself for allowing that lovemaking, and his even stronger rejection of her, had made the weeks that followed so much harder to get through.

She approached him, carrying a light blue pajama top—one that matched the pair he was wearing. "Here," she said, extending it.

Their fingers brushed as he reached out. She instantly pulled away.

"I—I'll find fresh sheets," she said, and escaped into the hall.

At the linen closet she paused for breath. She missed him. She missed him so badly it hurt. But dwelling on it did her no good. Tate would resist any attempt she might make. And she wasn't sure she could stand another devastating rejection. It was best, for now, to leave things as they were. To concentrate on helping him heal.

She secured her composure and presented herself back in the bedroom, fresh sheets folded over her arm.

Tate had yet to finish re-dressing. He'd managed to get up off the bed and discard his damp pajama top, but he hadn't yet covered himself with the clean one.

Jodie stopped abruptly, her newly determined resolve evaporating under an onslaught of feeling at the sight of him. The scarring where the bullets had torn through his body—three had penetrated the left side of his abdomen and chest and one had pierced his right shoulder—had been amplified by the work of the surgeons trying to save his life. A patchwork of splotches and welts—some white, some bright pink, some red—decorated his torso, both in front and back. Tate had undergone several surgeries during his initial hospital stay and later had returned for corrective procedures. Jodie had never seen his wounds without bandages. He hadn't let her.

Her breath caught at the uncontrovertible evidence of how close she'd come to losing him. She wanted to rush over and softly touch each and every mark as if her touch could act as a talisman against further danger.

He looked up, and the hurt etched on his face as he saw her standing transfixed, pale and trembling, was heart-wrenching.

"Tate." She wanted to say more but was unable.

"Just…get out, Jodie. Get out!" he ordered roughly.

"Tate!" she cried.

He took the two steps that separated them and jerked her hand to his left side, placing her palm flat against the abused skin. "Here," he challenged. "Is this what you want? To touch a scar? To feel one? I'm not the same man I was, Jodie. I'm barely a man at all. I can't even drink a simple cup of coffee without making a mess. Then I can't clean it up. You'll be better off finding someone else. Someone who can take care of you proper, make you happy."

All that Jodie felt for him was in her eyes. "I love you, Tate," she avowed softly.

"I don't love you."

"I don't believe you!"

He cast away her hand. "Then don't," he snapped coldly. "But that doesn't change a thing. Remember your promise—I come to the ranch, you file for divorce. I'll expect to see some papers soon."

Then he turned away.

He didn't seem to notice, or care, when she left the room.

JODIE DRESSED for her meeting with Mae in a haze of tears. Crying seemed all she'd done for the past couple of months. She had reason, but she knew she should be stronger.

She arrived at Mae's house a little after ten o'clock, too spent emotionally to be nervous. If Mae wanted to castigate her, let her. It couldn't be any more painful than what she'd already endured with Tate. Nothing could be more painful.

She walked straight to Mae's office and went inside. For Mae not to have specified a time meant she planned to be at work all morning.

As Jodie had speculated, Mae sat behind her highly polished rosewood desk, reading a letter. She looked up the instant Jodie presented herself.

Her gaze missed nothing. "You look like hell, Missy," she said as she put the letter aside. "Couldn't get any sleep among Darlene's frills, or was it something else?"

"I slept," Jodie said.

"How's Tate?" Mae demanded.

"Alive," Jodie retorted.

"You look like you've been cryin'."

"Can you blame me? I have something to cry about, don't you think?"

"No more'n Tate."

"It's Tate I'm crying about."

"And not yourself?"

Jodie lifted her chin. Dealing with Mae was never easy. "Maybe for myself, too," she admitted. "Things aren't looking real good right now, Aunt Mae. I'm sure you recognized that yesterday."

"I saw a lot of things yesterday. A proud man, a worried wife. I also saw a lot of other people ready to offer any kind of help they can give."

Jodie's hands were curled tightly against her sides. So tightly that her fingernails cut into the flesh. Still, she didn't relax them. She had to do something to help maintain control. If she didn't—

Mae came around the desk and, collecting Jodie's arm, led her to the sitting area off to one side. A wisp of a smile touched her lips as she settled beside Jodie on the green leather couch. "This feels like old times, doesn't it? How often have you and I had a little talk in here?"

"Since I first learned to walk, I think," Jodie said, and sniffed.

Mae handed her a tissue. "I always put our differences down to that red hair of yours. That and a good dose of Parker stubbornness."

Jodie laughed weakly. "I found my way into more than my fair share of trouble, I think."

"But never somethin' you couldn't get yourself out of if you put your mind to it."

"You usually had a few suggestions."

"I ordered you around, you mean."

"You order everyone around."

"I'm slowin' down a bit lately."

"That's not what I've heard."

Mae smiled again, pleased. She arched an eyebrow speculatively. "Would you like a little suggestion from me about Tate?"

"I'd like more than a suggestion."

Her reply caught Mae off guard. "You're *asking* for my help?" she questioned.

"Yours and everyone else's. I—I'm at the end of my rope, Aunt Mae. Tate's changed. You saw that."

"The way the boy looks shocked me!"

"It's like...he's given up and I can't get through to him. He won't listen to me, Aunt Mae. He won't—"

"When somethin' like this happens, people often strike out at the ones they love most."

Jodie hesitated. "He wants a divorce."

For the first time in her life she'd managed to surprise Mae into silence.

Jodie continued, her hands clasped tightly in her lap. "He says he doesn't love me anymore, but I don't think he means it. He's just saying it to— He wants to set me free, Aunt Mae, but I don't want to be free. I love him!"

"Of course he still loves you," Mae declared.

Jodie drew a shaky breath. "I agreed to do what he asked. It was the only way I could get him here. If I hadn't— I don't want him to die, Aunt Mae! Not after everything he's been through. It's like he doesn't care anymore. He stays in his room. He won't talk to me. He won't—" She stopped. She wouldn't go there. That Tate rejected her fully, in every sense of the word, was her own private pain. "If—if I have to...if there's no alternative," she said tightly, "I'll even go through with it."

Mae suddenly looked every day of her eighty-nine-plus years. She was quiet a moment, then said, "You know that I thought you two rushed things, that you were makin' a mistake marrying so soon. You'd just gotten back from your trip to Europe, and you still had a lot of growin' up to do in my opinion," Mae continued. "But I like Tate. I've liked him since he was a boy. You convinced me you knew what you were doing. And over time, you showed me that you did." Her usual determination returned with force. "So we can't let this happen! A divorce is simply out of the question."

Jodie shook her head. "It won't be that easy, Aunt Mae. Tate's…very determined."

"The boy's not himself. You said so."

"Yes, but he—"

"What he needs is some time to get well. That's why he's here."

"But he won't stay here if I don't—"

"So, you bring him some proof. We can get what you need from Ned Fowler." She named the lawyer in Del Norte the Parker family had used for the past thirty years. "He'll play along if I ask him."

Jodie was sure he would. When Mae said "Jump," almost everyone did.

"What you're suggesting is that we string Tate along," Jodie murmured. "I fill out the papers but don't file them." Deceiving Tate bothered her, but she could see no other recourse. "All right," she said. "But I want to talk to Mr. Fowler myself."

"There's no need."

"I need, Aunt Mae. I want to do it."

Mae shot her an estimating look. "How are you goin' to handle it if word leaks out?"

"Mr. Fowler won't say anything."

"Tate might. And once a secret's told, it spreads."

"I'll handle it," Jodie answered stoutly.

"What about the family? You gonna tell them or wait to see if they find out on their own?"

Jodie started to feel tense again. For a moment some of the pressure she'd been living with had lifted. Now it was back. Because she knew there still was something else she needed to tell Mae.

She must have looked pretty miserable, since Mae relented. "I had an idea earlier about somethin' that might help Tate. Marie reminded me of it this morning. Axel hasn't always been a cook. After he left the Marine Corps and before he came back to West Texas, he tried his hand working in a gym—a training gym for boxers. One of the things he did was give what's called a therapeutic massage. Now, I'm not real big on that kinda thing. It's sorta silly to me. If your muscles hurt, you should just get right back out there and do more of whatever it was you were doin', until the hurt stops. But it seems some of the boxers he worked with swore by it. It helped 'em with their aches and pains. Axel musta been pretty good at it, too. He says he's willing to do what he can for Tate…if Tate's willing. He still has a table—knows right where to find it, according to Marie."

Jodie shrugged. "I— Sure. We can ask."

"I was thinkin' I'd just send Axel over in a day or two and let him do the talkin'—man to man, you know. Tate might take to it better."

"Sure," Jodie said again. She was open to anything. And if nothing else, Tate might enjoy Axel's company.

Mae sat silent for a moment. When Jodie made no move to leave, she asked, "Is there somethin' else?"

Jodie's stomach plunged. "I—I just wanted to thank you, Aunt Mae," she hedged, "for asking us back. I was almost at the end of my wits, trying to find a way to—"

"Out with it, Missy. I know there's something."

"I—" Jodie stood up, no longer able to remain still. She crossed to the narrow table where a collection of family photos was on display. She saw what had to be the latest school photographs of Wesley and Gwen and Anna, along with an older photo of Harriet and LeRoy. There was one of her father and her when she was about twelve. Then a current one of Rafe and Shannon and their boys. Also, a family grouping of the Hugheses from the ranch's Little Springs division—Dub and his wife, Delores, seated in front of Morgan and Christine, while their teenage daughter, Erin, proudly held little Elisabeth. This portrait had to have been taken shortly after Elisabeth's birth, because the infant would be two this summer.

Jodie smiled as she remembered the frantic ride into Del Norte when she, Christine and Harriet tried to make it to the hospital before Elisabeth was born. Jodie had pushed the Cadillac as hard as she safely could and prayed.

She also remembered going with Mae to Little Springs a few days later, on the official welcome visit for the baby, who'd recently come home. And the way Christine had looked at Morgan—with all the love in her being, enhanced by the birth of their baby. At the time, Jodie had wondered if she'd ever look at a man with that degree of feeling… at Tate. Then she'd gone on to wonder if they might ever have a child together. *A child!*

She turned away, tears forming once again.

Mae moved near and with unusual tenderness lifted Jodie's chin. "Are you gonna make me guess?" she asked gruffly.

Jodie met her great-aunt's eyes, fearful at

first, then with growing relief as Mae smiled slowly.

"There's no way you can fool an old lady. Particularly *this* old lady. Just how far along are you, Jodie?" she asked. "When should we start lookin' for the next Parker baby?"

CHAPTER FOUR

"DOES TATE KNOW about this?" Mae demanded, seconds after receiving Jodie's answer.

"No."

"Why not? Because of this divorce thing? Maybe that'd help snap him out of it! A man, especially a man in his situation, should know he's about to become a father."

"He has all he can think about right now, Aunt Mae. I can't...add to it."

Mae frowned. "You make it sound like a burden."

"Aunt Mae—" How could she tell her great-aunt that she was afraid Tate might think she'd planned the pregnancy? That she'd pushed herself on him the one time in order to create some kind of hold? Blame wouldn't enter his mind in normal circumstances, but these weren't normal circumstances. Just as he'd misunderstood her reaction at seeing his scars, he would misunderstand her current condition. He wasn't thinking clearly. And because of that he might reject—

The prospect that he might reject the child as well as her sent a painful stab through Jodie's heart. The idea was numbing, but it must have lurked in the back of her mind all along.

"This isn't a secret you can keep forever, you know," Mae warned. "The man has eyes. He'll notice."

"I know," Jodie choked out.

"You should tell him."

For the first time since Jodie had been notified Tate was shot, anger flared in her. "Just leave it to me, all right, Aunt Mae?" she snapped. "You haven't lived with him for all these months. I have. I want to wait."

Mae sat down at her desk, her back stiff. "I think you're making a big mistake. But since when has that stopped you? You're a grown woman, Jodie. With a grown woman's full set of responsibilities. Not only to that baby, but to the man who helped you make it. You keep this secret for now, if you want. But just know, I think you're being foolish in the extreme."

"I've got the message, Aunt Mae," Jodie said tightly.

Mae retrieved the letter she'd put aside and began to read it, effectively ending their discussion.

Only, Jodie wasn't ready to be dismissed. "Promise me you won't tell him," she pressed.

Mae looked up. "You have my word."

Jodie's emotions had been all over the place during this audience. In her younger days she would already have stormed out. But age had broadened her perspective. She didn't want to leave things as they were between them—the atmosphere prickling with hostility.

She paused at the desk on her way out and bent to kiss her great-aunt's wrinkled cheek. "I meant what I said earlier. I do thank you for inviting us here and for being willing to help."

Mae's dark eyes sparked. "Missy, I'd fight the devil himself if it meant keepin' a member of this family outta harm's way. You most of all. I want things to be right for you."

"I do, too, Aunt Mae," Jodie murmured, and after bestowing a second short kiss, she let herself out of the office.

TATE WAS SHOWERING when Jodie returned to Darlene and Thomas's house. Since the simple ablution was now a drawn-out affair, hampered by his infirmity and his stubborn determination to brook no assistance, Jodie took advantage of the moment to finish the job she'd thought to do earlier—remake the bed—then she unpacked his things. Drawers had been emptied for their use, as had a large portion of the master-bedroom closet. She'd just finished emptying the last suitcase when Tate returned.

He stopped short, surprised by her presence. "I didn't think you'd be back so soon. Harriet told me Mae wanted to see you. What about? No, never mind. I can guess."

His ability to navigate generally improved after a hot shower. It took less effort for him to reach the bed. "My mother called," he said once he'd caught his breath. "She and Jack are on their way. They could be here any time."

Jodie looked anxiously at him. "You will see them, won't you? I mean— You won't—"

"Of course I'll see them."

There was no "of course" about it. How many excuses and evasions had Jodie been forced to deliver when they were in Austin because Tate refused to see visitors?

He glanced over to where the suitcases had sat. "You put everything away? Where'd you put my jeans?"

His jeans! Jodie's heart gave a hopeful little leap. Tate hadn't worn regular clothes since before his injury.

"Second drawer from the top in the large chest. Tate—"

"I'd like to dress now," he said, and tugged at the tie of his robe.

"You talked to Harriet?" Jodie asked, disinclined to leave him. Optimism bloomed on the slightest of encouragements.

"Mmm."

"Did she— Did you—"

"She left calling me a hero." He laughed caustically. "Some hero."

"Tate—"

He stood up with more difficulty, the benefits of the shower already wearing off. "Leave me alone so I can dress, okay? I don't wanna be standing here like this when Mom and Jack show up."

Jodie nodded and stumbled into the hall.

THE VISITORS GATHERED in Tate's bedroom. His mother sat on an overblown chintz-covered boudoir chair and Jack used one of the straight-backed chairs from the kitchen. A second straight-backed chair waited for Jodie, who'd gone to prepare something to drink. Tate reclined on the bed—at once his most hated, yet most comfortable, location.

He gritted his teeth at the scene. All he wanted was to be left alone, but that wouldn't happen until he let Jack and his mother have a good look at him. Then he could be assured that when he said he didn't feel up to company in the future, they'd believe him.

His mother's brown eyes, so like his own, touched him periodically in concern, as if at any second bits of him might fall off. He doubted she was aware of her action.

In her midfifties, Emma Connelly was still as slim as the young woman in the wedding photograph on her piano at home, who looked adoringly at the handsome man with a friendly open face—Tate's father. The dark brown had faded from her long wavy hair, replaced now by a short silver wedge. She was a proud woman, who'd instilled in Tate the value of hard work.

"I've told Jack, Tate," Emma said directly. "I've told him what you asked of Jodie, and he agrees with me. You shouldn't do it. Not now.

There's plenty of time for that kinda thing later, if it's still what you want."

"It's already done, so drop it," Tate snapped. His words were harsher than he'd planned. But he was tired of having his actions evaluated, as if he were a child. A muscle twitched in his wounded shoulder and in his cheek.

His eyes slid away and met Jack's, where he found rebuke.

Jack had been sheriff in Briggs County for over thirty years. His only interruption in service was the close to two years that Tate was sheriff, when Jack had thought he was ready to retire but learned differently once he actually had. Tate's recruitment into the newly organized investigative task force based in Austin had brought Jack back into office, where he once again thrived.

Jack had always been a large man—a good six feet and tipping the scale at over two hundred pounds. His body had softened as he approached his sixty-fifth year, but neither softness nor age stood in the way of him doing his job or upholding his reputation as one of the fairest, most ethical and toughest law-enforcement officers the county had ever seen. Jack came from a long line of impressive men. His great-grandfather had been among the first Buffalo Soldiers sent to guard the western frontier; his grandfather had fought in the same cavalry regiment alongside Teddy Roosevelt's Rough Riders at the Battle of San Juan Hill. Jack had yet to let down either.

"Your momma's been worried about you, son," Jack said levelly.

"She doesn't need to be," Tate retorted, the same muscle twitching in his cheek.

Emma spoke up. "I'm worried you're about to do somethin' you'll regret forever!"

When Tate didn't respond, she switched her frustrated look to Jack, then she stood up. "I'm goin' to see if Jodie needs help. Jack, you and Tate…talk."

Once they were on their own, Tate waited for more censure from his old friend. He didn't wait long.

Jack leaned back, folded his arms behind his head and said, "I never thought I'd see the day when you talked nonsense to your mother."

"It's not nonsense, Jack."

"Have you looked in a mirror lately?" Jack demanded. "Son, you're in no condition—"

"It doesn't matter how I look."

"It does to your mother. It does to me. 'Cause, son…you don't look good."

"Leave it alone, Jack."

"You ain't been hitched long enough to that little lady 'a yours to know anythin'! Maureen and me woulda been married forty-four years this July if she hadn't been called up to heaven. As it was, we made it to thirty-nine. Now, *that's* a long time. She knew me inside and out, and I knew her the same."

"I don't need a lecture, Jack."

"Well, maybe you're wrong about that, just like you're wrong about a few other things, too. And maybe I'm just the man to tell you about it! I promised your daddy I'd watch out for you and I am."

"I know what I'm doing."

"I hope so, but I can't help havin' my doubts. You didn't get hit in the head with one of them bullets, did ya? One didn't rattle around inside your brain and stir things up?"

Tate smiled grimly. "That's one place the bad guys seemed to miss."

"Then there's no reason you can't do a little work."

"Work?" Tate repeated, thrown off balance by Jack's change of course.

"Yeah. Case happened a few months after you left for Austin. Rawley Stevens. I'm sure you remember him—a distant relative of Harvey Stevens, our favorite complainin' car dealer. Never can do anythin' right in that man's eyes. Anyway, Rawley wasn't a bad guy, but he ran with a rough crowd. Well, he turned up dead out near our border with Debolt County. No signs of a struggle, just him and his motorcycle in a shallow ravine. Looks like the cycle ran over him. The coroner ruled the death accidental, but I keep havin' visits from Rawley's daddy and his brother, demanding that we take another look at it. They say it wasn't an accident. I keep tellin' 'em that there isn't anythin' else for us to go on. That's why we didn't do anything in the first place. But they keep insistin', and I ended up promisin' we'd give it another look." He paused. "I promised 'em you would."

"You shouldn't've done that, Jack."

"Like you said to your mom, it's already done. Won't take a second to redeputize you, if that's what's botherin' ya. I don't think you need it, but if you do—" Jack watched him levelly, not giving away any of his thoughts… as was his habit. "I could sure use a little help, son. You know how it is. I'm run off my feet so bad I don't have the time to take a long pee, much less—"

Tate smiled tightly. "Your little plan isn't

going to work, Jack. I don't care about investigating anything anymore."

Jack produced an expandable brown folder encircled with a wide rubber band. The case number and the decedent's name were printed in black ink on the flap. "You keep this for a while anyway, okay? It's sure not gonna get any kinda proper look-see at my place."

"Jack, I don't want it."

Jack slid the folder onto the bedside table. "Did you say somethin'?" he asked innocently, and once again leaned back in his chair.

EMMA'S EXPRESSION was strained when she joined Jodie in the kitchen.

Jodie expected some comment on Tate—an observation, a concern—but Emma appeared distracted. She offered to help, yet she stood at the window, staring into the backyard.

Jodie continued to gather cups and saucers, then place them on a serving tray, all the while remaining attuned to her mother-in-law's actions.

Finally, in a ragged voice Emma said, "I'm going to lose him, too, aren't I?"

Jodie almost dropped a cup. Porcelain rattled against porcelain.

Emma spun around. "I'm sorry. I shouldn't

have said that. Not to you. But I just— He's gone downhill again, hasn't he? When I was in Austin last—it couldn't have been over a month ago—he seemed…not exactly better, but— Should he be seein' a doctor, do you think? Could somethin' else have gone wrong inside him?"

"He saw his doctor last Friday. There's nothing physically wrong with him."

"Nothin' more than bein' torn apart by four bullets!" Emma burst out.

Jodie looked down. The extent of Tate's wounds was seared in her brain.

Emma again sounded regretful. "I don't need to tell you that either, though, do I? We were there together, you and me, day after day, hour after hour." Her throat tightened. "I thought we were through the worst of it when he finally was moved out of intensive care. I never expected Tate to just— He's quit, hasn't he? Just gone and…quit." Her gaze moved over her daughter-in-law's tense body. "This has to be agony for you. You bein' so worried, and him bein' so—" she searched for an appropriate word "—so sick. Then for him to say what he did to you!"

Jodie glanced instinctively in the direction of the low male voices coming from the other room. She wanted to confide in Emma about the plan she and Mae had devised, but she couldn't take the chance that Tate might overhear. She wondered if she should tell her about the baby. Maybe knowing of the pregnancy would help the other woman hold on. But that, too, was something she couldn't take a chance on. Not here, not now.

"Maybe we should go back?" she suggested, and motioned to the readied serving tray.

"You're right," Emma said. "Jack's probably had all the time he needs. He came up with an idea to get Tate movin' again. At least, to get his mind on somethin' more than his problems. It's a case no one could work anythin' out about. Jack thought it might tweak Tate's interest. I guess it's worth a try."

Jodie nodded as she added the percolator to the tray. The two women then rejoined the men in the bedroom.

EMMA AND JACK'S VISIT lasted for the better part of an hour. When Tate drifted into sleep, they quietly filed out of the room. After a short exchange of supportive words, Jodie walked with them to Jack's patrol car, so poignantly familiar because it used to be Tate's.

"He's gonna be fine," Jack stated firmly,

settling behind the wheel once he'd helped Emma inside. "I've seen this kinda thing happen before. Main object is to keep him busy. Don't let him have time to feel sorry for himself."

"He still hurts a lot, Jack," Jodie pointed out, defending Tate loyally.

"I know that. I know the boy, too. He needs somethin' to chew on. That's why I brought along that old case—did Emma tell ya? Maybe he can get a handle on somethin'."

Jodie smiled, murmured agreement and, stepping back, waved them off.

As the patrol car pulled away, Emma still looked worried.

SOMEONE CALLED Jodie's name as she turned to go back inside. When she looked around, she saw Shannon striding toward her across the courtyard. No trace remained of the limp the other woman had once sustained, not even the slightest hitch.

If ever there was a person who could offer hope for Tate's eventual recovery, it was Shannon. Jodie had been nearing eighteen when Shannon arrived at the ranch. None of the family had known her except Mae, who'd met her only once, briefly, as a child. Mae knew her father, though—Nathan Bradley, a high-up in the opposition political party Mae occasionally butted heads with. Following the crash of the light aircraft that had killed all on board except Shannon—including Shannon's father and her fiancé—Mae, in her usual imperious way, had insisted that she recuperate at the Parker Ranch. Of course Mae had had an underlying plan. To her mind, Rafe needed a wife, and she was out to get him one.

Both Mae's plots had worked, much to the good of the family and to Shannon. Rafe, in spite of his stubborn determination not to, had fallen in love with the frail young woman, and she had found her strength again and the will to live.

When Shannon drew close, Jodie reacted to her hug with a little more enthusiasm than the moment called for. She'd seen her yesterday, after all.

Shannon's blue eyes held concern as she drew back. "I saw Emma and Jack leaving. Is everything all right?"

Jodie pushed a fall of hair away from her face and tried to smile. She'd been through a lot that morning, had too many ups and downs. "I— Everything's fine. As fine as can be expected, I suppose."

"Is Tate still up?" Shannon asked.

"He's asleep…the company—"

"Wore him out. I know. It doesn't take much when you're convalescing." She nodded toward Harriet's house. "I was on my way over for a little girl-chat. You want to come along?"

Jodie considered the prospect of returning to the house and sitting quietly so as not to disturb Tate's rest. She nodded in agreement. "I'll just be a minute. I want to leave Tate a note so he won't wonder." As if he would. But she'd feel better having left one.

The two women parted company and a few minutes later Jodie tapped on Harriet's back door. Shannon was already seated at the long country-style table, which stood opposite the nicely appointed food preparation area. Harriet was putting the finishing touches on something she was about to pop into the oven. Harriet loved to cook and loved to have people around, and her kitchen reflected it. The room was large and open, obviously the heart of the house. Jodie remembered many a warm exchange that had taken place here.

Harriet smiled a welcome. "Make yourself comfortable. I just put the kettle on and as soon as these calzones bake, we can dig in. You haven't had lunch yet, have you?"

Jodie shook her head and settled into one of the comfortably padded captain's chairs.

After setting the timer, Harriet joined them at the table. "Did you say the boys are over at Little Springs?" she asked Shannon.

Shannon grinned. "Christine called and invited them. I told her I wasn't so sure she'd want Ward and Nate as influences on little Elisabeth, but she said they'd be fine. She worries about Elisabeth not being around other kids enough," Shannon explained in an aside to Jodie. "She even told them they could bring Junior." Junior was the yellow Labrador mix that had been a part of Rafe and Shannon's family since shortly after his namesake, Shep, had died at the great age of nineteen. "Shep, Jr." was the name the children had given the new puppy. Over time, it had been shortened to Junior.

"She's obviously a glutton for punishment," Harriet teased, winking at Jodie.

"So I have a free afternoon!" Shannon said.

"We're honored you're spending some of it with us."

"Well, honestly, I wouldn't be if Rafe could've gotten a little time off. But he couldn't, so—"

"Eight years and two boys later and the two of you are still actin' like newlyweds," Harriet teased, shaking her head.

"Maybe one of these days we'll get lucky and have a little girl for Elisabeth to play with," Shannon said cheerfully. "Someone to dress in bows and frills and have girl-talks with when she gets older."

Harriet laughed. "You hope! I had my one chance with Gwen. She's always liked girly things. But Anna…I've given up!"

"I think Rafe would like a baby girl," Shannon said, smiling softly to herself.

The kettle whistled and Harriet went to pour the hot water into the coffee press. A short time later she passed around steaming mugs, saying, "Since Anna started school, LeRoy's made some noises about us having another baby, but at least this time Mae hasn't said anything, thank goodness. Last time I wasn't sure that she didn't have as much to do with me gettin' pregnant as LeRoy did! And I resented it."

"I remember," Shannon murmured.

Jodie felt their surreptitious glances. They were carrying the conversation, waiting for her to feel relaxed enough to join them. But what could she say? The talk was about making babies.

She cleared her throat. "I imagine Elisabeth has grown a lot," she managed to say.

"Like a weed!" Harriet exclaimed. "She's the cutest little thing. All that golden-blond hair, just like Morgan's. Dub and Delores are crazy about her. So's Erin."

"Erin's really bloomed," Shannon said. "She's still quiet and shy and acts much more mature than her age—you'd think she was in her twenties already, instead of just sixteen. She's been an 'old soul' since she was born, Christine says. But she's— It's like she's finally let herself believe she's a part of the family. That no one's going to come along tomorrow and take it all away from her. It helped when Christine married Morgan, and when Morgan formally adopted her. But it was Elisabeth's birth that finally set things right."

"It was all that post-to-pillar living she did when Erin was small," Harriet said. "Christine was doing her absolute best, but it wasn't until they came here—"

"Erin was what then…eight?" Shannon asked.

Harriet nodded. "One year older than Anna is now. Hard to believe, huh?"

"I'll say." Shannon glanced at Jodie, who still hadn't managed to relax. Harriet did, too. Then the two women looked at each other and exchanged a silent message.

"Jodie," Harriet said after drawing a deep breath. "We want to know what we can do to help. We know you need it, so don't pretend you don't."

"That's right," Shannon said quietly. "We're the people you should call on. We're your family."

"Yeah, like, where's Tate at?" Harriet asked. "His physical condition, I mean."

Jodie shrugged. "He's doing as well as can be expected, I suppose. His wounds have... healed. His doctor cleared him for the trip out here—he saw him last Friday."

"He doesn't seem to be very strong, considering." Harriet said.

Jodie shook her head. "No."

"But he can get stronger," Shannon murmured.

"Only if he wants to."

"And he doesn't want to," Harriet surmised astutely.

Jodie's nod was anguished.

Shannon said, "Getting well is a battle of the mind as much as of the body. When he starts to feel better—"

Jodie clasped her hands. "That's what everyone says!"

"And it doesn't help," Harriet said.

"Not when I see him. Not when I made him come here because I was afraid he was going to *die* in Austin! I didn't know what to do. How to stop it. How to make him—" She halted her near-hysterical rush of words and took a breath. "I'm afraid. Afraid of what's going to happen tomorrow. I never used to be, but I am now. And I'm not the only one who feels this way. Emma does, too. When she saw Tate today, it made her afraid."

Shannon placed a hand over hers on the table. "We won't let that happen, Jodie," she said firmly.

"There's nothing anyone can do!" Jodie moaned.

"You must have thought someone could," Harriet countered. "Otherwise, why would you have brought him to the ranch? It's not his home. It's *yours*."

Unshed tears made it impossible for Jodie to speak.

"Jodie, what did Mae say this morning?" Shannon asked. "Did she have a plan?"

"She—she's sending Axel over to give Tate massages."

"That's good. My father tried to schedule one every day, particularly during a heated campaign. He'd be exhausted and tense, and afterward, he felt much better."

"Anything else?" Harriet asked curiously, referring back to Mae.

Jodie hesitated, remembering her great-aunt's challenge—*What about the family? Are you going to tell them or wait until word leaks out?* Or words to that effect. "Tate's asked me to end our marriage," she said quietly. "He wants a divorce. That was the only way he'd agree to come here. I said…yes."

Her words were met with stunned silence. Once again, she'd shocked her listeners.

"Will you go through with it?" Harriet asked. The oven timer buzzed, but she ignored it.

"I'll do anything as long as it helps him get better."

"But you just said—" Shannon started, and stopped.

"I'll take that chance! I have to do something."

"Mae has an idea about that, too, doesn't she?" Harriet guessed, at last getting up to see to the buzzer.

Jodie nodded.

"Then do it," Harriet advised. "Whatever *it* is. As much as I hate to admit this, Mae has some really good instincts. She'll do anything to protect this family. Especially you, Jodie. You're her soft spot."

Jodie hesitated. "You won't say anything outside the family, will you? And nothing to anyone about Mae's plan. Tate can't— I don't want him to hear a thing. Otherwise—"

"Mum's the word." Harriet pressed a fingertip to her lips.

"There's a plan?" Shannon questioned facetiously.

As they'd been talking, a wonderful aroma filled the kitchen. When Harriet took the savory-filled Italian turnovers from the oven and slid them onto a plate that she then brought to the table, the wondrous smell increased. Even Jodie experienced a stirring of hunger.

Now that she'd shared her burden she no longer felt so alone. Even if it was only for the moment, she had confidence that everything would work out to the good.

Harriet slid plates and forks into place for each of them and distributed paper napkins. The napkins had some kind of cartoon animals printed on them. "All I have left at the moment, ladies," she explained.

Shannon held up hers. "My favorite!" she teased. "I have some just like these at home."

Harriet grinned, then said in an aside to Jodie, "Don't laugh. Just wait until you and Tate have kids. And you will. I have all kinds of faith in that. One day you'll look back at this time and wonder how it ever could've seemed so bad." She paused. "I guess what I'm tryin' to say is, you and Tate were meant for each other. And nothing, not him gettin' shot, not the troubles you're goin' through now, can change that."

"I always knew you were a closet romantic, Harriet," Shannon said fondly. "And I agree, Jodie. I know it sounds trite to say that Tate will look on things differently when he feels better, but he will. I know. I've been there. All we have to do is get him to feel better as quickly as we can. Get him outside, sit him in the fresh air and sunshine, encourage him to go for little walks." She laughed lightly. "Even get him up on a horse. That's what everyone kept urging me to do. As if that would fix everything. Funny thing was, though, it did help." She grew more serious. "And another thing—he may look breakable, but don't treat him that way. I didn't get any concessions from Rafe for being convalescent. He irritated the heck out of me from the first time we talked...and I think I got better just to show him I could."

"Okay! Now that that's settled," Harriet said positively, "let's dig in before our feast gets cold!"

Shannon laughed and took a bite of calzone, only to widen her eyes and waggle her hand in front of her mouth.

"It's not cold yet?" Harriet murmured.

For the first time since last September, Jodie enjoyed a good laugh as Shannon shook a playful fist at their hostess.

CHAPTER FIVE

TATE SPENT another restless night. He could find comfort in no position. His side hurt, his middle hurt, his shoulder hurt. He would've gone into the bathroom and stood in the shower to let the hot spray ease some of his misery, but he didn't want to wake Jodie. He knew from past experience that as soon as she heard him up, she would come to check. Anyway, he probably couldn't remain standing long enough to do that much good. What he needed was one of those shower seats he'd used in his latter days at the intermediate-care facility. He'd hated having to use one, but it was better than a bed bath, though not by much. Both were indignities he'd never thought he'd suffer at his age.

As muscles protested and nerve endings continued to sing off-key, he lay there, waiting. For the night to be over? For the pain to ease? For the Grim Reaper to put in another appearance?

He smiled sardonically. Whatever bargains he'd struck with that entity while his life had hung in the balance must have been solid, because he couldn't seem to go back on them. No matter how much he might want to.

What use was he to anyone? As always, the question begged an answer. *Not much!* came the reply. Again…as always.

He'd wanted to work in law enforcement his entire life. It was all he'd known since his earliest days. He'd spent most of his free time as a young boy in the Briggs County Sheriff's Office, hanging around with his father, with Jack, and the other deputies while his mother handled communications. When he'd gone off to college, naturally he'd taken courses in law enforcement. Then he'd moved on to street patrol in Dallas, doing all the hard physical labor of chasing down miscreants. His mother's battle with diabetes had brought him back to Del Norte—literally, to wear his father's badge. It was an old-fashioned five-pointed Texas star, which he'd continued to wear as sheriff. He still had it…put away. After that he'd joined the task force.

Tate groaned, careful to keep the sound

light so it would remain in the room. Despite all the soul-searching he'd engaged in at the time about the best thing for him to do, he now wondered if it had been a mistake to go to Austin. His father would've stayed here, loyal to the community in Briggs County to the end, but he wasn't his father. Even his mother had encouraged him to accept the opportunity if it was what he truly wanted. And Jodie—

Jodie.

She meant more to him than anything.

Memories played in his mind. His and Jodie's closeness, their love—he'd thought himself the luckiest man in the world. And now?

Well, Eden always has its snake, just as heaven has its hell. The day arrived when their life together was shattered, and their happiness came to an abrupt end.

A muscle tightened in Tate's midsection, creating another spasm. He instinctively curled onto his good side and held his arms tight against him. Once again, he waited.

Why hadn't he or his fellow investigator, Billy Vance, sensed what lay ahead? Cumulatively, they'd had over thirty years' experience. Yet how could they have known? They were targeting a big-time fencing operation that had been active in the state for several years. The perpetrators had managed to escape arrest because they were careful not to use guns or violence. They bought and sold their stolen goods with seemingly appropriate paperwork and pretended to be normal businessmen. He and Billy had been working a weasel of an accomplice who, for his own reasons, was ready to talk. They'd arranged to meet him in an auto-wrecking yard on the outskirts of a small town in Hays County. They'd just arrived at the appointed spot and were waiting for the weasel to show...when all hell broke loose.

Either someone from the fencing operation had learned of the meeting and decided to put a stop to it, or the weasel had ticked off someone in one of his numerous other "enterprises" and that person, having decided to play rough, had mistaken him or Billy for the weasel.

In the melee the weasel escaped—Billy had seen him scurrying away as he himself dived for cover. Tate, hit first in the shoulder, had been spun around to present an even better target to the assailants.

He'd remained conscious for a long time after crumpling to the ground. Heard Billy yell his name as Billy returned fire. Then all had gone quiet. Billy had rushed over to see how badly he was hit, then he'd fumbled in his pocket for his cell phone to call for help.

Tate remembered wondering if his father had felt the same way after being shot. The sudden numbness. The unreality. Then pain had swept through him like an out-of-control inferno, and he found it difficult to breathe.

In his last few seconds of consciousness, he'd thought of Jodie, of his mother, of Jack. After that…nothing. He had no memory of the next two weeks. When his recollections started up again, they were floaty. He seemed to drift in and out of a dream—or nightmare—filled with grimly serious strangers. Except he saw Jodie, and his mother, even Jack once. Mostly he remembered Jodie—her sweetly beautiful face hovering close, her jewel-like yellow-green eyes glittering with moisture, while her copper-red hair was bright like the sun against her pale skin. She'd always seemed to be there.

He drew a deeper breath as the muscle spasm subsided.

Their marriage had been a gamble from the first. In every sense, they came from different worlds. He was "town"; she was "ranch."

The only family he and his mother had to rely on were each other; Jodie was a member of the wealthy and influential Parker clan. He'd worked constantly after his father's death to help his mother and himself survive; Jodie had always been cared for and protected. A status he'd vowed to maintain. A vow he could no longer honor.

Like all the Parkers, she was loyal and stubbornly determined to keep her word. But the playing field had changed radically. A gunman's bullets had seen to that.

He had to set her free. She shouldn't be tied to a cripple by an overactive sense of obligation.

He had no idea what the future would hold. If he'd ever be well enough to function normally, much less go back to law enforcement.

He was doing her a favor by bowing out of her life.

The only positive in the situation was that they had yet to start the family they'd talked about.

A chill passed over him at the thought.

DAWN BROKE AT LAST. Tate heard when Jodie got up, showered and went back to the second bedroom to dress.

He forced himself to get up, as well. Forced himself into the bathroom. Forced himself through his agonizingly slow morning routine.

The hot shower felt good on his tense and aching muscles, but not as good as he'd hoped. Discomfort had become a fact of life, pain something to measure in degrees. He changed into fresh pajamas and started back to the bedroom, exhausted from his effort. But he heard Jodie in the kitchen and was drawn to her, even though he knew he should resist the contact.

She hummed as she prepared coffee and toast and set up his tray. She wore faded jeans and a short T-shirt. Her flame of hair was caught away from her face, a face that bore no makeup and needed none. Even from the doorway he could breathe her fresh sweet scent.

He'd always thought of her as an exotic flower, unique among her surroundings. With her gamine looks, she was like none of the other Parkers, who were all so strikingly similar—black hair, black eyes, strong chiseled features. He'd seen a drawing of her mother, the woman who'd walked away from her in infanthood, and the resemblance between them was amazing. Her mother, too, had been exotic. Only, that was as far as their similarities went. In character, Jodie was a Parker, even if she'd spent much of her life fighting the label.

He remembered her in her younger years—feisty, fiery, determined to have her way. He remembered when he'd come close to tossing her off the school bus for behaving like a brat. She'd been twelve or so and he'd been working to pay for his first semester at college. It was a moment anchored in her memory, as well. They'd laughed about it years later when she'd confessed that at the time, she'd had a crush on him and acted up only to attract his attention.

Tate turned away, his recollections of both distant and near past causing him too much pain.

She must have sensed his presence, though, and still smiling from her private thoughts, she glanced around to say, "Tate?"

Tate stopped. Everything inside him urged him to go to her, to drink in her essence, as if time and trouble had never interrupted their lives....

"I was going to bring breakfast to you," she said. "But if you like, we can eat in here."

Tate maintained his grip on the door frame, holding himself in place. "The bedroom's fine," he said gruffly. He knew that the answer excluded her. It *had* to exclude her! He turned away again, but again she stopped him.

"I'm going into Del Norte today—" her voice had changed, lost its sunny inflection "—to talk to Mr. Fowler. To ask his help in getting things started."

Ned Fowler was one of the county's two attorneys. The second was Ned's daughter, Nicole. "All right," Tate agreed.

"He's the family's lawyer."

"I don't care who does it," he said tightly.

"This could take some time, you realize," she cautioned. "I don't know the rules or regulations, but there has to be some sort of waiting period."

"I don't have anything else to do."

Her expression grew more miserable, presenting further proof to Tate that dealing with him was damaging her. The sooner she got away from him the better.

"Would you like someone to come stay with you while I'm in town?" she asked. "Harriet or Shannon, or even Aunt Mae. I'm sure any one of them would be glad to."

"I'm not a baby," he said coldly.

"I didn't imply that you were."

"Just...leave it, okay? And just leave me. I'll be all right."

"There's more of Marie's stew in the refrigerator if you want it for lunch."

"I doubt I'll be hungry."

Tate's conscience pricked him, but he held firm. The deed had to be done.

"I'll—I'll let you know before I leave. Then maybe when I get back, we can sit out on the front porch? I don't know if you saw them or not, but there are a couple of chairs. Or, if you want, you can sit there by yourself. I'll find other things to do."

Tate shrugged, and this time finally managed to break away.

The return walk down the hall was harder for him now that his muscles had stiffened. He shuffled slowly to the bedroom, like an old man, then closed himself in. The bed, his ultimate destination, seemed a long way off, but he made himself start toward it.

Would anyone watching him believe that he was only thirty-three?

JUST AS SHE'D PROMISED, Jodie stopped by to tell Tate that she was on her way into town—she was borrowing the Cadillac from Mae, she said—then she asked if he wanted anything from the stores.

Tate, who normally was so good at reading people, couldn't read her. He'd never been able to. All he could do was note the obvious—a slight hesitation to meet his eyes, and she seemed a little jumpier than usual. She was dressed more conservatively, in a skirt and blouse, with her hair brushed down over her shoulders. She looked beautiful.

"I wish you'd come with me," she said, yet her tone acknowledged the uselessness of her plea. "Daddy said everyone in town has been asking about you. If you'd like, we could—"

"I'll be here when you get back," Tate cut in coolly.

"Some of them might want to drop by to say hello."

"Tell them I'm not ready yet."

"Some of the deputies—"

"You heard what I said."

She'd been about to add something, but stopped herself. Then she left.

Tate glanced at the small television set his father-in-law had brought over the evening before. Gib had hooked it up at a comfortable angle from the bed, slid a DVD in the player and Tate had seen his first movie in months.

He hadn't wanted to watch anything, or read anything, or be entertained in any way. But Gib had pulled up a chair and watched the old movie with him, laughing at the antics of Danny Kaye as he and a merry band of Sherwood Forest types went to rescue a baby from the clutches of a greedy king.

Before leaving, Gib had pulled more DVDs out of a bag and stacked them by the television. He'd even loaded another one for Tate's use later. Tate had ignored it, until now. After pushing some buttons on the remote, the screen flickered to life, and Laurel and Hardy began hatching another of their impossible schemes.

Tate was just getting involved in the story when someone knocked on the front door. The door opened and a distinctive thin voice called out, "Hey, Tate? You in there? Sing out if ya are!"

Tate struggled to sit up. "In here!" he called, grimacing.

Axel Douglas's imposing form soon filled the bedroom. He carried what looked to be a folding table under one arm. "Mae sent me," he announced. He noticed the TV. "Ah, Laurel and Hardy! You musta got that from Gib, right? He loves those old comedies."

Tate switched off the movie. "Can I help you?" he asked. Not exactly friendly, but not unfriendly, either.

Axel swung the table around and unfolded the legs. When set up, the top was long and padded, with a head extension. "I'm ready when you are," he said confidently. "I thought we'd start kinda slow and easy, just to let ya relax. Then maybe in a few days, we'll move a little closer to the real thing."

"You're here to give me a massage?" Tate asked.

"Yep, didn't anybody tell ya?"

"Not a word."

"Ah...well, then...I guess I just did."

Tate smiled grimly. "I don't want a massage."

"You're hurtin', ain't ya? I can see it in your face."

"Axel—"

"Mae said I was to give ya one," he maintained stubbornly.

"Mae's wrong."

Axel's round face broke into a grin. "Better you say that than me."

"Why? Because she won't hit a helpless man?" Tate challenged sourly.

"Nope. You're family. Family's the only

ones that can get away with sayin' somethin' like that."

"You're family, too, or so Jodie's always said."

"Honorary family's not the same as the real thing." He patted the cushioned table with a broad hand. "C'mon. I'm gonna hav'ta get back out to the cookhouse to check on things shortly."

"What good is this gonna do?" Tate demanded. "All the therapy in the world can't put me back like I was. So what's the use?"

"This ain't therapy. Not like what those doctors was probably doin' to ya. This is more... relaxation. You just lay there and I do all the work. I guarantee you won't hurt as much after."

Tate had never had a formal massage in his life. He'd never seen the need. Rubdowns, yes. In high school, after a football game. "I don't know," he hedged.

Axel grinned. "Just give it a try. I'm not gonna charge you."

Tate cocked his head. "The only way I'm gonna get rid of you is to do this, right?"

"Mae gave me my marchin' orders," Axel maintained.

Tate swung his feet to the floor and stood

up. He moved forward creakily under Axel's watchful eye, but the camp cook didn't try to help him—at least, not until he got to the table.

"I brought a sheet," Axel murmured, assisting him up. "It's best if you take off your shirt. Actually, it's best if you take everythin' off, but that's up to you."

"Just the shirt'll do," Tate said tersely. It was enough to reveal his scars. He peeled off the pajama top and waited for Axel's comment.

The other man gave a low whistle. "No wonder you're hurtin'," he said ruefully. "You eat anythin' lately? It's best if you haven't."

"Not since breakfast, and that wasn't much."

"That'll do."

Axel helped him stretch out on the table on his stomach. It felt odd at first, uncomfortable. The injured muscles and scar tissue, both in front and in back, protested.

Then Axel started to work. After rubbing a little oil between his hands, he smoothed them down either side of Tate's spine, moving lightly yet firmly, before going up again along his sides to his shoulders and neck. He repeated this action several times, using long strokes, careful of the still-angry remnants of Tate's wounds.

Tate was tense at first, until he discovered that he felt almost no pain. Axel's strong, educated hands worked his flesh like magic. Axel began to push gently with the heel of his hand and to pull back with his fingers in a lifting and scooping motion that he alternated from hand to hand. At the top of Tate's shoulders, even the injured one, he carefully repeated the movements on the thick muscles, before moving down his back again.

Axel never said a word, intent only on his job.

Tate started to lose reality. He dozed; he drifted. Time passed in a haze.

Axel woke him gently. "I gotta get back to the cookhouse, but whatcha think? You want me to come back tomorrow?"

A moment passed before Tate could speak.

Axel grinned in the silence and said, "How about this same time? One o'clock?"

"Sure," Tate agreed, sitting up. With assistance, he stood. The areas of his body that Axel had worked felt warm, soothed. And when Tate moved toward the bed, he found his muscles loose in the way they were after a shower.

Axel handed him his pajama shirt, which he put on prior to stretching out. He watched as the other man folded the table and tucked it under his arm.

"Hey, Axel," he said as the camp cook turned to leave. "Thanks."

Axel smiled and shrugged, and a few seconds later Tate heard the front door close.

For a time he lay there, enjoying a pleasant peacefulness. He moved his arms, rocked his head and lifted his shoulders, all without the usual accompanying aches. Then he drew a deep breath and closed his eyes, and almost immediately he fell asleep.

JODIE'S RELUCTANCE to do what she'd planned made the long drive into Del Norte feel even longer. She'd contacted Ned Fowler, arranged an appointment and set off on her way—all with a sense of dread. As she passed through the outskirts of town and into the town proper, her apprehension increased.

To her eyes, Del Norte never changed. With a fairly steady population of twelve hundred, it was Briggs County's largest settlement. Two other towns appeared on the county map, but they were so small they were little more than outposts.

Del Norte was the hub for residents of the surrounding ranch land. It was where they found schools, a small hospital, a car dealership, a motel, a hardware store–lumberyard and numerous other small businesses that catered to their needs. The town also had its own small police force, separate from the sheriff and his four deputies, who protected the rest of the county's six thousand square miles. Because Del Norte was the Briggs County seat, the courthouse, the sheriff's department and the jail were located there. Which, in turn, brought lawyers.

Jodie parked the Cadillac in a slot across from the courthouse and directly in front of a brick-faced building that might have come from another era. The entire downtown was more reflective of the 1930s or 1940s than the new millennium. A discreet sign on the door announced the offices of Fowler and Fowler, Attorneys-at-Law.

Jodie had been in this building only once before, and that was years ago when she'd accompanied Rafe into town on business. They'd stayed for barely fifteen minutes, but Ned Fowler had made a lasting impression on her as a man who could be trusted. If she'd been alone at the time, she might even have confided to him her growing teenage discomfort at being a Parker, with all that entailed. Maybe if she'd talked to him she could have avoided future embarrassments. But then, every mistake she'd made in the process of growing up had pointed her toward Tate and allowed her to appreciate him even more.

The secretary looked up, smiled in recognition and murmured for Jodie to go through the closed door and into the office on the left.

That room was crowded with cabinets and tables, all groaning under the weight of numerous stacks of legal papers. Multiple bookcases, which nearly obliterated the walls, were packed top to bottom with law books and references. The contents almost overshadowed the man at work behind the desk.

Ned Fowler rose to greet her. "Jodie Parker!" he said in a sincere, friendly way, coming around the desk to take her hand. "It's been years and years. What brings you to Del Norte, Jodie? And to see me? I have to say… I've been intrigued since getting your call."

Ned was a relatively small man—Jodie was several inches taller than he was—in his sixties, with fine brown hair, a kind face and the same world-weary look that she remembered.

After seeing her into a chair, he returned to his cubbyhole behind the desk.

"Actually," Jodie said "it's Connelly, Jodie Connelly. I'm married to Tate, remember?"

"Of course," he said, his smile quickly fading. "How is Tate? We've all heard that you've come back to the ranch."

"He's why I'm here," she said tightly.

He gave her a penetrating look. "Maybe we should get you a little refreshment. I'll ask Renee to—"

"No, I'm fine, thanks. I'd just as soon—"

The door behind Jodie opened and a pretty, young woman in her late twenties, with fine dark hair and large blue eyes, leaned into the room. "Before you get started— Oh, I'm sorry. You have already. Dad, I apologize. To you, too, Jodie. I didn't mean—"

Ned smiled tolerantly. "By the time you get through apologizing, you'll have had time to say whatever it was you wanted two or three times over."

Nicole Fowler was the second member of Fowler and Fowler, Attorneys-at-Law. She, too, was delicately made, but showed none of her father's world-weariness. "I just wanted to ask Jodie if Tate might like to have a few visitors. People have been wondering, and I'd love to see him myself." She grinned. "Catch him up on the latest shenanigans of some of our favorite ne'er-do-wells."

"I—"

"Not for very long," Nicole assured her. "And not all at once. Just now and again, one or two of us could stop by. We wouldn't even have to talk shop."

"Tate's not— He—" Jodie didn't know what to say. The young lawyer hadn't settled in Del Norte until after she'd passed the bar exam some five years earlier. She'd been raised elsewhere by her divorced mother, and had rarely come to visit her father. Tate had had numerous dealings with her in his work and had spoken highly of her, but Jodie didn't know her very well.

"Or not. Whatever you think best." Nicole had been quick to sense Jodie's unease.

"Maybe we could give it just a little more time?" Jodie murmured. "Tate's not ready yet."

Nicole frowned. "It frightens me when I think about what happened to him. It frightens everyone." She glanced at her father for confirmation.

As he nodded, Nicole said, "Tell Tate we're pulling for him," then she closed herself out of the room.

"Have you changed your mind about that refreshment?" Ned asked quietly.

Jodie shook her head.

Ned shifted into a comfortable position, not about to hurry her.

Jodie looked down at her hands. She was clasping them so tightly that the knuckles were pale. Finally, she looked up. "I've come to ask about a divorce. Not a real one. I just want the papers to show Tate."

"Not a real one," Ned repeated, surprised.

"The only way I could get Tate to come back to the ranch was if I agreed to file for divorce. So that's what I'm doing. Aunt Mae and I thought—"

"Mae's in on this?"

"Yes."

"I'm amazed she didn't tell me herself."

"I asked her not to. I thought— Well, we thought that I could pretend to get the paperwork started but not go through with it. Not file anything. Just let Tate think I had."

"I'm not so sure I can do that." When Jodie blinked, Ned explained, "Ethically, I mean."

Jodie's hands tightened even more as a mild

panic set in. What would she do if— What would *Tate* do if—

"Would you like to tell me what's going on?" Ned requested, cutting into her thoughts. "Why doesn't Tate file the petition himself if he's the one who wants a divorce? Why send you? What do *you* want?" He smiled kindly. "As you can see, I'm confused."

Jodie stood up. The office was small and starting to feel smaller. She needed to move around. She walked the few paces to a credenza and retrieved a small hand stapler left on top of a stack of papers. Then, unsure what to do next, she brought it to Ned's desk and sat down.

"I don't want a divorce," she replied bleakly. "I don't want anything to do with one. This is Tate's idea. He thinks I should be set free. Because he—he's not doing very well, Mr. Fowler. In fact, Emma and I are worried that he—" Her chin quivered before she could control it. "There's more than one way for a person to die. It doesn't always take a violent act."

"Are you saying Tate wants to die?" Ned asked incredulously.

"He would if he could. If he can't, he'll settle for sending me away."

"He needs to see a counselor."

"He won't talk to one."

"A minister."

"Same thing." She looked at him pleadingly "Our only hope is that he'll soon start to feel better. And that if he does, he'll let go of this crazy idea. He thinks of himself as a cripple now."

"Has Jack seen him?"

"Like everyone else, Jack says he needs some time." She paused. "That's what I'm trying to do…buy time. If he sees the filled-out forms, sees that I'm keeping my word, then maybe he'll relax and quit being so—" She stopped. No matter how trustworthy the lawyer might be, no matter how long he'd worked for the family, she couldn't bring herself to be disloyal to Tate. She wouldn't complain about him. Not in this instance or in any other.

Ned looked at her consideringly. "I thought Tate was doing a great deal better. That's too bad. He's a good man." He reflected some more, then pulled a legal pad out of a desk drawer and opened a pen. "All right," he said. "What we'll do is get things started. We'll fill out the complaint all legal and proper, but, as you suggested, nothing in law says we have to file it. We'd have to send it to the courthouse in Austin, anyway, since you're both residents of Travis County. You do still list Austin as your legal residence, don't you?"

Jodie swallowed. She'd just thought about not complaining, then the lawyer had used the word in a legal context. "Yes. Yes, we do," she said quickly. "At least, that's where our apartment is."

"Are you registered to vote there?"

"Yes."

"Okay, so we fill this out, just as if it's going to go through the process. Then we sit on it. Let Tate get back to a better frame of mind, regain his equilibrium, so to speak, along with his health." He smiled at Jodie. "Then we'll see what's what. Nothing wrong with that."

"Will I get a copy to show him?"

"I'll make sure you do." Ned looked at her from under his eyebrows. "There are no children from this union, I presume."

Jodie panicked again. What should she say? "Ah—no. No children." In her mind she added, *Not yet!*

The lawyer stared at her long and hard because of her hesitation. Instead of ducking her chin and looking away, as she was wont to do lately, Jodie held her head high and returned his study. *That* was something she was not going to confide, either.

"All right, then," he agreed at last. "Let's get started. I'll have Renee type up the paperwork and you can have an extra copy to take home to Tate. Will that do?"

"It'll do nicely," Jodie answered, and for the first time since her world had been thrown so far off center, she felt a little more like her old self.

CHAPTER SIX

JODIE LEFT the law firm with her copy of the divorce petition folded neatly in an envelope. Just outside the front door she stuffed the envelope in her purse, hoping that out of sight, out of mind would lessen the impact of what she'd just done. Even though the petition was based on pretense, the words were still there on the page.

She restarted the Cadillac and reversed out of the parking slot, but instead of heading straight back to the ranch, she turned the car in another direction. She had one more errand to perform: she had to talk to Emma.

Her mother-in-law wasn't at home when Jodie stopped by the small two-bedroom house where Tate had grown up, so she continued to the sheriff's office.

Like the town, little about the place had changed since before the Second World War.

The walls were painted an institutional green; the lighting was a weak fluorescent. In the reception area an ill-used couch and a long wooden bench provided seating, while in a far corner a scarred table was set up as a self-serve coffee bar.

A deputy, dressed in the Briggs County uniform of long-sleeved tan shirt, tan pants and dark brown tie, stood at the table, filling a mug from an ancient aluminum multicup coffeemaker. When he glanced up and saw Jodie, he grinned.

"I heard y'all were back," he drawled. Then, in a change in expression that Jodie was fast becoming used to, his grin shifted into a concerned frown. "How's Tate doin'?" he asked.

"He's working at getting well," she lied. What else could she say?

"All right!" the deputy said approvingly, his grin returning.

"A call for you, Bob," Emma Connelly said from the doorway of the dispatch room.

The deputy waved an acknowledgment, dipped his head politely to Jodie, then disappeared down the hall, carrying his cup.

Jodie's gaze followed him. She'd never noticed that Bob Stewart and Tate were so physically similar. Both were long and lean; both moved with fluid ease. In uniform, Bob might have been Tate...Tate as he once was. A yearning for the past swelled in Jodie's chest. She drew a constricted breath.

Emma placed an arm across her shoulders. "Were you comin' to see me?" she asked. "We can't talk here. The phones have been ringin' off the hook all mornin'. I'll see if Rose can cover for me." She consulted the short woman seated behind a glass partition. "It's okay," Emma said on returning. "She will. C'mon, let's go."

Once they were seated in a small café down the street, Jodie apologized, "I'm sorry. I just didn't expect—it was the uniform and the way Bob—"

"He's given me a turn or two, as well," Emma confessed. "I never saw the resemblance before. Bob's always been Bob. It's from the back that he looks the most like Tate. You'd never mistake them head-on."

"No." Jodie sniffed, and controlled her emotions.

"How's Tate doin' today? I thought I'd wait until later this evenin' to call him."

"He's the same. My dad brought some old movies over last night and they watched one, but this morning—" She shrugged and repeated, "The same."

"Has he looked at the case Jack gave him?"

"Not that I know of."

There was a pause, then Emma murmured, "You two aren't sharin' the same bed, are you?"

Jodie froze. She didn't want to answer. The truth was too personal, too hurtful. But it couldn't be escaped. "No," she said quietly. "We're not."

Emma sighed. "I thought not. It didn't make sense that he'd ask you to get a divorce and still— Tate's not like that. Once he makes up his mind, he sees things through."

Jodie remained silent for so long that Emma said in a concerned voice, "What is it? What's happened? Why are you in town?"

"I had an appointment with Ned Fowler. We filled out the paperwork for the divorce. I have a copy…in here." She patted her purse.

Emma looked at the purse as though it contained a hornet's nest.

Jodie went on. "That's what I need to talk to you about. I did what Tate asked, and I'm bringing him a copy to prove it. But the petition won't be filed. Ned's going to hold it. If

Tate asks—*when* Tate asks—why it's taking so long, I'll make up an excuse. And I'll keep making excuses until he gets better."

"You'll lie to him?" Emma said.

"If I have to."

Suddenly Emma looked years older, the weight of worry sagging her skin and drawing down her features. "I'd do the same," she conceded sadly. "I'll *do* the same. Whatever it takes. Just tell me what you want me to say."

Jodie again debated telling Emma about the baby. There was no reason for anyone besides Mae and herself to know until after she started to show, and that wouldn't be for another month, possibly two. Even then she could camouflage her thickening waist and bulging tummy to gain a little more time. *Don't tell anyone!* a part of her mind warned, echoing Mae's admonition about a secret once told. She also had to consider the real possibility that once Emma knew, she'd tell Tate, thinking the news might save him. Yet, witnessing her mother-in-law's deepening despair, Jodie realized she couldn't continue to keep her in the dark.

"Emma," she said, leaning forward. "There's something I—"

The waitress arrived with their soft drinks, and as she was serving them, Jack ambled up to their table.

"I thought I recognized that old black Caddie out in the parkin' lot. Then Rose told me you two had come down here. Mind if I join ya?"

Jodie's attempt at disclosure became lost in the flurry of Jack settling down and the waitress teasing him about the sameness of his lunch order. She could have picked up where she'd left off, but she didn't. She respected Jack, and understood that he, too, wanted only the best for Tate, but she'd been nervous about increasing the number of her confidants to two, much less three.

Emma smiled at her old friend. "No one can beat you at trackin' someone down, huh, Jack? Unless it's Tate. He used to be pretty good at it."

"That he was," Jack agreed. "Still is."

As sheriff, Jack wore the same uniform as his deputies, just as Tate had done. In fact, it had been at Jack's behest that the force changed to professional uniforms from the good-ol'-boy jeans and white long-sleeved shirt of the county's earlier years—only one of the improvements Jack had pushed through.

The area's population was becoming increasingly mobile, he'd insisted, and not everyone knew who their lawmen were. Jack didn't want anyone mistaking one of his men for someone else, which could create a danger for all involved.

He peeled off his hat and placed it on the table, then rubbed a hand over his short salt-and-pepper curls. "I been thinkin'," he said as he accepted his steaming cup of coffee from the waitress. "Maybe I shoulda given Tate an active case—somethin' he could really get his teeth into—instead of one from the inactive file. I didn't mean to insult him. You think he took it that way?"

Jodie glanced at Emma, before offering Jack a tight smile. "I doubt it. I don't think he cares much either way. It was a good idea, though."

"But you don't think it's gonna work," Jack said.

Jodie shrugged. "I hope it does. Just…it may not."

"I'm startin' to think that what that boy needs is a good swift kick to his rear end."

Jodie murmured, "Shannon says we shouldn't treat him like he's breakable, but—"

"I didn't mean a real kick," Jack denied.

"We know that, Jack," Emma said. "We're all tryin' to figure out what to do for the best."

"Gotta make him care again," Jack said firmly. "It breaks my heart to see him the way he is."

"Breaks all our hearts," Emma agreed. For added reassurance, she clasped his hand resting on the table.

The bond between these two old friends touched Jodie profoundly. Tate had told her how Jack had helped them in every way he could after Dan Connelly's death. How, over the years that followed, he'd looked out for Tate and Emma as if they were his own.

Emma and Jack were Tate's family—all he'd had until he married her.

She hesitated, conscious that what she was about to do could be interpreted as intrusion. Still, she reached out to place her hand over theirs in what she hoped would be received as a show of unity.

Her gesture was readily accepted.

JODIE HAD COMPLETED most of the drive back to the ranch when an oncoming car flashed its headlights as a signal for her to pull over.

She recognized the vehicle instantly and tapped her brakes, slowing the Cadillac until her speed was low enough to pull off the road. The other car did the same. They drew to a stop directly across from each other.

Jim Cleary, Jennifer's father, hailed her. "Jodie! Hello! Are you just getting back from town? That's where I'm headed. Little Angela needs some carrots. Won't eat just any kind, mind you. They've got to be a certain brand or she'll refuse 'em." He laughed. "I'd nearly forgotten what it's like to have a baby in the house. They sure keep you hopping!"

Even sitting in his full-size Buick, Jim Cleary looked a large man. He had a booming voice and bright blue eyes, and a little under two years ago had retired from his construction business in Dallas to live exclusively on his ranch. Cattle always had been an afterthought to the Clearys. Unlike the Parkers, they relied on an overseer to run every aspect of their ranch.

"If I'd known, I could've picked up what you wanted," Jodie said, smiling.

"I need to stop by the post office anyway. It's been a week since I checked our box." He paused. "Actually, I talked to Mae earlier. She told me Tate's not doin' so good."

"No," Jodie answered dutifully.

"I was wondering something, Jodie," Jim Cleary began. "I know it's an imposition, with you involved in your own problems and such, but do you think you could find a few minutes to give my Jenny a call? Maybe even come over to see her? Things are a little rough for her right now. It's that no-good husband of hers. He sure fooled me. Fooled her, too." Jim scowled. "Anyway," he said, forcing the dark look away, "maybe the two of you could talk for a while. She could sure use a friend right now, and, from what Mae says, you could, too."

Jodie's first instinct was to decline. As Jim Cleary said, she had enough problems of her own. But his expression held such worry Jodie wondered just what kind of trouble Jennifer was in with her "no-good" husband. "Sure," she said. "I'll be glad to call her."

A smile eclipsed Jim's worry. "I'll tell her to be expecting it," he boomed; then, waving, he checked the still-empty lanes for traffic and rolled back onto the narrow highway.

Jodie accelerated in the opposite direction, avoiding the dust kicked up by his wheels. At the same time she kicked up a thin dust cloud of her own.

So Jennifer's baby was named Angela, and she liked a certain brand of prepared carrots.

Jodie had watched her cousins with their babies, and baby-sat for them and others on numerous occasions. She'd done a lot of that as a teenager, in a vain—and she later learned—wrongheaded attempt to separate herself from her family. But the children had never been *personal* to her. How would it feel to have her own baby? To discover all the things that were good for the child and made him or her happy—

Him or her! She hadn't let herself think about the child's sex. A boy? A girl? Which did she want most? She didn't know. Her pregnancy didn't feel real, even though a doctor had confirmed it.

She'd experienced no morning sickness or wildly swinging moods. She tended to cry easily, but that undoubtedly was due to Tate's condition…though she remembered reading somewhere that quick tears were a natural occurrence in early pregnancy.

Maybe when her body started to change in less subtle ways, she'd feel pregnant. Yet she dreaded that stage, especially if Tate was still determined to carry through with the divorce.

It would mean her plan had failed and he was still in bad shape.

This should be one of their happiest moments. Together, they'd created a new life. But what kind of world was this baby going to enter? One where his father rejected both his mother and him?

Jodie tightened her grip on the steering wheel and didn't relax it, not even when she turned onto the private road that led to the heart of the Parker Ranch.

TATE AWOKE, conscious of having slept better than he had in months. Normally, his rest consisted of what he could get in fits and starts. He stretched slightly and immediately his muscles tightened. Along with the tightness came discomfort. His respite had been only temporary.

He checked the bedside clock. It was after four. Had Jodie gotten back yet? He listened carefully. The house was quiet.

He sat up and swung his feet to the floor. Nature called; otherwise he would stay in bed.

When he started to walk, he still felt groggy. Had Axel's massage allowed him to sleep so deeply? Or had it simply been exhaustion?

The human body could withstand only so much and then it shut down. The trip here had been difficult, so had the time after their arrival—getting used to a new environment, adjusting to different ways of doing things. A person with ease of movement could breeze in and do what he wanted almost anywhere. When each step or each reach was difficult, the world became a much more complicated place.

Once in the hall, he again skimmed the wallpaper with his fingers, using the light touch for balance. This time, though, his fingers bumped into something and dislodged it. He muttered a short curse and tried to catch whatever it was, but the object went crashing to the floor.

Jodie rushed out of the living room, which answered his earlier question. She bent to retrieve the larger pieces of what had once been a showcase for a pair of sea horses.

"Stupid froufrous," Tate growled, scowling at the frame decorated with numerous tiny shells.

"I'll get a broom," she said, straightening.

"Good. Sweep me out with the rest. We're all damaged goods."

Jodie saw beneath his acid words. "Darlene won't blame you," she reassured him.

"She probably prizes everything she has. Why would she keep it if she didn't?"

"She'll likely come back from this Australia trip and hang up all kinds of new things. She's my aunt, remember. I know how she thinks. This—" she glanced at the shattered bits "—won't matter to her."

"It matters to me," he said flatly.

He started to walk away, but his bare foot came down on something sharp. "Ahh!" he yelped, and a second later wished he hadn't, as Jodie instinctively stepped closer to offer assistance. Her free hand was soft and warm as it clasped his arm.

"What is it? You've hurt yourself?" she asked in concern.

"I can handle it," he said tightly.

"Let me help you, Tate. There's no broken glass, but one of the shells—"

He slid his foot on the floor and dislodged the irritant. "I'm fine. I was on my way to the bathroom. I'll see to it there."

His breaths were short as he closed himself into the small room and leaned back against the door. The imprint of her fingers still burned his arm. He had to struggle to keep from going back to her. Even in his debilitated state he wanted to touch her. Nothing else, for that moment, mattered.

Once he regained control he limped over to the toilet. The bottom of his foot stung as he swung the lid down and settled on it, using it as a chair.

Blood smeared the floor where he'd stood and could be traced back, footstep by footstep, to the door.

An expletive passed his lips as he tried to inspect the damage. He couldn't do it! Couldn't bend forward enough, reach far enough or lift his foot high enough to see the bottom.

He had only one alternative. "Jodie!" he called. *"Jodie!"* He didn't want another infection. He'd already had enough trouble in that department. The initial damage a bullet did to tissue and bone as it tore through a body was only part of the package. The other part was infection that frequently overwhelmed the victim.

Jodie didn't respond. He leaned over as far as he could and managed to open the medicine chest above the sink. He could see a bottle of rubbing alcohol on one of the shelves, but he couldn't reach it.

He'd just started to get to his feet when Jodie tapped on the door.

"Tate?" she asked. "Did you call? I thought I heard—"

"Yeah. Come in. I need—"

The door swung open and her beautiful eyes swept over him. They widened at the blood smears on the floor. "You *did* hurt yourself!" she exclaimed, and quickly divested herself of broom and dustpan to hurry over to him. "Here, let me see."

She held his foot gently and turned it so that she could give it a proper examination. She made a small sound in the back of her throat.

"Just put some alcohol on it," he recommended, uncomfortable once again at being so close to her.

"We have to do this right. If we don't—"

"Do what you have to," he ground out, cutting her off.

Jodie washed her hands, then found some cotton balls and the alcohol. "They don't have any other kind of antiseptic. This will burn," she warned.

Tate grimaced. "After everything, do you honestly believe a little alcohol's gonna bother me?"

She dampened a cotton ball and carefully

cleaned the bottom of his foot. "I see the spot. It looks as if—" She reached for a pair of tweezers, which she also cleaned. "There could be a bit of shell," she explained, before going back to work.

The cold touch of steel brought back unpleasant memories. He'd been poked and prodded so much and for so long in the hospital and in the intermediate-care facility that he finally got to the point where he couldn't stand it any longer. Some of his wounds had needed to heal from the inside out—an agonizingly slow process. Once they'd healed, he'd rejected all further indignities by refusing to endure more treatments.

He must have winced, because Jodie looked at him in quick concern. His gaze slid away as he braced himself for another attempt.

This time she sounded pleased when she drew back. She placed a tiny fragment of shell on the sink ledge.

"There," she said. "We got it." She didn't wait for a response but dabbed at the cut with more alcohol, then covered it with a wide plastic strip. "It's all clean now. It should be fine."

"Thanks," Tate murmured.

When she didn't immediately straighten, Tate watched her warily.

"Would you like something to drink?" she asked. "Some water, some coffee—"

"How about a beer?"

His answer surprised her. Not because he'd never imbibed before, but because this was the first time he'd requested one since he'd been shot.

Tate frowned slightly, wondering why the idea of a beer suddenly appealed.

"I'll look in the refrigerator," Jodie said. "If there aren't any, I know good and well someone on the ranch will have a bottle."

She smiled and Tate's heart lurched. His hand lifted, seemingly of its own volition, to touch the creamy smoothness of her cheek. Her softness was only inches away, but, unaware of his intent, she stood up.

"Would you like me to help you to your room?" she offered.

"I'll be fine," he said. His stock line.

She took a moment to sweep a path clear in the hall. Then, as he made his way to the bedroom, he heard her in the kitchen. Seconds after that, she went out the back way, probably to the house next door.

By the time he'd resettled himself in bed,

she'd returned with one of LeRoy's special microbrew beers. "He has a standing order," Jodie explained. "Harriet says she hopes you enjoy it."

"It didn't have to be special," Tate said.

"Why not?" Jodie replied, grinning.

She'd already opened the bottle, so he had a long sip. Beer was a beverage he drank on occasion, seldom as everyday fare. In his line of work he'd seen too many tragedies caused by people who weren't disciplined in their drinking.

The taste was smooth on his tongue, full-bodied and cold. He had another swallow, then slid the bottle onto the bedside table. It wouldn't take much in this state to undo him.

"Tell her I like it," he said. "And tell LeRoy thanks, too."

"Why don't you tell them yourself?" Jodie asked.

"You'll see them first."

"Maybe...maybe not."

He could already feel the effect of two swigs of the strong brew. He was so out of condition, so weak. He suddenly longed to be left alone again. He closed his eyes, hoping Jodie would take the hint.

She didn't. "Tate?" she said. "I need to talk to you."

He opened one eye, then the other when he saw that she was serious. "What is it?" he asked.

"I want to tell you about today."

He'd forgotten, and when he remembered, he didn't *want* to hear about it—at least, not right then. He pretended confusion, which wasn't all that difficult at the moment. "You did something?" he murmured. "What'd you do?"

"I saw Mr. Fowler. We filled out the papers."

"Good."

"He asked about you. So did Nicole. So did Bob Stewart. I saw him, too."

"Okay."

A moment passed. "Do you still want your copy?" she asked.

"Of what?"

"The divorce petition."

"You can...put it over there." He motioned vaguely to the dresser.

She frowned. "A lot of people asked about you. Some really want to come see you."

"I told you, I don't want to see them."

"They care about you, Tate."

"So?"

"So, I'm tired of making excuses. Since you're the one who doesn't want to see anyone, *you* can tell them. I quit!"

Tate looked at her. It had been a long time since she'd shown him any anger.

She lifted her chin, and he couldn't help the twitch of his lips. Her fiery spirit had always delighted him.

"Are you laughing at me?" she demanded, again like the Jodie of old.

At one time he could hold his own—win even, on occasion. But his supply of energy had hit rock bottom. "Jodie," he said tiredly, "do what you want. I don't care."

His answer only irritated her more. She strode from the room in a display of Parker temperament, then came back. She marched straight to the bed, opened an envelope and let the legal papers inside rain down on him.

"Here," she said fiercely. "You wanted me to do it. Now you get to live with the consequences. You can't pretend it didn't happen, Tate. It did. And here's the proof!"

After which she spun around and stomped out again, this time slamming the door behind her.

Tate flinched at the sharp crack.

JODIE REALIZED what she'd done, what she'd said, how she'd left him, immediately after closing herself in the hall. The noise the door had made echoed in her ears, as did her words. *Now you get to live with the consequences,* she'd shouted. At Tate! Tate, who she was terrified had decided he didn't want to live. *Consequences*…as if he didn't already have enough of those!

He'd made her angry and she'd exploded. All the while that she'd been keeping such scrupulous rein on her emotions, had she also been hiding them from herself? And when she'd found them again…pow!…he'd borne the brunt?

It wasn't fair, though. She hadn't been hurt in the shooting. She hadn't had to suffer his pain, his frustration—

She became very still. Or had she? In her own way, hadn't she suffered through everything with him? Faced it all, except for the actual gunshots?

She and Tate were a unit. If he hurt, she hurt. Wasn't that what love was all about? She was hurting, too! But he wasn't at the point where he could see it.

She placed a hand over her still-flat stomach and thought of the baby growing inside her. Their baby.

She'd been mistaken in thinking she had no control over the type of world their child would enter. She did. She had choices—she could either let the forces presently at work have their way, or she could fight them.

By coming to the ranch, hadn't she already decided to fight?

It was only now, though, that she realized she couldn't rely solely on the others to solve her problem for her. She herself had to take a more active role.

CHAPTER SEVEN

JODIE PHONED Jennifer the next morning. With everything that had happened, she'd forgotten to call last night. They had a nice light conversation, not touching on anything of importance, but Jodie could hear the strain in her onetime close friend's voice.

"When can I see the baby?" Jodie asked. Maybe Jennifer was feeling the same reticence as she was.

"Whenever you want," Jennifer replied.

"How about this afternoon?"

"Angela usually naps from twelve to two."

"How about if I come over about one, then we can catch up a little."

"Daddy told me he'd talked to you. Jodie, you don't need to—" She paused. "You have so much to deal with already."

"One it is," Jodie said. "Unless you'd rather not."

"No, one will be fine."

Jodie had heard Tate switch on the shower shortly after she'd dialed the Clearys' number. The water was still running when she hung up. She decided to take advantage of the moment to change his bedding and quickly straighten up the room. Those chores were easier when he wasn't there. She didn't feel so much like an intruder.

She'd just finished her work and was in the hall, carrying an armload of sheets to the laundry room, when he stepped out of the bathroom.

He'd stayed in bed for most of the evening yesterday and had done little more than grunt when she'd brought him his dinner. Then, when her father had come over to ask if he'd like to watch another movie, Tate had begged off, saying he wasn't up to it. But he himself had refused Gib. He hadn't fobbed off the duty on her. Jodie's conscience pricked her, but she bolstered herself by focusing on the appropriateness of her decision. It would do Tate good to face the consequences of his actions, to deal with the very people he didn't want to see. At the very least, he'd communicate with them, however briefly.

Tate was wearing his robe and smelled of shaving balm. For a period after leaving the care facility, he'd worn a beard. He hadn't been steady enough to shave himself with his favored safety razor and he wouldn't allow anyone else—her—to do it for him. Then his fellow investigator at the shooting, Billy Vance, had heard from Drew Winslow that Tate could use a little encouragement, and he'd dropped off an electric razor as a present. "Tell him it's so I'll recognize him the next time I see him," Billy had said. He'd spoken jocularly, but Jodie knew how badly Billy felt that he'd escaped injury and Tate hadn't.

Jodie offered a tentative smile.

Tate returned her look coolly and murmured, "'Morning," before he continued on his way. They might have been mere acquaintances. Neither with any claim on the other.

She loaded the sheets in the washer and started the machine running. No matter how Tate felt about the situation, she couldn't leave him to fend for himself. He didn't realize how many things she did. If she stopped doing them— She wouldn't stop doing them.

She collected the alcohol, some cotton

balls and a fresh plastic strip, then tapped on Tate's door.

"Tate?" she called. "May I come in?"

She thought she heard him answer yes, but when she pushed inside, she saw that he'd just started to dress.

"I'm sorry," she apologized. "I thought I heard— I knocked." Her gaze slid away from his embarrassment. A situation that was as natural as breathing for other couples was anything but for them.

He secured his pajama bottoms at the waist and tried to shield the scars on his torso with his shirt. In the end he had to slip the shirt on.

Jodie turned away as he did.

"All right," he said gruffly, signaling her to turn back.

What she wanted most in the world was to go to him. He looked so ravaged emotionally, *was* so ravaged physically. The scars didn't matter to her! She wanted to shout that out so everyone could hear, but she held her tongue. Tate wouldn't believe her.

"I— Your foot," she explained. "I thought—"

"I hardly feel it."

"Still."

He eased himself onto the edge of the mattress. She went over, kneeled on the rug and lifted his foot to examine it. "The spot's still red," she said, her fingers gently caressing his foot before she could think about what she was doing.

"Just…put something on it."

A curiousness in the way he spoke made her look up, meet the unsettled flash of yearning in his eyes.

Jodie came alive to every sensation. She wanted so badly to reach out to him, to show him how much she loved him. But she held back. This time the first move had to come from him.

Her hope died as she saw his face turn to stone.

"Take care of my foot, then get out of here," he directed shortly. "I don't want— You gave me some papers last night. You told me to live with the consequences. Well, I am. And you will, too."

A tremor passed over Jodie's body. "Tate—" She breathed his name, a plea.

He shut his eyes and murmured tightly, "I can't do this by myself!"

Jodie glanced at the first-aid materials. She might have been seeing them from a distance. She shook her head, then quickly ministered to his injury, careful to keep her touch sparing. When she was done, she stood up and took a step back.

"Like I said…go. *Go!*" he repeated more harshly when, for a heartbeat, she didn't move.

Jodie hurried out the door, then she pressed herself back against the nearest wall, stuffing a fist to her mouth to keep quiet.

She wasn't sure what she wanted most—to laugh or to cry. He wasn't as indifferent to her as he pretended! Not even when he'd sent her away.

I can't do this by myself! His declaration revealed a chink in the wall he'd built around himself. He needed her help in caring for his injury, but he also needed it in keeping her at bay.

She laughed softly, unsteadily.

Since keeping herself at bay definitely wasn't in *her* better interest, hadn't he just handed her a tool that she could use to her advantage?

AS TIME APPROACHED for Jodie to leave for the Clearys' she debated whether to tell Tate in person that she was going or to leave a note. In the end she decided on personal contact.

She made the choice purely on instinct, not yet having had time to reflect on her prospective actions. By coupling last night's realization—that she needed to take a more active role—with what she'd gleaned this morning—that he needed her help to keep her away—she felt she was on the right track. Stay in his face so he couldn't harden himself against her, yet not to the point where he would cut her off altogether.

She tapped on the bedroom door, and this time waited several seconds after receiving his permission to enter. In order to build goodwill? She smiled faintly to herself as she stepped into the room.

He was propped up in bed by several pillows, and the nearest lamp was switched on. Yesterday's newspaper was folded where she'd left it on the bedside table, but some of the pages were ruffled, as if he might've read it.

"Tate, I'm going over to the Clearys'. I'm not sure how long I'll be gone. Jennifer's home."

He shrugged.

"I didn't want you to wonder where I was. Are you sure you're not hungry? I could take a minute to—"

"I'm fine."

"Some water? Another beer? Harriet sent some more over."

"Go."

Exactly what he'd said earlier. When his frown deepened, she wondered if he, too, was remembering this.

She moved toward the door, conscious of his eyes on her, conscious of the way her voile print dress complemented her coloring and her still-lithe figure.

The dress was one that Tate had helped her pick out last spring, when they'd both had a three-day holiday coming up and were planning to spend it in West Texas. It was one of the most romantic getaways they'd ever had together.

Her smile strengthened as she let herself out of the room.

Let him remember that, as well!

ONLY IN A VAST AREA like the West Texas ranch country could someone who lived such a distance away be considered "a next-door neighbor." The Cleary Ranch and the Parker Ranch bordered each other on one side, but the family homes were separated by a number of miles.

The differences in outlook of the two families were immediately apparent. The Cleary house stood by itself and was much showier, its sprawling architecture far more modern. It had tennis courts, a swimming pool and an impeccably kept paddock next to a formal horse stable. The working heart of the ranch—ranch headquarters—lay a good two miles away. From there a manager oversaw the operation. Jim Cleary had always been a gentleman rancher, and Jodie doubted that even in retirement, he interfered with the day-to-day decisions of his manager.

A maid answered the doorbell. The woman—in her early sixties, with white hair, a thin face and a strong assertive nose—looked at Jodie blankly, before breaking into a smile. "Miss Jodie?" she questioned. "Jodie Parker? As I live and breathe. It *is* you!"

"It's me, Edna," Jodie said warmly. "Only it's Connelly now. Jodie Connelly."

The maid motioned her into the house. "Miss Jenny told me she was expectin' someone, but I had no idea! Come in. Come in. I'll go tell her you're here." But she didn't move away. She continued to look Jodie up and down and smile. "I can't believe how much you two girls have grown. I remember when you both weren't any higher than my elbow.

You used to come over here and swim every chance you got."

"It has been a long time," Jodie acknowledged, grinning.

"I remember now. When you and Tate got married it kinda took everyone by surprise."

Jodie's smile tightened. "Us, too," she agreed.

Edna glanced over her shoulder at the young woman who'd approached them quietly.

Jodie and Jennifer hadn't set eyes on each other for close to ten years. Jodie had no idea whether Jennifer found her familiar, but she couldn't have mistaken Jennifer for anyone else. She had the same narrow face, the same blue eyes, the same burnished brown hair. The only difference was that she no longer wore her hair held back at the crown by a barrette. Beneath her new maturity, though, was a sadness Jodie found disconcerting.

A soft smile tilted Jennifer's lips and Jodie smiled in return. The years of detachment melted away in an instant as the two young women stood across from each other again.

Jodie took her hand. "Jennifer...I'm so glad—"

"Me, too," Jennifer whispered.

Edna sniffed and blew her nose on a tissue

she'd pulled from her pocket. "I'm so happy," she said.

Jennifer's and Jodie's smiles deepened. Edna had always been an easy touch, just like Marie.

"Could we have something to drink, Edna?" Jennifer asked. "Or, have you had lunch yet, Jodie?"

"I've eaten, but go ahead if you like."

"I've eaten, too," Jennifer said.

"Like a bird, she eats," Edna complained. "Only not as often. I don't know how she has the energy to look after that little angel of hers. A mother has to take care of herself. For the sake of her baby."

"Angel...Angela," Jodie mused.

"Wait until you see her." Edna beamed. "She's beautiful...and so smart! She's able to—"

"Something to drink, Edna?" Jennifer prompted.

"Ha! I could talk about that little one all day, I sure could. Just get me started!" But she hurried off, not needing another request.

The interior of the house was just as modern as the exterior. But possibly because the Clearys had never lived in the house full-time and frequently had used it to entertain

Jim's associates for long "ranch weekends," it felt more like a showpiece than a home.

Jennifer invited Jodie into the sitting area, which was down two steps in the center of the large open room. She offered her a seat on a cinnamon suede couch, then took one herself not far away.

"Needless to say, Edna's in love with Angela," she murmured.

"It kind of sounds that way," Jodie teased.

"She is an angel…you'll see. Unless she wakes up cranky, which she does sometimes when she's cutting a tooth."

Jodie shook her head. "I can't believe you have a baby. The last time—the last *real* time—we talked, you were worried about a show-jumping competition, not a baby tooth."

"I know. So much has happened." Sadness again overtook Jennifer's pretty features.

Jodie wasn't sure how to broach the subject, or even if Jennifer would allow her to pursue it once she did, but, true to her nature, she plunged right in. "Would you like to talk about it? Your dad said—"

Jennifer laughed hollowly. "Oh, I can imagine what Daddy said."

"He's worried about you." Jodie sat forward.

"What is it, Jennifer? I thought—we all thought you were happily married and—"

"Living a *nice* life with my *nice* husband." Her laugh was hollow. "I know. I did, too!"

Jodie had had enough recent experience with intense emotional pain to recognize it in others when she saw it. She'd been that distraught, that panicked...and not too many days ago, either. In some ways she still was. Had Jennifer come back for the same reasons? For comfort, for help? Was she hoping to heal her marriage—or was it the reverse, and she wanted her marriage to end?

Jennifer quickly apologized. "I'm sorry. I'm just— This isn't something you should have to worry about, Jodie. My father should never have asked you to call. I'm fine. I can deal with this."

Jodie asked quietly, "What's *this?*"

Jennifer looked at her. "Alan—my husband. My father knows only a part of the story, so don't—"

"I'm good at keeping secrets," Jodie murmured. "I've got a few of my own."

"It's embarrassing, but it was all over the local Boston news. How could it not be? He was so *stupid!* I don't understand how he ever thought he could get away with it." She took a breath. "Alan was involved in embezzling money at the private high school where he teaches. Him and another teacher. He says it was the other teacher and that he had nothing to do with it. I believed him at first. I stood by him. Then I found the emails between the two of them. I know he did it."

"And the police?"

"They're investigating."

"Did you turn the emails over to them?"

"Not yet." She bit her bottom lip. "I just found them a couple of weeks ago. I panicked. I packed everything I could for Angela and me, and we left Boston. Daddy flew up to get us. I haven't talked to anyone there since."

"Are you planning to turn them over?"

"I— Yes. Yes, I think so. Alan can't be allowed to get away with something so awful. Only, Daddy doesn't know about the emails."

"Is Alan aware you found them?"

She shrugged.

"Does he know where you are?"

"He's called, but Edna tells him I'm not here."

Ordinarily, Jodie would advise Jennifer to talk to Tate. He'd know best what she should do and how she should do it. "Have you talked to Jack?" she asked. "He might be able to—"

"I don't want anyone here to find out. It was bad enough back in Boston. All the neighbors, the reporters. People were angry. And I don't want Angela...she has to grow up somewhere!"

"No one here would hold what her father did against her, or you."

Jennifer's gaze was level. "Jodie, you're a Parker. You belong. I don't. I've been a visitor out here for most of my life. It's different for me."

"You're mistaken about that."

Jennifer shook her head.

"Is there something else?" Jodie probed, sensing that there was. What she'd been told was bad, but not bad enough to tie her friend in such emotional knots.

"I—I'm not sure how stable Alan is. It's like— Jodie, I thought I knew him! We met at the university, we dated, we fell in love, we got married. We had a child. But it's like he's had this other life. And his two lives are coming together now, and—" she paused, then added rawly "—I'm not sure his life with me is the real one!"

"Has he threatened you? Been violent?"

Edna cleared her throat as she carried a tray in from the kitchen. Two glasses of lemonade sat on white paper doilies, and were accompanied by a plate of chocolate-dipped cookies.

"Now, don't either one of you tell me you're too full to eat at least one of these cookies. I bought 'em special, just for you, Miss Jenny. And Miss Jodie, I remember you used to like 'em, too."

She placed the tray on the low square coffee table fashioned from dark marble and waited for an answer.

Jodie spoke first, giving Jennifer time to collect herself. "They've always been my favorite. Thanks, Edna."

Jennifer echoed Jodie's response, then took a sip of her drink.

Edna went away satisfied.

"You didn't answer my question," Jodie said. "Has he been violent?"

"He pushed me once and slapped Angela… hard…when she wouldn't stop crying."

"Oh, God."

"But he was under a lot of stress then, Jodie. The story had just broken in the news and the school was forcing him to go on leave. The police had just questioned him, too, and told him they'd be back. A lot was going on."

"Still—"

"I don't think he meant it."

Jodie narrowed her gaze. "But you're afraid there could be more. That's why you left him."

Jennifer nodded and looked away.

"I'll talk to Tate," Jodie said. "You won't mind if I do that, will you?"

"I'd rather you didn't!" Jennifer moaned.

"You don't have to worry about Tate. He'll help in any way he—"

"I've heard how he is, Jodie. Mae told Daddy and Daddy told me. I don't want to bother either one of you with my silly little worry, but especially not him. He's been through enough. I can take care of my own problem. I can handle it."

"At least tell your father."

"I don't want him to worry any more than he already does."

"He knows you're holding something back, Jenny. Why do you think he asked me to talk to you?"

Jennifer looked at her. "Are you going to tell him?"

The question echoed back over the years to when Jennifer had told Rafe where to find Rio Walsh, and Rafe, Shannon and her father had traveled to New Mexico to bring him back. Jodie had recognized right away that her friend had done the right thing, but it still hurt that Jennifer had betrayed her. Now, it seemed, Jennifer was asking if she wanted to even the score.

"No," Jodie said, "I won't tell him. But I think you should. You're his daughter, his only child. Think how you'd feel if Angela needed your help."

"I'm already doing that," Jennifer asserted. "Everything I'm doing is for Angela."

Edna carried an adorable curly-haired little blonde into the room. The child clung to the neck strap of the maid's apron with one hand and rubbed at her eyes with the other. Her bottom lip quavered.

"Look who woke up early this fine afternoon," Edna said. "She must have known Mommy had company and wanted to come meet her."

Jennifer reached for her daughter and the

child accepted eagerly, wrapping her arms around her mother's neck as she changed women. She peeked at Jodie from beneath her arm.

Jennifer gently introduced them. "Angela… this is Jodie. Jodie…Angela."

"Jo-die," the child repeated.

The pronunciation was far clearer than Jodie had expected. The little girl drew back, glancing at the other adults.

Jennifer and Edna grinned.

"I said she was smart," Edna bragged.

"She was talking a blue streak at a year. Four-and-five-word sentences. And she knows what she's saying," Jennifer said.

"How old is she now?" Jodie asked.

"Sixteen months."

"Angel hungry," the little girl said. "Angel wants a cookie."

"Good heavens," Jodie murmured.

Jennifer hugged her daughter close, causing Jodie to wonder if the action stemmed from pride and love or if some of her ongoing worry had slipped in.

A loving mother protecting her child. Jodie had never experienced that kind of love first-hand because her birth mother had abandoned her early on. But she'd felt a form of it from Mae, and she knew the emotion could be fierce.

Fierce enough to be firmly in place even before a child was born.

CHAPTER EIGHT

AXEL SHOWED UP at exactly one o'clock, and just as he had the day before, he carried the table under one arm and set it up near Tate's bed.

This time Tate made no protest. He was curious, in fact. He wanted to see if the good rest he'd gotten after the previous massage was due to it or to some other cause.

"How'd you sleep?" Axel asked, rubbing oil between his hands while Tate removed his pajama shirt.

"Pretty good, actually," Tate murmured.

"That's what I thought."

Tate stretched out on the table and positioned his head, knowing that Axel would turn it from time to time as he worked. The strong hands began to smooth the muscles on either side of Tate's spine, then along his sides and onto his shoulders. Moments later, Tate released a long sigh. "Where'd you learn to do this?" he asked, trying to stay awake.

"In a fight club."

"A gym for boxers?"

"Yep. Right after I left the marines."

"You were in the marines?"

"Yep. Doin' what I do here—feedin' people."

Tate glanced at the arms on the large man. "What'd you do at the gym?"

"Anythin' and everythin'. Helped with the trainin', did a little fightin' of my own. But not much. I got a glass jaw. Hit me in the right spot and I'm out like a light."

"How'd you get started giving massages?"

"Regular guy had to leave. He gave me a few lessons and I took over. The fellas seemed to think I did a good job. Somebody was always hurt. Some worse than others, dependin' on how bad their matches went." He laughed. "Some were pretty bad even when they won."

"How long did you do this?"

"A coupla years. Then I came back here, met Marie, settled down."

"You miss the gym?"

"Nope. Mind if I ask you a question?"

Tate could hardly refuse. "Nope," he echoed.

"What kinda bullets you get hit with? Musta

been some 'a those that go clean through, huh? Which is bad enough, but it coulda been worse if they'd been those nasty types that leave a lot bigger holes comin' out than they do goin' in."

Tate had stiffened at Axel's first question.

Axel must have felt it, but he continued to talk, even as he continued the slow smooth strokes. "I'm askin', 'cause I was wonderin' if you'd realized yet what a helluva lucky fella you are. You coulda been dead on the spot. I knew a young boxer once. He got hit with a coupla those bad ones. Didn't live an hour. Tore him up somethin' awful. Then another boxer—he was older—he got hit in the stomach. But you know what? His muscles were so hard and tough from his trainin' that those bullets as good as bounced off. Just like he was a superhero!"

Tate had discussed his injuries with no one except his doctors. Not even any of his fellow task-force members. He hadn't wanted to relive the shooting, which was exactly what he would've had to do over and over.

Axel continued to work, smoothing the muscles. Pushing, pulling, scooping.

Slowly, Tate began to relax again. "Well, I guess I'm not a superhero," he murmured.

"Who is?" Axel returned, and went on plying his magic.

Tate was dozing when Axel finished, but he was able to stir himself enough to suggest that the camp cook find a place in the closet for the folding table. If he was going to return the next day, there was no reason for him to carry it back and forth.

Axel made no comment, just did as he was directed, then said he'd see Tate the same time tomorrow.

Tate's rest was undisturbed after Axel left. But once again, when he awoke, his respite proved temporary…although a pain-free few hours, even if spent in sleep, were worth it.

Axel had kept his promise. His massages helped. Which also meant Mae had been right to send him over—something that, if she wanted to use it later, could be turned into as much of an irritant as a blessing.

A stirring of hunger drew Tate to the kitchen. He rummaged in the refrigerator and found the sandwich Jodie had prepared for him, plus another bottle of LeRoy's favorite brew. Then, carrying them with him, he made his way slowly back to the bedroom, where he resettled himself, took a few bites…and took a few more. For the first time in a long while food tasted good to him. So did the brew, but again he was careful with the portion.

He switched on the small TV, but after a few minutes switched it off again. Still vaguely dissatisfied, he reached for the newspaper... and his gaze fell on the case folder Jack had left behind. He immediately wrenched his eyes away and tried to concentrate on some light reading, but little by little the too-frilly room began to close in. The chintz curtains, the ruffles, the busy wallpaper, the profusion of candy-box colors were more than his senses could handle.

He moved tentatively into the hall. So far he'd seen only three rooms—his bedroom, the bathroom and the kitchen. Curiosity made him move toward what must be the bedroom Jodie was using, open the door and look around. The room was a jumble of unrelated objects—little better than a storage room really, but with a single narrow bed. Though Jodie had unpacked for him, the majority of her clothes remained in her suitcase. Only a couple of her dresses hung in the closet, because there wasn't room to hang up more. It was already overstuffed. As must have been the chest drawers.

Tate stared at the suitcase for a long time.

The Parkers had expected Jodie and him to share the master bedroom, so they hadn't cleared out the other room. Which meant Jodie hadn't confided in them. Did they know even now? They had to.

He turned away, his discontent increasing as he went across the hall to the arched doorway of the living room. It, too, had been decorated with a heavy hand, but in a less obviously feminine way. Thomas must have insisted.

A second doorway on the far wall led from the living room into the kitchen.

So much for the tour.

Tate sighed. He was tired, he needed to rest again, but he couldn't go back to that bedroom. Just thinking of the overblown flowers and frills made him twitch.

The front door was only a few steps away. Jodie had said there were chairs on the porch. He reached for the doorknob, then remembered how he was dressed.

Possible embarrassment about wearing pajamas weighed against overblown flowers... and the pajamas won. He was on the Parker Ranch, not in the middle of downtown Austin. If he sat on the porch stark naked, only a few people would be around to protest.

Once outdoors, he had to shut his eyes against the glare. The overhanging roof offered some protection from the afternoon sun. But the brightness hit with force. Tate could barely remember the last time he'd been outside for pleasure. His recent forays had all been medical necessities.

He spotted the chairs. One was a chaise longue, the other an outdoor tubular upright. Comfortable cushions covered both.

Tate moved to the chaise. By the time he'd settled himself, he was puffing and his muscles were protesting.

He hated the weakness that gripped his body. Hated the invalid he'd become. He couldn't *do* anything anymore. On the job, he never hesitated to plow into fights and separate the combatants, before hauling any or all off to jail. Never thought twice about chasing fleeing felons or wrestling drug dealers to the ground. His effectiveness had come through his strength as well as his acumen. Even when he was sheriff—particularly when he was sheriff—the power of his word lay in his ability to back it up physically.

His task-force duties had been less physical, the emphasis being more on detective work than hands-on functions. But he'd still needed to take care of himself, and to support his fellow investigators when necessary.

"Hey, Tate!"

Tate looked up to see Rafe a short distance away, at the end of the path that led from the business heart of the ranch to the living compound. As usual, he was dressed in dusty jeans, scuffed boots, a long-sleeved Western shirt and hard-used Stetson.

Rafe had worked on the ranch his entire life, doing the same jobs as the hired help. He was as good at it as they were, if not better. And to this day, even as ranch manager, he worked just as hard.

Rafe strode down the gravel drive and onto the walkway, not stopping until he reached the porch. His dark eyes, as black as night, gave Tate a quick assessment. There wasn't much you could put past Rafe. Tate had always respected him, and had come to respect him even more after marrying into the family.

"You enjoin' the fresh air?" Rafe drawled.

Tate answered honestly. "Got tired of all the ruffles."

A smile tugged at Rafe's lips. "Yeah, Darlene's a surprisingly ruffly person. I don't know how Thomas stands it."

"Maybe that's why he enjoys traveling so much."

Rafe considered. "You know? I never thought about it like that. Maybe it is. Maybe he's just tryin' to get away." He chuckled. "I'm gonna have to tell that one to Shannon. She'll get a kick out of it. But she'll probably defend Darlene. Say she's gotta have somethin' female to cling to out here."

"I suppose so."

Rafe hung a boot on the first step. "You, ah, feelin' better, are you? You look a little better."

"Not particularly."

"Would you like a good book to help pass the time? I got one. A mystery by that guy from England who used to be a jockey. He writes about horses and horse racing sometimes. They do things different from the way we do here, but his books are usually pretty good. I'll get Ward to bring it over."

Tate nodded, though he doubted that he would read the book. "Sure. Thanks."

Rafe straightened, sliding his boot back to the walk. "Well, you need anything else, you just let one of us know."

"I'll do that," Tate answered.

Rafe tipped his head and turned around.

But instead of heading back up the U-shaped drive, he took a shortcut through the courtyard to his house, which was directly opposite Darlene and Thomas's place.

Tate grew sleepy again, and after a few adjustments to his position, he dropped off. What seemed only seconds later, he opened his eyes to a smaller copy of Rafe. The young boy was looking at him in the same estimating way.

"Daddy said I was to bring you this," Ward said, handing Tate a book whose cover had a distinctive drawing of a jockey in bright silks mounted on a racehorse.

Tate grimaced as he tried to sit up. "Thanks," he said tightly.

He felt the boy's eyes move over him.

"Daddy said you got shot."

"He's right."

Ward tilted his head. "How? Did a bad guy shoot ya?"

The curiosity of a six-year-old knew no bounds. Tate had been around the boy off and on during the first year of his and Jodie's marriage, but since he'd never had much to do with children, he hadn't made all that much of an effort to get to know him. Or Ward's younger brother, Nate.

"Yeah. It was a bad guy."

"What'd he shoot you with? A rifle?"

Rifles were common in this section of the state. People needed weapons here. They had to be able to take care of themselves, dealing mostly with unwanted critters on their ranch land—occasionally, of the human variety.

"Yeah," Tate confirmed. "Of a sort."

An even smaller version of Rafe ran up onto the porch—four-year-old Nate.

"Momma says to come home, Ward. The ice cream's ready. It's gonna melt."

"'Kay," Ward agreed, but he held back, still curious. "You got any scars?" he asked.

"Scars?" Nate repeated. He instantly forgot his mission.

"A few," Tate said.

"Can we see 'em?" Ward asked. His brother pushed closer, excited at the prospect.

When Tate wasn't much older than Ward, he remembered how one of the deputies had accidentally shot himself in the arm. The first thing he'd done when the deputy returned to work was pester him to see the scar until the man had let him. But since his own scars were much worse than the deputy's, Tate refused.

"Why not?" Ward persisted.

"Are you two botherin' Tate?" Harriet

demanded, coming up on them from inside the house. "Tate, you just send 'em home when you've had enough. Shannon won't mind. She'd say the same thing." She explained her presence in the house. "I was on my way back home and thought I'd stop by for a minute, but Jodie wasn't there and neither were you—" she grinned "—so I started lookin'."

"The ice cream!" Nate squealed in remembrance, his eyes wide. Both boys took off across the courtyard.

Harriet laughed. "What those two won't do for somethin' sweet!" She looked at Tate. "Jodie off visiting somewhere?"

"Over at the Clearys'. She should be getting back soon."

"It's a wonder I didn't see her on the road, then." She pulled a face. "I had to go into Del Norte. Wes got into trouble at school again. Honestly, I don't know what I'm goin' to do with that boy. He's been talkin' back to some of his teachers and tellin' me and his daddy that none of 'em know enough to come in out of the rain. LeRoy's talked to him. Rafe's tried, too. Wes listens, but—" She sighed. "I'm sorry. I didn't mean to involve you in this. It's probably just one of those stages kids go through and he'll be over it soon enough.

Anyway, I tried to make peace with his principal, told him it wouldn't happen again, but I know I was mostly talkin' through my hat and so does he."

"How old's Wes now?" Tate asked.

"Fourteen. He'll be fifteen this summer."

"That's a hard age."

"Don't I know it! I went through a bad time myself about then, but I never talked back to a teacher! Kids today—"

Just then, the black Cadillac turned into the drive and continued slowly until it stopped in front of Mae's house.

"Jodie's back," Harriet said, an extra warmth entering her voice.

Tate saw his wife's bright red hair—always a dead giveaway—as she stepped out of the car. She waved when she saw them on the porch and jingled the keys, a signal that she would return them to Mae before coming to the house.

"I wonder if she's picked up any idea about why Jennifer's back. Did she tell you? Jennifer just showed up a couple of weeks ago, baby in tow, and that's all anyone knows."

"No, she didn't," Tate said shortly. He struggled to stand up.

Harriet reached to help him and he suffered her aid without snapping.

"You're goin' back to bed?" she asked solicitously.

"Yes."

"Jodie won't be long."

Tate didn't answer. He couldn't. If he could live on his own at this point, he would. It was so hard being around her, seeing her, dealing with her...missing her.

Jodie and Harriet entered the house a short time later. He heard the two of them talking. Then she came to check on him.

To protect himself he growled at her. It was the act of a wounded animal, but the result was the same. She left him alone.

Which was what he wanted. Wasn't it?

THE HOUSE GREW QUIET again and he tried to sleep. This time he couldn't. His body felt like a coiled spring—tense, tight.

There was a commanding tap on the front door, and Mae soon stood before him.

"I saw you outside a little while ago," she said. "About time you stopped hidin'."

Typical Mae. Always the aggressor. Always seizing the upper hand.

Tate answered tiredly, "If you have something to say, Mae, spit it out."

"I don't have all that much," she denied. She looked around the room, taking in the book, the newspaper, the TV. "You seem to be doin' all right for yourself. Settlin' in."

She leaned on the cane she'd been using for nearly two years. In one way she seemed frail…in another, anything but. She might have been a cougar on the prowl for prey.

"Don't see much that belongs to Jodie in here," she said. "In fact, I don't see a thing. And that's a little strange in the situation, don't you think?"

"Mae, what Jodie and I do—"

Her dark eyes snapped. "It's what you *aren't* doin' that's important! Jodie told me what you asked. She also told me what she did. And I don't like it."

"It's not up to you, Mae."

"I get to have my say, don't I? Divorce isn't somethin' I take to easy, son. You've known that from the beginning. So does every person who marries into this family." She looked for a place to sit down, spotted the boudoir chair and, after a moment of quiet disdain—ruffles and overblown flowers weren't Mae's style, either—dragged it closer.

"Things…happen," Tate said stiffly.

"Then you ride 'em out. Does your momma know about this?" she demanded.

"She does."

Mae frowned. "I can't think she'd be happy."

"She's not. But she's staying out of it."

"Like I should," Mae finished, smiling. But her smile wasn't comforting. It was more like a smirk before a pounce. Mae tapped the tip of her cane on the floor, then spoke up. "For me to stay out of it—not fight you on this—two things have to happen. One, Jodie has to be let down easy. She can't come out of this with a broken heart. *That* I will not stand for. Two, you have to be able to take care of yourself. Otherwise, Jodie will worry. That'll break her heart. And that'll bring me back into it." She paused. "You understand what I'm sayin'? I like you, Tate. I've always admired the way you handle yourself. You're a good strong man with good solid principles. But Jodie is my first concern. I've helped raise that girl since she was a baby, and that as good as makes her my own. I don't want to see her suffer any more than she already has." She paused again, her eyes moving over him, noting the tense way he held himself. "You've been through a lot. Had some real bad times. Are *still* havin' some bad times. But Jodie's been through every bit of it with you. She deserves to be treated kindly. You do that...you help her through this thing...and I promise I won't stand in the way."

Tate felt too weak to fight. And what was there to do battle against anyway? His goal was the same as Mae's—that Jodie not suffer any longer. "All right," he said wearily. "It's a deal." Then he held out his hand.

Mae's expression was unreadable as she accepted it.

JODIE WAITED impatiently in Harriet's kitchen. When she'd dropped off the car keys, Mae had informed her that she had another plan. But this time she wouldn't say what it was. Mae had instructed her to go straight through Darlene's house to Harriet's and wait there.

Jodie couldn't sit still. She went to the window and peered outside, then paced back to the counter, before moving away again.

Harriet's gaze followed her. "She didn't give you just the tiniest hint?"

Jodie shook her head. "Only that she's worked something out."

"That could be anything."

"I know. I—"

Mae tapped on the back door and opened it almost at the same instant. "Well," she said, stepping inside, "I did it. I think it's gonna work. I'll be surprised if—"

"What, Aunt Mae?" Jodie demanded. "What did you say to him?"

"We made a deal. I won't interfere with the divorce if he promises to be nicer to you and tries harder to get well."

Jodie slid slowly into the nearest chair, disappointed.

Mae seemed puzzled by her reaction. "Think about it, Missy. That's a lot!"

"Aunt Mae, he only agreed so you'd leave him alone. He's done that before…with me."

"No," Mae disagreed stubbornly. "It was more than that. He meant it. We shook hands."

"Aunt Mae—"

"Bein' nice to you isn't a bad thing," Harriet said. "Neither is him gettin' well."

"*Think* about it," Mae urged.

Jodie held her great-aunt's gaze. Mae never acted without considering every angle. When she set out to maneuver and manipulate, she did it with full reason. The person who was the object of her intentions seldom knew what was going on until much later—if then.

What was she telling her?

Little by little, Jodie worked it out. Mae had maneuvered Tate to a point where he thought that if he did as Mae asked, he would get what he wanted—when, in fact, if he did as Mae asked, he would be following Mae's plan to thwart the divorce.

"Aunt Mae," Jodie said, her smile blossoming. "Maybe you have done it. As bad as things are, it can't hurt. It's worth a try. Oh, Aunt Mae, thank you! Thank you!"

Mae accepted her great-niece's hugs and the kiss she planted on her cheek, but she soon brought Jodie back to reality. "Now, don't get your hopes up all the way. 'There's many a slip…' you know the old saying. A lot of what happens in this is goin' to be on your shoulders. You think you're up to it?"

"I'll do whatever it takes," Jodie swore.

Harriet was confused. "The pair of you have left me so far behind! I don't have the slightest idea what you're talking about. At least, not beyond what you talked about at first."

Mae said gruffly, "Jodie knows, and that's what's important."

"So, he still wants a divorce?" Harriet asked.

"Oh, at the moment he thinks he does," Mae murmured dryly, and broke into one of her rare full smiles.

Once Mae left to go back to her house, Jodie hugged Harriet. "I'll tell you all about it one day, I promise. But right now—"

"The way Mae's carryin' on, I'm not sure I want to know," Harriet teased. "Poor Tate. One day he's gonna wake up and wonder what—" She paused. "I was about to say 'hit him,' but I don't think I should. You know what I mean, though." She frowned. "I'm beginning to wonder now if Mae had a hand in gettin' LeRoy and me together. I met her at a party with my mother once and we talked for a few minutes. Then, about two months later, I met LeRoy. Do you think—" She shook her head. "No...surely not. Mae wouldn't have—"

Jodie grinned. "Maybe you should have a little talk with LeRoy. See what was going on with him about that time. But then, the way Mae works things, he probably wouldn't have the slightest idea that she'd set things up, even to this day." She hugged Harriet again. "If she did, though, aren't you glad? I am. And

LeRoy...LeRoy still worships the ground you walk on."

"I wouldn't say that," Harriet protested, pinkening. "But I'm glad you did!"

Jodie turned to leave, but Harriet stopped her.

"Jodie, Tate said you were visiting the Clearys. Did you see the baby?"

Jodie smiled. "Little Angela...they call her Angel. She's a sweet little thing. I played with her for at least an hour."

"And how's Jennifer?"

Jodie hesitated. "She's...fine. She's left her husband and it doesn't look good for the marriage. But she doesn't want word to spread. She needs to be on her own for a time, without him bothering her. So, don't tell anyone what I said, okay?"

Harriet was quick to divine that there was more to the story, but she didn't probe further. Jennifer had been Jodie's friend for so long while they were growing up that Harriet looked upon Jennifer as an extension of the Parker family. It would take an act of God to get any information out of her.

CHAPTER NINE

JODIE'S NEXT DAY started with a phone call from her mother-in-law.

"Jack's comin' out your way in a couple of hours and I'm catchin' a ride," Emma said. "Tate keeps tryin' to put us off, did you know that? Every time I've talked to him—Jack, too—he says he's too tired for company. But I'm not company. Neither's Jack. So we're comin'…unless *you* have a reason for us not to."

"Not at all. I think seeing the two of you would be good for him."

"So do I," Emma said with determination. "Whether he likes it or not."

After hanging up, Jodie went back to finish the breakfast dishes. There were so few that washing them and putting them away took nearly as little time as loading them in the dishwasher.

While she worked, she reflected on the course of action she'd spent hours in bed last night deciding on. She would continue to follow her instinct—keep challenging Tate. The strategy dovetailed perfectly with Mae's unspoken instruction to make him remember why he had married her in the first place. Yet instinct also warned her to be careful how she did it. Every action and reaction—what she felt, what she said—had to be genuine. Because even in his misery, Tate would be quick to spot an inconsistency or falsehood.

She experienced a moment's trepidation but quickly fortified herself with the memory of whose blood coursed through her veins. She came from a long line of people who didn't give up, who held their ground, no matter how fierce the opposition. They did what had to be done and didn't look back.

She would do the same.

TATE WAS DISPLEASED to hear that his mother and Jack were coming to the ranch. He'd rather they left him alone, and had done his best over the past couple of days to discourage them. But they wouldn't be put off. He doubted that their visit would be lengthy. As sheriff, Jack was always on call. But it would inevitably last through the time of his scheduled massage. That soothing half hour, and the rest he could have afterward, were something Tate had started looking forward to, especially following last night's meeting with Mae.

He worried how he could get word to Axel. As far as he knew, the cookhouse didn't have a phone, and he hesitated to call Mae's house on the off chance that she might answer the ring herself.

In the end, he mentioned the problem to Jodie. She'd been in and out of his room several times already that morning—bringing his breakfast, picking up the tray, delivering the message about the visit, straightening the bed and the area around it while he was still lying in it.

Her frequent intrusions had started to get on his nerves. Ignoring her was hard enough when she looked so pretty all the time, but doubly hard when she smiled at him.

She was coming to herself again—back to being Jodie. As if her return to the welcoming womb of her family was starting to dispel the dull gray pall his shooting had cast over her life.

Which only underscored the rightness of

what he was doing, he told himself. Jodie needed people around her who put her well-being first. She also needed security. He was able to give her one but not the other. It was time to let go.

"I need to get word to Axel about something," he said when she entered the room yet again, this time carrying a small vase with a couple of bronze-and-red flowers.

She set the vase on the dresser. "You do? What about? I can tell him."

"Tell him we'll either have to cancel or postpone. He'll know what."

She watched him levelly. "I know about the massages, Tate. Aunt Mae told me. I've also seen the table in the closet. Have they been doing any good?"

His smile was sour. "Mae didn't tell you that, too?"

"I think she's saving it for a special treat," she quipped. "Come on, Tate. You give her more credit than she's due. I'd really like to know. Have the massages helped?"

He shrugged his uninjured shoulder. "Maybe a little."

Her smile grew. "Well, that's something, isn't it?"

"I didn't say a lot," Tate murmured.

"Neither did I," she retorted. "So, do you want him to come over later?"

Tate's frown darkened. "No. Tell him to forget it."

"Okay," she agreed. And made no attempt to change his mind.

Tate *couldn't* read her. He couldn't tell what she was thinking. When she wanted to, she could be maddeningly enigmatic.

She started out of the room and his gaze unwillingly followed her.

What good was him missing the massage going to do? Refusing the only moments of peace he'd found in all these long months.

"Jodie?" he called, stopping her at the door. "Ask him…ask if three o'clock would be all right today. As long as it won't interfere with anything else."

"Sure," she said, and flashed him another smile. Then she continued on her way, seemingly oblivious to the havoc she left behind her.

A COUPLE OF HOURS LATER Jodie saw Emma and Jack into Tate's bedroom. He was stretched out on the covers, but once again he'd dressed in jeans and a shirt.

"Would you like some coffee? Some lunch?"

Jodie offered. "Marie sent over soup this morning. I haven't looked to see what kind, but it sure smells good. I'm thinking it might be chicken vegetable."

When the visitors declined, Jodie left the room...something Tate hadn't expected.

The seating arrangement copied that of their first visit—his mother perched on the boudoir chair and Jack, in uniform, made himself comfortable on a straight-backed chair from the kitchen.

They seemed disinclined to talk at first, as if they were having difficulty finding the right words. Tate let the moment draw out, then challenged, "Did you come all this way just to look at me?"

His mother folded her arms. "I suppose what we'd like is an explanation. Why didn't you want to see us, Tate? What possible harm can it do for us to talk? We're not your enemies, you know."

"I never—"

"Well, you certainly act like it!"

"Are you punishin' us for some reason?" Jack demanded. "That's the only conclusion we can come up with when you cut yourself off like this."

"I talk to you—both of you—almost every day."

"Might as well be in Austin," Jack grumbled. "Telephone doesn't let us see with our own eyes how you're doin'."

"So…how do I look?" Tate asked. "Any different?" He'd seen himself in the mirror this morning as he shaved. Very little, if anything, had changed. His face was still gaunt, his eyes tired, haunted.

His mother tipped her head. "I think there could be somethin'. You don't look quite as tired."

"Well, I am," Tate snapped.

Jack leaned forward. "I don't care how much you hurt, son. You don't talk to your mother that way. Your daddy wouldn't like it."

Tate grimaced. "I'm sorry."

"Tell *her* that," Jack instructed.

Tate looked at his mother, who gazed back steadily. "I'm sorry," he repeated, then he shot Jack a resentful look. "I'm not five years old, Jack. Don't talk to me like I am."

"I talk to you like the age you're actin'," Jack retorted. "Five seems about right."

"So, you came to pick a fight."

"I'm not pickin' nothin'," Jack denied. "You're the one who's spoilin' for trouble."

Emma intervened. "Jodie looks better," she said. "More like she used to." When that met with silence, she tried something else. "Has Jodie seen Jennifer yet? It's all over town that she's back at her father's ranch. They used to be such good friends."

"She saw her yesterday," Tate said.

Emma, who Tate knew liked nothing better than a good gossip about any matter unrelated to her job, asked, "Did she say why?"

"You'll have to talk to Jodie."

Jodie appeared in the doorway. "I'm sorry to interrupt, but Emma...Mae's asked to see us. I wonder if you'd mind—I doubt it'll take long. She probably just wants to say hello."

Emma glanced at Tate, who sensed her hesitation. But a request from Mae when you were on Parker land was a request from the Queen of the Realm.

For a moment he recalled the strong misgivings his mother had always had about the Parkers. Them being "town," compared with the Parkers "ranch"; them always having to struggle financially, compared with the Parkers having revenue from a number of oil and gas wells in addition to a hugely productive cattle business. All of which, Emma believed, firmly fixed the two families on different social levels. She'd told him never to let himself think that he wasn't good enough to be a member of the family, but her hesitancy about the sides mixing had been evident. And maybe she'd been right.

Emma seemed disconcerted by the even deeper sadness that entered his eyes, but she did her best to answer Jodie's question. "Ah—yes. Yes, of course. When?"

"Now?" Jodie returned.

Emma stood up, and they walked together out of the house.

Jack resettled in his chair, having stood as the women left, his politeness ingrained. "A command performance," he observed dryly. "But I like ol' Mae. When she wants somethin', she sure don't let mucha anythin' get in her way."

"She's easier to appreciate at a distance," Tate murmured.

Jack's keen eyes crinkled at the corners. "Sounds like the voice of experience talkin'."

"Try being married to her favorite niece."

Jack fiddled with his flat-brimmed hat, which he'd balanced on his knee instead of setting aside. "She not takin' to the idea of you two gettin' a divorce?"

"Not in particular, but she won't stand in the way. She's told me so."

Jack frowned. "Now, that don't sound like Mae."

"Maybe she's just facing reality, Jack. Like you and Mom should do. It ain't right keeping Jodie in this marriage for any longer than she has to be. So, I'm not."

Jack shook his head. "Have you ever asked Jodie what she thinks?"

"She's got it all mixed up with that Parker honor stuff."

"They do set a big store by it."

"Damn straight they do. But I'm not gonna let her ruin her life."

"What if she still loves you?"

"She'll get over it."

Jack smiled sadly. "I thought you were smarter than that, son."

Tate's frustration broke through. "I thought I was too, Jack, but I'm not. I'm not much use in any kinda way. I'm not much use as a man!" He ran a hand through his hair. It still came as something of a shock to him that it had grown so much longer. "Try to see this my way. What am I gonna do with myself?

The only thing I know in life is being a cop… and I don't know if I can ever be one again. The way things are now—"

"Like I said before…nothin's happened to your brain."

"It takes more than that and you know it! How can I put any kinda force behind what I say when the bad guys know all they have to do is give me a little shove and I'll fall over? You think they're gonna listen? No, they'll do what they want and I'll just have to watch 'em walk away. Who wants a cop like that?" He glared at his old friend. "You want a deputy like that? One you can send into the Watering Hole, or a place like it, and know he won't even be able to corral a friendly drunk?"

Jack studied his hat, mulling over his reply.

Tate went on, "Jodie's used to having men around her who can take care of themselves. Look at Rafe. Look at Morgan Hughes. Even at her old friend Rio. He might've been a waste of space in a lotta ways, but he could sure do that. Rafe said he was a damn fine cowboy. Well, I used to be a damn fine lawman. Now I'm not."

"You just need to give yourself a little more time," Jack said.

Tate took him up on it. "I'll do that. But I won't do it to Jodie."

Jack narrowed his eyes. "I still say, have you asked her? Does she get to have a say in any 'a this? Or have you—"

"I don't *need* to ask her," Tate interrupted him sharply.

"You know best, huh?" Jack returned, his irritation increasing.

"In this? Yes. I do."

"You're makin' a big mistake, son. You're throwin' away somethin' precious because of your pride. You can't take not bein' you at your best. Maybe Jodie'd like to have you as you are, though, instead of not here at all. You didn't see her at the hospital when things were so dicey for you. She wouldn't leave your side, not for a second. Then afterward, all she could think about was gettin' you home."

"That was before she knew what she'd be getting back."

"Your momma's really come to admire Jodie. And I do, too. From everythin' I heard, from everythin' I saw and see now, that girl's a keeper. But you're too stubborn to admit it."

"I know she is!"

"Then act like it, and drop this tomfool idea!"

Tate suddenly felt depleted. He didn't know how he'd withstood the argument for so long.

He drew a shaky breath, partially exhaled it, then said quietly, "Mind your own business, Jack."

Jack gazed at him for a long, long time. Long enough for Tate to drift asleep. When he woke up again, Jack had gone…so had his mother. And Axel was setting up his table.

JODIE HAD LOOKED in on Tate shortly before his mother and Jack started back to town, and found him still fast asleep. She'd hugged them both, her feelings of closeness to them increasing. Jack told them the gist of his conversation with Tate, but it was nothing Jodie hadn't heard before from Tate himself. After exchanging mutual encouragement, the two visitors got back into Jack's patrol car and set off.

Jodie couldn't face going inside the house to sit and wait, so she searched for her father and found him in his painting studio—an old shed he'd converted in the roughest of manners, keeping nail kegs as seats and leaving much of the contents that had long ago gone into disservice hanging on the walls and lining some of the shelves.

A number of canvases had been set on edge and were leaning against each other on the floor. The air smelled of oils and turpentine, which took Jodie back to the times in her childhood when her father would come home, his clothes bearing those mysterious scents.

Gib hadn't painted openly then, having hidden his talent because Mae disapproved. But little by little, he'd come out into the open, especially over the past few years, when his work had been recognized by critics and become popular. He'd sold a number of paintings and could have sold many more, but he wasn't much interested in that part of the business, preferring instead to paint to please himself. Galleries were constantly pleading for him to send more work, but he didn't seem to care.

He looked calmer and happier now than Jodie had ever seen him. The twilight years of his life were being good to him. He sat back from the easel and put away his brush.

"Hi, little girl, you lookin' for a place to hide out?"

Jodie smiled. After a number of years of

emotional strain, she and her father had come to an understanding. The bond that now connected them was stronger than it ever had been. "Just for a little while. Tate's asleep."

"Did I see Jack's patrol car out in front?"

Jodie nodded. "You could've stopped by to say hello."

Gib shrugged. "I'd just as soon leave Tate's family to have time with him in peace. No use me pokin' my nose in."

"I'm not so sure how peaceful it was," Jodie murmured. "I think he and Jack had a tiff."

Gib's eyebrows lifted. "Takes energy to have a tiff."

Now it was Jodie's turn to shrug. She examined the painting he'd been working on when she'd interrupted him. It was a ranch scene, his specialty. Cattle were grazing on a portion of rolling range, with a dark red cliff jutting into the sky. She recognized the spot instantly as being in Indian Wells, one of the nine divisions of the Parker Ranch. The ranch was so large, measuring in hundreds of sections, that some sort of location mapping had needed to be devised. Anyone who knew the ranch well could name in a second the exact location of each of Gib's paintings. "This is nice," she said.

Gib gazed at it consideringly. "Yeah. I like it, too." He got up to pull a notebook from a stack of others on a shelf and handed it to Jodie. "See what you think of this."

Jodie opened it, smiling. Then she totally forgot to smile as she turned page after page of drawings of the most wonderful little animals, all done whimsically in watercolor. A family of ground squirrels, a coyote, a rattlesnake, even some calves. "What is it, Dad?" she asked, looking up.

"Somethin' Harriet's asked me to try my hand at. She's been wantin' to write a children's book—one for little kids, not the older ones like she's done before. This one's about a little coyote who's lost his way, and all the animals and such that he meets as he finds his home again. It's kinda cute. She let me read it."

"And you're doing the illustrations? What a great idea!"

"I've kinda enjoyed it. It's a change."

"I'm sure. Dad, they're wonderful. The little kids are going to love them. They look so real, yet at the same time…cuddly. Their expressions are perfect!"

Gib closed the notebook and put it back on

the shelf. "Got a couple more to do yet. Some birds and a bunny. Then we'll see."

"I never expected—" She hugged her father. "You're a very surprising artist, Gib Parker," she murmured. "And so's Harriet."

"It's amazin' what a person can do when you let yourself." Gib grinned and added, "And nobody tells you that you can't. I'm not complainin', though. If I'd been doin' this all along, I mighta quit by now. Gotten bored by it. Mae mighta done me a favor by bein' against it all those years."

"I think she still owes you an apology," Jodie said.

"She's already given it to me," Gib said quickly. "Then, to top it off, she asked if I'd do a painting of ranch headquarters from up on cemetery hill, so she could hang it over the mantel in the main house. She asked if I could have it ready for her birthday. Number ninety, comin' up next fall. I've already started makin' sketches."

"That's wonderful, Dad. You must be so proud."

"Yeah, it does kinda make me proud." Her father stuck out his chest a little.

Jodie settled on a nail keg and watched him paint. They talked about this and that, but not about Tate. Gib seemed to sense, without being told, that she needed a little time away from her worries.

JODIE MET AXEL at the front door. He was coming out as she was going in.

"'Afternoon, Miss Jodie," he greeted her before hurrying down the walkway.

A warm pleasant scent of sesame oil trailed after him, which she followed all the way to the back of the house and Tate's room. She'd noticed it over the past few days, but never so intensely as she did now. But then, she'd never been at home when Tate received his massages.

He was on his feet when she entered the bedroom, his back to her as he buttoned his shirt. For a moment, she could have forgotten that time had passed since last September. He held himself as he used to—straight, tall, proud. A man to be reckoned with.

He swung around. Was his movement easier than it had been before? Their gazes met, held…then he looked away.

"Where've you been?" he asked.

"With my dad."

"Mmm," he said.

He moved over to the edge of the bed and

sat down. This, too, looked more easily performed. Was he finding the same benefit in a massage as in a shower? Was his face, when she studied it, less stricken?

She wished she could ask but knew better. Instead, she said, "Your mother said to tell you goodbye. Jack, too."

"Mmm," he said again.

"Aunt Mae asked after you."

That got his attention. His head came up. "What was it she wanted with my mom?"

"Like I thought…just to say hello."

"Mae never does anything *just* to do it."

"This time she did. She likes Emma."

"And how did my mom take it?"

"Fine. Tate, why would you think—"

"You know how my mother feels about the Parkers."

"I know how she used to feel."

"She still does."

Jodie walked past him and reached for something on the nightstand. When she turned, she was holding the case folder. "Jack's asked about this twice. It's starting to hurt his feelings that you haven't even looked at it."

"I told him not to leave it."

Jodie put the folder back where she'd found

it. When she turned around again, she saw that Tate was still watching her. His gaze was purposefully unrevealing, but she had an idea more was going on inside him than he was prepared to admit. She'd been about to leave but decided to stay for a bit.

Her gaze dropped to his foot, and she made a small sound of distress.

"What is it?" he asked gruffly, frowning.

"The cut. We didn't put anything on it this morning."

"I forgot about it."

"Let me see." She dropped to her knees in front of him. He still wore the jeans and shirt he'd put on for his visitors. She wondered if that, too, was a good sign. Wrapping her fingers around his bare ankle, she urged him to lift it.

He kept his foot solidly on the floor. "I don't feel a thing," he said. "There's nothing wrong."

"Then it won't hurt for me to look."

They had a brief battle of wills, during which she used an unfair weapon—her smile. After a moment, he relented.

She examined the cut. "Good news. It's barely pink and looks to be healing nicely. Would you like a Band-Aid?"

"It's fine as it is," he said gruffly.

Jodie sat back on her heels. She tried to think of something else that would give her more time with him.

"You know I saw Jennifer yesterday," she said.

He nodded.

"She has a problem I wish she could talk to you about."

"What kind of problem?"

"It's her husband. Tate, I think she's afraid of him."

His expression quickened with interest, which he immediately schooled. "Why tell me?"

"She's not. I am. She doesn't want anyone to know, not even her father."

"What's he done?"

"You want to know the whole thing? They live in Boston, remember, where Alan—that's his name—is a teacher at a private school. He and another teacher stole money from the school. He denied it, of course, and Jennifer believed him…then…" She paused.

"Then?" he prompted.

"Then Jennifer found some emails that implicated him. He doesn't know she found them and she brought them with her…here."

"She didn't give them to the authorities in Boston?"

"Not yet."

"You told her she should, of course."

Jodie nodded. She switched places and sat on the bed, careful not to get too close. She rubbed her knees, as if they were the reason for her change of position.

"That still doesn't explain why she's afraid," Tate said.

"He got rough with her and the baby. Pushed her, slapped the baby. It happened after the police questioned him."

"He slapped his child?"

Jodie nodded. "When she wouldn't stop crying."

"How old's the baby?"

"Sixteen months. Tate, Jennifer says he's changed. Like he's two different people. And the real one isn't the one she married. It frightened her. I still don't think she's told me everything."

"Does Jim know?"

"He knows only what the press does—about the money. She won't tell him the rest."

"He's gonna have a hard time protecting her if he doesn't know the truth."

"I gave her my word I wouldn't tell him.

It's—it's something that goes back a long way between Jennifer and me. I can't do it."

Tate met her look. "But I can."

Jodie touched his arm lightly, then withdrew her hand. "There's no one else. To Jennifer's mind, it's bad enough that people in the Boston area know about him. She said it made all the news programs there and will probably make a lot more before it's over. Particularly if she turns over the emails and he goes to trial. Whatever happens, it'll be noisy. She's worried for the baby—for little Angela—and wants to keep it quiet out here. She says her daughter has to grow up someplace."

"No one here would blame her."

"That's what I said, but she's afraid, Tate. I've never seen her so afraid."

"You say she's willing to turn these emails over to the police?"

"She thinks she is. She will."

"Then Jim has to know. If that husband of hers is as unstable as she's making out, he could come after her."

"Edna tells him they're not here when he calls."

"I'm sure he believes it," Tate said dryly.

"Jim's already worried. He's the one who asked me to talk to her."

Tate cursed beneath his breath. "Maybe you shoulda told all this to Jack. I'm sure as hell not gonna be able to do anything if there's trouble."

"I suggested that. I knew you weren't—"

The hurt look that flashed into his eyes wounded her, as well. For the first time since he'd been shot, they'd been having a conversation that lasted more than a minute. A conversation about something other than the end of their marriage. Then she'd ruined it!

She tried to make amends. "She told me not to bother you. She knows what happened, how badly you— I told her we needed to tell you!"

Tate stood up and moved across the room. He wasn't as bent as he had been previously, but he still walked slowly. He caught hold of the open door and held on to the knob. "I'll think about it, Jodie. I may tell Jack myself."

"Jim's the one—"

"And Jack can tell Jim."

Jodie stood up. He wanted her out of the room. *He* was waiting to see *her* out of the room. A first! "That would work," she agreed. "Jennifer will know it came from me, that I told you, but that's okay, as long as I don't tell Jim. He's the one I specifically promised not to—"

"You're willing to go to any length to keep your word, aren't you? Well, Jodie, sometimes a person just can't manage that. Sometimes the real world takes a hand and it comes down to a choice between honor and having a life."

"I don't understand. I'm not— It's Jennifer who—" Her gaze was puzzled as she stepped into the hall.

"Think about it," he advised, then he shut the door.

CHAPTER TEN

TATE HAD NO IDEA whether Jodie had heeded his advice to "think about it," because the next morning, after bringing his breakfast tray, she announced excitedly that she was going riding with Shannon. It had been a long time, she'd said. Too long. She'd missed it.

Her eyes had shone at the prospect of getting back on a horse; her face had been aglow. Her beauty had nearly robbed Tate of breath. He hadn't wanted her to leave! But he'd done nothing to stop her.

That image of her haunted him as the morning wore on. He returned to it repeatedly—but that only increased his frustration, until the confines of the small house, with its many frills and flowers, once again drove him outdoors.

He fled to the porch and stretched out on the chaise longue, glad that instead of donning fresh pajamas after his shower, he'd pulled on jeans and a T-shirt. Being in regular clothes yesterday had felt good, and it did again today.

He could hear children playing. They sounded as though they were in the yard next door—at Harriet's—which would stand to reason if Shannon was out riding with Jodie. Only, he heard a young girl's voice, as well. Probably Anna. Then he saw Harriet come outside with Wesley and point to various spots in the flower beds. That was when Tate realized this must be Saturday. No school!

He had lost track of time during these past months. The days of the week held little importance to him. One day—one month—was much like another. He had no reason, no cause, to notice.

Harriet saw him on the porch and walked over.

"'Mornin'," she said brightly. "It's a nice day, isn't it? I love the spring. My favorite time of the year. Looks like it's gonna be another early one this year, too. Flowers I didn't expect for another month are already startin' to bloom. And the weeds!" She glanced at her tall, dark-haired son, who was dejectedly beginning his assignment. "I set Wes to work gettin' rid of 'em. I thought that would be a fitting punishment for him talkin' back to his teachers. He hates it. Thinks it's beneath him."

"He's doing it, though."

Harriet grinned. "He knows he'd best." She motioned to the newspaper Tate had brought with him. "Thought you'd do a bit of readin', hmm?"

Tate shrugged. "Somethin' to do."

Harriet grinned. "You better be careful what you say. I could set you to work, too... if you're bored."

"I'm not that bored. Anyway, the weeds'd probably win."

"I wasn't thinkin' about makin' you weed. Wes can do Darlene's flower beds. No, I was thinkin' of somethin' else." She paused. "Like maybe, when he comes over here to weed, you could have a little talk with him. Everyone else has had a try, and it hasn't done much good. Maybe you— You were always pretty good with kids when you were sheriff. Maybe he'd listen to you."

"I was pretty good at taking 'em in when they needed it. I didn't deal much with kids who stayed outta trouble."

"Wes is in trouble."

"Not the kind I'm talking about."

Harriet agreed, "No, you're right. Not that kind. But that doesn't stop me from worryin'. One thing could lead to another, then before you know it—"

Tate surrendered, lifting his hands. "I'll talk to him."

Harriet looked pleased.

On her way back into her house, she paused to say something to her son. Wes glanced toward the other house, nodded, then got back to work.

Tate sat for a long time, enjoying the fresh air and the warm morning sun. His thoughts moved to Jodie again, but he purposefully kept them light. He wondered if she was enjoying her ride. Then he answered his own question. She'd learned to ride a horse at almost the same age as she'd learned to walk. She was a Parker, on Parker land. Of course she was enjoying her ride!

He reached for the newspaper, but his fingertips scraped the tougher paper of the case folder underneath, which he'd also brought along. Jodie's rebuke about Jack's being hurt because he'd yet to look at it had resonated inside him.

He doubted that Jack put great store in his

coming up with anything to further the case when so many others had already combed through it, but the least he could do was read the file. As he'd said to Harriet, it would help pass the time.

He removed the rubber band and slid out the paperwork. Photos of the autopsy and the scene slipped loosely onto his lap. Curiosity made him examine them first. The initial autopsy display showed a man in his late forties, Rawley Stevens, a big bear of a man, with several colorful tattoos and a couple of body piercings that must have been uncomfortable to live with. He was stretched out on the coroner's table, pale and still, looking nothing like the raucous individual Tate had had several run-ins with over the years. There were numerous close-ups of bruises and abrasions on his limbs and torso, and several views of a tire track that cut across the middle of his belly. The scene photos showed the same tracks in the same position between his short vest and black leather pants. His big heavy motorcycle lay on its side a distance away.

There was good reason to believe Rawley had come upon his death accidentally. For one thing, he was known to drive through sections of isolated ranch land like a madman.

For another, the tire track. The autopsy report stated that death was due to internal injuries, complicated by his not having been found right away.

Tate read the scene report, read the follow-ups, read the medical and toxicological reports. Rawley's blood-alcohol level had crossed the legal limit. He would have been cited for operating a motor vehicle under the influence if he'd been stopped on the highway.

The paperwork pretty much spoke for itself. Rawley Stevens must have been on one of his usual tears, done something stupid and paid the ultimate price. There were no signs of foul play. Just him and the bike at the bottom of a shallow ravine, as if he'd ridden straight off the upper level, gotten separated from the bike and somehow been run over by it.

Tate examined the scene photos again. The bike had been carefully photographed—the angle at which it had come to rest, the damage to its structure, the distance from the body.

Tate frowned. Something…wasn't right. He couldn't quite put his finger on what it was, but something—

"Ah—Tate? Will it bother you if I—"

Still frowning, Tate dragged his gaze away from the photographs and met Wesley's dark eyes. He was a lanky boy, handsome as all the Parkers were, and on the verge of manhood. His voice had lowered, his chest had deepened and he'd already acquired the look of someone who'd been tested and had prevailed. Yet there was still enough boy in him that he needed approval.

Tate stuffed the photos back in the folder. Autopsy and scene photos were sometimes hard to take, even for a lawman accustomed to them.

Wes took up his question. "Will it bother you if I work in the flower beds now? Mom wants me to do 'em before I start on the ones in back. I can come again later, though."

"Work away," Tate said agreeably.

Wes dropped stoically to his knees and started pulling weeds.

Tate watched him for a time, then he said, "This seems like hard labor. Is it? Or do you enjoy it?"

"Who in their right mind would enjoy it?" Wes retorted, suppressed anger tightening his tone.

"Somebody must. The bushes and plants all look pretty nice."

"Mom usually does it."

Tate teased, "Isn't that funny? Harriet's

always impressed me as being in her right mind."

"I meant for a ranch hand."

"Ah." Tate nodded understanding. "You've been on what, two roundups?"

"I go on my third this May," Wes said proudly.

Tate whistled softly, impressed. Roundups were rough, dirty work. There was no place in them for people who didn't pull their own weight. "Then how do you come to be doing this?"

The young man's expression darkened as he sat back on his heels. "It's Mom's idea of a joke."

"Looks more like punishment. What'd you do?"

Wes shrugged.

"Rather not talk about it, hmm?" Tate guessed.

"Not really."

"Well, since I'm not exactly the busiest person around, if you feel like talking sometime, you just come on over. I'll be here."

Wes resumed his work. He didn't answer, but in Tate's experience, boys his age wouldn't say a word until they were ready.

After Wesley finished weeding the front

beds, he moved around back, which freed Tate to bring out the photos again and study them.

Something about this case bothered him. Something he couldn't—

"Who's that?" a young girl's voice demanded. "Is he sleepin'?"

Tate had been concentrating so hard he hadn't heard anyone approach. He quickly put the photos away. This time when he looked up it was into the curious gray eyes of Wesley's younger sister, Anna. Rafe and Shannon's boys stood beside her, one at each side.

"Yeah, he's sleeping," Tate said.

"Why does he look so funny?" Anna persisted. Her black hair was naturally curly and held back by a wide plastic band.

Harriet would have his ears if she knew what her daughter had inadvertently seen. But at least it wasn't one of the more gruesome photographs. Rawley Stevens did appear to be sleeping peacefully.

"Because he's a funny-lookin' man," Tate returned.

He had even less experience with children of this age. They seldom got into trouble, and if one went missing or was caught up in a battling-parent home, his longest time with them, once they'd passed into his care, had lasted only until he got them to the station, and to whoever took them from there.

"Can I see him?" Nate begged. "I didn't get to see him!"

"Me, neither," Wade agreed, joining in.

Tate noticed the length of rope in each child's hands. "What are y'all doing with the rope?" he asked, hoping to divert their attention. It worked.

"Practicin'," Wade said, and promptly twirled a loop and tossed it over Tate's feet, catching them neatly.

"Me, too! I can do it, too!" Nate bragged.

The four-year-old made a less practiced loop but did manage to snare Tate's feet. He giggled proudly as he released him.

"I can, too," Anna said. "But I'm not a show-off."

"Can't!" Wade and Nate cried in unison.

"Can!"

"Can't!"

Anna sighed, rolled her eyes at the stupidities of males, then expertly twirled her loop and caught Tate's feet. "See?" she said. "I told you I could."

She then wrapped the ends around each hand and converted the lasso into a jump rope.

The boys groaned at her girlish whim, while she skipped faster and faster, until she missed a step.

The children continued to play on the porch, occasionally talking to Tate but mostly not. He knew they had to be curious about him. This time, though, the boys didn't mention his scars, obviously having been told by their mother not to. And Anna either had been forewarned or didn't know about them, because she didn't make any requests, either.

Axel interrupted the nap Tate had slipped into shortly after the children ran off to play somewhere else.

"It's one o'clock already?" Tate asked, surprised. Then he thought of Jodie and a slight frown marked his brow. Was she still out riding? She hadn't said when she'd return, but wasn't this length of time unusual? Should he raise an alarm? Then he realized the hypocrisy behind his thoughts. He couldn't expect her to report to him each time she came and went. If he wanted to end the marriage, the end of their accountability to each other went along with it.

He got up to go inside, and while Axel was giving him his massage—this time starting to work the muscles a little deeper—Jodie came home. She explained that she and Shannon had stopped by to see Christine at Little Springs and ended up having lunch.

Jodie's face still glowed. He couldn't remember her any more beautiful, except maybe on the day they married. He had to swallow hard to keep himself from telling her that.

She walked up to the massage table, bent close and sniffed. Then she filched a little of the light oil from his back and rubbed it on her hands.

"This is nice," she said.

Tate's muscles where she'd touched him jerked spasmodically.

She giggled. "Did that tickle?"

Tate made a noise deep in his throat and closed his eyes against her.

Axel said nothing. He just continued to work.

Only when she went to take a shower was Tate able to relax. Axel, of course, was aware of that, as well.

"CHRISTINE SAID to tell you that she's sorry they haven't been able to come see you yet. Several of them have been trading a cold, and they didn't want to give it to you." Jodie had showered and changed and was now back in his room. "She said to tell you they send their love."

Tate nodded.

"We had a picnic outside so Harriet and I wouldn't be exposed. But, like Harriet said, when you're around young kids a lot—" She stopped abruptly.

When Tate looked at her, she had a funny expression, as if she'd just remembered something whimsical yet at the same time serious.

"What is it?" he asked.

Jodie blinked. "Ah…nothing. I was just— I was wondering— When I said that about young kids— Have you talked to Jim Cleary yet?"

"Not yet," Tate replied.

Her body gave a little twitch, and she stood up. "Let me get you something to eat. What would you like? Some soup?"

She seemed to want to get away from him. Away from his curiosity.

"Soup's fine," he said.

She left the room without looking back.

What was it? he wondered. Had something happened to her out on the ride? Or during her visit to the Hugheses? He knew she was covering for something, hiding a truth. But what?

When she returned with the soup minutes later, she'd collected herself. She smiled at him confidently, warmly…and if Tate had been in a less probing state of mind, he might have believed it, because he wanted to believe it.

Jodie was good at keeping secrets. Hadn't she hidden Rio away the entire time the Hammonds, the relatives of the girl the ne'er-do-well cowboy had been suspected of killing, were on the lookout for him? Not to mention himself and his deputies? Did she have another secret she was keeping? But…was that possible? He and Jodie had been living in each other's pockets for all these months.

A thought struck him. She wasn't seeing Rio, was she? The cowboy hadn't shown up on the ranch from out of the blue and started making a play for her, had he?

The only time Tate could remember being jealous in his life was when Jodie had stubbornly protected Rio. She'd even enlisted Tate's aid in helping him. That she'd been proved correct—Rio hadn't harmed the Hammond girl—had done nothing to mitigate Tate's situation. But she'd sent the cowboy away, then told *him* that she loved him—only him—and he'd believed her.

Hypocrisy had begun to rear its ugly head again, he realized, because just as setting her free released her from accountability, it also freed her to find comfort in the arms of any man she chose. Even Rio.

Tate groaned. That image hurt too much to think about! How could he watch it happen? How could he let her— But then, how could he not? She was too young, too vital, to remain tied to a person who could give her so little. He loved her far too much to condemn her to that.

"Tate!" She must have said his name more than once because she was looking at him with deep concern. "Are you all right? You made the most awful sound. Are you in pain?"

Tate shook his head, denying everything, even as he continued to dwell on what had hurt him the most. How would he be able to stand seeing her with Rio or with anyone else? He shook his head again, attempting to clear it. He had to stop thinking this way or he'd drive himself crazy! He struggled for control.

"I'm fine," he said tightly, to her, to himself.

"Maybe you should lie down for a while. Not try to do so much. You don't want to set yourself back."

Tate remembered his promise to Mae. To be kinder to Jodie and to get himself strong enough to stand on his own feet so Jodie wouldn't worry when they parted. What happened after they parted wouldn't matter. After they—Tate couldn't bring himself to form the word: *divorced.*

"I'm fine," he repeated, and made himself smile for added reassurance.

He started to eat the soup, more for something to do than because of real desire. Then he found, to his surprise, that he was hungry. He even asked for a second bowl.

JODIE WENT TO BED early that night. She'd burrowed out a little more space for herself in the spare bedroom, hung up a few more of her things and emptied a drawer in one of the packed chests. She was still living partially out of her suitcase, but spreading out a bit made the situation easier.

Nothing made dealing with Tate easier, though. This afternoon, she'd almost done it! She'd almost blurted out that she was pregnant. She'd been regaling him with what Harriet had said to Christine about catching various ills from your children, when she'd almost slipped into saying that that was something she and Tate would soon find out for themselves. It had seemed the most natural thing. A mother talking to a father about their coming child.

He'd been suspicious when she'd stopped talking, then grown introspective, and afterward, he'd moaned in some kind of terrible pain—a pain he wouldn't admit to. As Emma had asked the first time she'd seen him, should they get him to a doctor, just to be safe? But would he even go? *I'm fine,* he kept repeating. But was he?

Encouragingly, his appetite had picked up. She'd noticed less food being returned to the kitchen over the past couple of days. He also seemed to be sleeping easier, for longer periods of time.

It was hard to wait. Harder still to keep this secret. But telling anyone else now—even Emma, she'd ultimately concluded—was too much of a gamble. The balance was too delicately struck to chance disturbing.

Emma would forgive her. So would her

father, Harriet, Shannon, Christine and the others. The baby, when he or she was born, would melt even the hardest heart.

Which, hopefully, would include the father's.

TATE MOVED around his room, lurching from this to that. He couldn't get the thought of Rio Walsh and Jodie out of his mind. She'd told him how they used to communicate with a special Mexican silver coin. Would Rio know to hang the coin from a nail head outside her window in this house? She'd have told him which room, of course.

Jealousy spread through Tate like a fever... until he remembered that Rio had given the coin to Jodie as a keepsake before he'd left West Texas. She could have given it back to him, though. She—

Tate dropped into a chair. *He had to stop this!* It wasn't good for him. It wasn't good for Jodie, either. His unfounded suspicions didn't speak well of his opinion of her...and wasn't accurate. Their...separation...wasn't her idea. It was his. He was the one holding back, pushing her away. In Jack's opinion, throwing away something precious.

Thinking of Jack prodded Tate to thoughts

of his father, something he hadn't let himself do since the day he'd been shot. He'd avoided it, just as he'd avoided talking to his fellow task-force members.

The two men had suffered strikingly similar wounds, only Tate had had advantages that his father hadn't. Modern techniques and technologies doctors could only dream about twenty years earlier had saved his life. If his father had those same advantages, he'd probably be alive today. Still, there were instances, as in the Rawley Stevens case, when modern medicine arrived too late. And sometimes even with the very best of care the patient died.

He himself had come so close!

Tate started to shake. He shook so hard that his teeth chattered. And he could do nothing to stop it as a memory from that time rushed over him, one that until now he hadn't acknowledged. A floaty period—when he seemed above it all, watching himself as strangers in surgical gowns and masks fought to bring him back to life. He had died then. And had done it more than once over a period of days. His mother had tried to talk to him about it later, but he'd been too afraid to listen.

Too…terrified.

Tate continued to shake, not from cold but from horror. From seeing himself lying there…dead.

He should have dealt with it earlier but had hidden from it, instead. Just as, when he was a child, he'd hidden from the news of his father's death. Jack and his mother had wanted to tell him themselves, before he found out from someone else. But Tate had already overheard two townspeople talking. To his young mind, if it didn't come from the people he was closest to, it wasn't real…so he'd avoided both Jack and his mother, and thereby avoided the truth. Eventually, though, Jack had rooted him out and told him.

Was he less of a man than his father for looking back on his own death in fear? His training had taught him to survive as well as to protect, to defend and if necessary to die. But die like that? For no reason? Because some two-bit hoods hiding out in an auto-wrecking yard had confused him with another two-bit hood the men wanted to silence?

His father had been killed when he'd noticed a car's broken taillight and made a traffic stop. A pair of escaped felons, who didn't want to go back to prison, had shot him.

Had he, Tate, imagined himself somehow magically protected because an act so devoid of reason couldn't possibly happen twice in the same family?

But it had happened. His father had made the traffic stop and been shot; he and Billy Vance had walked into the wrecking yard and been fired on.

Tate continued to shake, but little by little his tremors slackened, until finally they stopped.

Then he dragged himself to bed, where after a few numbed seconds he fell asleep.

CHAPTER ELEVEN

MAE HOSTED a big family meal at her house midday on Sunday. Tate declined the invitation, but Jodie had to go, though she couldn't stop thinking of him. He'd been quieter this morning than in recent days, his manner slightly different. There didn't seem to be as much anger, as much defiance. It was as if something within him had altered. Only, she didn't know what. And she wasn't sure how to respond. She begrudged the time away from him, which she might have used more constructively.

When the obligatory part of the meal was over and custom called for everyone to move from dining room to living room for after-dinner coffee, she lingered for a private word with her great-aunt. "I should leave now, Aunt Mae. I need to get back to Tate."

Mae eyed her, assessing her disposition. "Are we startin' to make any headway yet?"

Jodie shrugged. "It's hard to tell."

"It might help if you stopped looking so glum."

Her great-aunt always had been able to disconcert her. Jodie stammered, "I'm not— I don't—"

Mae smiled and patted her arm. "I'm just teasing you," she said. "Trying to get you to smile. Go ahead and do what you need to. Everybody'll understand." Then she went to join the others.

Before Jodie could follow, Marie entered the dining room from the kitchen. When she saw her, the housekeeper's face lit up with a smile. Jodie had made a special point earlier to thank Marie for all the meals she'd sent over. True to her nature, Marie had dismissed the kindnesses.

She picked up quickly on the fact that Jodie was about to leave. "Wait just a minute. I have something for Tate." She disappeared back into the other room, then hurried out to hand Jodie a covered plate. "There's plenty of food left over from dinner and I know Tate loves fried chicken and cream gravy. I added some vegetables, but tell him if he doesn't like 'em, not to worry. I won't have my feelin's hurt."

"Marie," Jodie protested, "you've already done so much."

"I enjoy cooking. I'm good at it. So, why not?"

Jodie hugged her. "Still," she said, emotion tightening her throat as gratitude for what everyone was doing washed over her, "I appreciate it."

Marie drew back. "Axel tells me he thinks Tate's startin' to look better. That the massages are helpin'."

"I know Tate enjoys them. If he didn't, he'd stop."

"That's what Axel says, too."

Needing to hear the encouraging words once again, Jodie prompted, "Axel…thinks Tate looks better?"

"He sure does. He says Tate was all one knotted-up muscle when they first started. Worse he'd ever seen. But now…he's not nearly so bad."

Jodie hugged Marie again, then let her get on with preparing the coffee, while she braved the gauntlet of good wishes from her family as she passed through the living room to the front door.

INERTIA HAD STARTED to get to Tate.

Maybe what he needed was to have the whole divorce thing over with. See things settled. Or maybe, he was just tired of being tired.

He moved restlessly around the house while Jodie was at dinner. Then, bored with that, he studied the photos from the Stevens case, only to give up again in irritation.

He'd like to go sit out on the front porch, but with the entire Parker clan at Mae's, he'd soon be inundated with well-wishers when they saw him outside. If he'd wanted that, he could have gone to dinner.

Eventually, he ended up in the kitchen. On a whim he picked up the phone and dialed Jack, but Jack was out on a call. Next, he dialed his mother—he knew she wasn't planning to work this Sunday—but she was out, as well. Probably doing something with her women's club. As a last resort, he consulted the phone book for the Clearys' number.

An older woman answered—Edna Hardy, the Clearys' longtime housekeeper. Tate knew her sister, Marybeth, better than he knew Edna. Marybeth Hardy was the perennial president of his mother's women's club. He'd dealt with her on numerous occasions when the club had planned an event.

"Edna," he said crisply, slipping back into his official tone. "This is Tate Connelly. Is Jennifer around?"

"Of course," Edna said, and hurried off.

Moments later another voice answered. "Tate? This is Jennifer. Is that really you?"

Tate's hand tightened on the receiver. She sounded as if she might be talking to a ghost! "It's really me," he said.

Jennifer laughed somewhat nervously. She didn't ask his reason for calling. "You— I— You don't have to do this. I told Jodie you shouldn't be bothered. I know you haven't been well, and—"

Tate cut into her gush of words. He didn't know Jennifer all that well, but that didn't matter. She and Jodie were friends, and Jodie had asked for his help. "Jodie told me what you said. She also told me you seemed unsure about what to do. You don't have a choice, Jennifer. If the emails you found incriminate your husband, you have to turn them over to the Boston police. Otherwise, you could be charged with a crime yourself."

She made a small strangled sound.

Tate softened his tone. "Do you have the

name of the detective handling the case? If you do, give him a call. Tell him. He'll do the rest."

"I have it," she said tightly.

Tate sensed a lingering hesitancy. "Are you afraid your husband'll do something bad if he finds out?"

"He might," she admitted.

"Tell that to the detective, too. He should know."

Jennifer laughed unsteadily. "I'm probably just being silly. I don't— Alan doesn't—"

"Jodie told me what he did to you and to the baby. She's worried."

"I shouldn't have told her."

"Would that make it go away?"

"No," she breathed. "But I wish it would."

Tate knew the feeling. Life would be so much easier if you could just wish away the bad parts.

He sighed.

She must have heard him. "I truly didn't mean to bother you with this, Tate. I told Jodie—"

"Jodie did exactly the right thing. And you should, too. You should tell your father so he can watch out for you. If this husband of yours takes it into his head to make trouble, you're gonna need help. Tell Jack, as well. He'd wanna know."

"No," she said quickly. "I'm...probably exaggerating things. Making them worse than they really are. Alan wouldn't come here. He wouldn't—"

"If you don't tell your dad, I will." Tate delivered the ultimatum.

It elicited a little moan. "I'm afraid of what he'll do when he finds out! Daddy idolizes Angela. If he hears that Alan slapped her—"

"All the more reason he should hear it from you." Tate paused. "Would you like me to ask Jack to pay a visit out to your place tomorrow so he can be there when you tell your dad what happened? He'll be able to defuse any problem. And he won't tell a soul."

"He'll have to alert his deputies. Then other people will find out, then more and more. Pretty soon Angela and I won't be able to—" She broke off. "Could you do it, Tate? Could you be here when I tell Daddy? I know it's a lot to ask, but...I could come get you and bring you back. It wouldn't take very long. Jodie could come, too."

"I'm not up to paying calls yet," Tate said flatly. He'd had to pull up a chair and drop into it shortly after starting this conversation. Right now, all he wanted to do was lie down.

"Then could we come over there? I'll tell Daddy we'll be visiting you. He's been wanting to do that anyway." She hesitated. "He's going to be upset, and when he's upset, he won't listen to me. He'll want to jump into the plane and go to Boston himself. Then he'll go looking for Alan. Tate...I won't be able to stand it if anything happens to him. He's all Angela and I have left!"

"Your father's never struck me as a rash man. I'll be glad to do what I can, though." He hoped his quiet confidence would quell her agitation. "When do you think you'll be coming over? Jodie'll want to know."

"Would this afternoon be all right? If I'm going to do it, I shouldn't wait too much longer to call Detective Logan."

"I'll tell Jodie."

"Thanks, Tate," Jennifer said softly, and hung up.

Tate sat very still, wondering what he'd let himself in for. Wondering *why* he'd let himself in for it.

As a favor to Jim Cleary? He knew Jim mostly in passing, the older man having lived at the ranch more off than on before his retirement.

No, it was for Jodie, who he couldn't stand to see concerned about anything.

"Tate?" She said his name from the doorway.

He turned to find that she was wearing another light summery dress, sleeveless and pale green—a green that uncannily matched the green in her eyes. She'd pulled her mass of copper-colored hair into some kind of twirl at the back of her head and let bright tendrils escape onto her neck. She was nothing short of gorgeous.

"Were you on the phone?" she asked.

"Ah—yes," he said, grappling for control. "I was talking to Jennifer. She and her dad will be coming over later. Jennifer wants me around when she tells Jim about..." His words petered out as Jodie came closer.

"Are you sure you want to do this? I thought you were going to tell Jack and let him—"

"She asked me to."

Jodie slid a covered plate onto the table at his side. She smiled wryly. "Another offering from Marie. Fried chicken this time. I can vouch that it's good."

"Is she trying to fatten me up or something?"

Tate murmured. Much to his relief, Jodie moved away after delivering the dinner.

"If you're hungry, it's probably still warm."

Tate wanted to refuse but couldn't. For the first time in months he sat properly at a table to eat. It didn't take long for him to make inroads into the delicious meal.

Jodie grinned. "Would you like me to go get seconds?"

Tate pushed away. "No, that's it. Next time you see Marie tell her thanks."

"I already did. She says she enjoys it."

Tate glanced at the wall clock, an action that felt odd to him. For so long he'd had no need to know the time. "Did you see Axel?" he asked. "He's late."

Jodie shook her head. "Only Marie. Axel's probably barbecuing something special for the hands' dinner and got held up. You want me to go check?"

"No," he answered. "If he's held up, he's held up. He'll be along."

He felt her study him as he stood up, taking in the fact that he was again wearing regular clothes. "I got tired of pajamas," he said uneasily. "They're comfortable, but..."

"I can imagine," she answered softly when

his explanation trailed off. With a quick smile, she announced that she was going to change.

Tate watched her leave. He wanted to accompany her into the crowded room—to take her in his arms and kiss her like he used to, like he couldn't get enough of being close to her. But what good would that do either of them?

Tate steeled himself to stay where he was.

AXEL HURRIED to the house, a little over an hour late and full of apologies. Jodie would've kissed him if Tate hadn't called him into the bedroom. Ever since her conversation with Tate in the kitchen, she'd started to feel a tingle of encouragement. She was afraid to let herself be too optimistic, but she couldn't help it.

Tate was up and about more now. He moved with less pain, talked to her with more ease. And, as she'd noticed this morning, he didn't seem as angry or as tense. Also, his appetite continued to improve. All combined, it meant he was growing stronger.

She knew his agreement with Mae could have had something to do with it, but even if that was the case, it gave her something to work with. She could see flashes of the old Tate. And if she could see them, didn't that mean the old Tate was actually there? The Tate she loved, and who, she knew, loved her in return?

Axel was still in the bedroom with Tate when the Clearys arrived. Jennifer and Jim and the baby. Jodie could see the dread in her friend's eyes as well as a little spark of anger aimed at her. Jennifer probably resented the fact that Jodie had brought Tate into the dilemma, which in turn had forced the issue. But she wasn't going to apologize. She'd kept her word about not telling Jim.

She saw them into the living room and took Angela onto her lap. The little girl was dressed in her Sunday best—a ruffly pink dress with a white petticoat and shiny white patent-leather shoes. A barrette shaped like a rabbit was caught in her curly blond hair.

"Jo-die!" the little girl cried.

Jodie was surprised that she'd remembered her.

Jennifer smiled tightly. "I told her we were coming to see you and she's been saying your name ever since."

"Jo-die!" Angela repeated in her thin treble.

"I would have left her with Edna, but her sister called from town and she had to go in. I hope you don't mind."

"Not at all," Jodie said.

"Bunny!" The girl pointed to her barrette. "White bunny! White shoes!" She pointed to her feet. "Jo-die!" she said again, giggling as she burrowed her cheek against Jodie's chest.

Jodie laughed in shared delight, while Jim nearly burst with pride.

"Paw-paw," Angela cried, reaching for him. Jim, of course, happily took her. "Mommy... Angel." The little girl enjoyed being the center of attention.

Jennifer pulled a children's picture book from a satchel. "Read this to yourself, sweetheart. Paw-paw and Mommy want to talk to Jodie."

Amazingly, Angela accepted the book and did as she was told. She needed only occasional help from her grandfather as she studied the pages and identified everything on them—softly, to herself.

"Is Tate asleep?" Jennifer asked. "I suppose we should have called. Dad wanted to, but I didn't think..."

Jodie spoke into the pause. "Actually, Axel's

giving him a massage. He gets one every day."

Jim brightened. "I used to get those all the time. Really helped when I was in the middle of contract negotiations."

Jennifer sprang to her feet. "Maybe it would be better if we came back later. You were right, Dad. We should've called before we left. Jodie, I'm sorry we bothered you."

But as she reached for Angela, Axel spoke from the arched doorway into the hall. He was on his way out. "All done, Miss Jodie." He included the others. "Mr. Cleary, Miss Jennifer…and who's this little dolly? Is she your baby, Miss Jennifer?"

"Angel," Angela promptly introduced herself. She wasn't the least bit intimidated by the stranger's size. She looked Axel straight in the eye and grinned.

"Well, that you are, little dolly," Axel said, his huge smile stretching from ear to ear. "That you are!"

Jodie excused herself immediately after Axel left, to consult Tate. "They're here," she said. "Jennifer and her dad, and she brought the baby, too." She paused briefly. "Do you mind?"

Tate finished tucking his shirt back into his jeans. "You mean about the baby? No."

Jodie nodded, her heart thumping. She wished she'd been talking about their baby and that he'd taken the news with such equanimity.

"I'll bring them in," she offered.

Tate refused. "I'll come to them."

Jodie tried not to show her surprise.

There was a slight awkwardness as Tate met the Clearys. They did their best not to assess his health too obviously, and he did his best not to act as if he felt like a bug on display. They were the first people in the area outside of the family to see him. Jodie suspected this was an important moment for him.

Jodie let Tate decide where he wanted to sit. He chose Thomas's leather recliner, where he wouldn't have to sit fully upright. He had to be tired and wanting to rest, but he carefully schooled his expression.

More pleasantries were exchanged, as well as lamentations about Tate's shooting and long recovery. Then Jennifer, the instigator of the ploy to deceive her father about the reason for their visit, reached the point where she could stand it no longer.

"Daddy," she said quickly, "we didn't come here just to see Tate. There's something else. Something I asked Tate to—" Her glance at Tate held panic.

"Jennifer has something she wants to tell you, Jim," Tate said quietly, calmly.

Jim grew very still.

"It's—it's about Alan," Jennifer said.

But before explaining further, Jodie saw her friend glance worriedly toward her daughter. Jennifer was hesitant to discuss the matter in front of the child, even at Angela's young age. Jodie volunteered, "How about if I take Angel outside to play? Would that be all right?"

Jennifer was relieved.

"Outside!" Angela cried, and waved at the others from Jodie's arms as they left the room.

Everyone, including Tate, waved back.

As the child explored the courtyard, Jodie couldn't help pondering the expression on Tate's face as she'd held little Angela. Had he been thinking about the child they'd once talked about having? The children they'd once given thought to? As only children themselves, each had wanted more than one.

Jodie drew her fingers lightly across her belly. Here, inside her, was that first child.

What did destiny now have in store for them?

TATE FELT COMPLETELY worn out by the time the Clearys left. Both because Jim had proved more volatile about taking out after Alan than Tate had expected and because it had been hard to watch Jodie minister to the child. It brought home again just how much they'd lost from his inability to sustain their marriage. They'd wanted children. But he could only thank the gods that they'd gone no further than talking about it.

He couldn't imagine what their situation would be like now with a baby to consider. A divorce wouldn't be so easily obtained. How would he be able to walk away from them? But then, how could he provide for them, either?

He made his way back to the bedroom and stretched out on the mattress, covering his eyes with his bent arm.

Within seconds he felt Jodie's presence, but he couldn't look at her.

"Are you asleep?" she asked softly, testing.

"No," he replied.

He heard the whisper of her steps as she came nearer.

"I…was just wondering how things went. How did Jim take it?"

"Like any father would, like any grandfather."

"And Jennifer?"

"She was right to ask for help. Getting him to settle down took a lot of convincing. But he did eventually. You saw him when he left."

She laughed lightly. "He was still a bit pink at the edges. But Jennifer didn't look as angry at me."

Tate moved his arm. "She was angry?"

Jodie shrugged. "She never said anything, but I knew." She came closer to the bed, not stopping until she was at its edge. "Tate, thank you. I know this was hard."

"It wasn't that hard."

"Still—"

She stood there, gazing down at him. In the soft afternoon light, diffused by the ruffly curtains, *she* might have been the angel.

Tate couldn't help himself; he reached for her hand. And with a little catch of her breath, she bent forward, letting him draw her closer…closer…until they shared the same breath. Nothing existed outside of them. No sound, no presence, except for the rapid beating of their hearts.

His fingers skimmed the soft skin of her cheek, curved under her chin, passed over her lips. "Jodie?" he whispered huskily.

He thought she breathed his name. Or maybe it was a meeting of their minds in the seconds before their lips met, tentatively at first, half-afraid, with all the uncertainty of new lovers. Then the kiss deepened, became needful as denial and loss were cast aside.

His hands were in her hair and he rained kisses on her face. She wrapped her arms around him, smoothing his shoulders, his chest, his back. Then her fingers brushed a cluster of scars.

All movement stopped.

"Oh, Tate," she whispered brokenly, tears welling in her eyes. "I don't care! I don't care!"

But he'd had enough. For a moment, he'd forgotten. "No," he said gruffly, pushing her away.

"Tate, please!" Tears slid onto her cheeks as she tried to stay where she was, beside him.

He pushed harder. "No, Jodie. We can't do this. I told you before. It's not right."

"I'm your wife!" she cried. He succeeded in getting her onto her feet.

"Not for long."

"I don't want a divorce!"

"Nothing has changed."

Tears rolled freely down her cheeks. "I'm going to fight you on this, Tate," she swore. "I'm going to—"

"*Nothing* has changed," he repeated harshly. "I'm still the same, you're still the same. So's the situation. Just now…was a mistake. It won't happen again."

"How can you be so sure? If we love each other, what makes this so wrong?"

"That's not the way it works, Jodie."

"Other people wouldn't care."

"We're not other people."

"I don't understand you, Tate!"

"Good," he said tautly, and covered his eyes with his arm again.

CHAPTER TWELVE

THE DAYS IMMEDIATELY following the Clearys' visit were difficult for Jodie. She existed in a state of limbo, unsure how to proceed. Was there any significance to what had happened between her and Tate? Had she won some points or lost some? Had he?

The only thing she'd done was get close to him—a little too close. But she would have moved heaven and earth—any obstacle!—to be with him.

Since then, her emotions had gone up and down, depending on the smallest reaction from Tate. He hadn't become withdrawn and angry as she'd feared, but neither was he forthcoming. He might have forgotten all about the encounter, except that the ease between them had all but disappeared.

Once again Jodie heeded instinct. She left him alone as much as she could, doing nothing to provoke him. Yet she knew that at some point this impasse must end. Time was slipping by. Her window of opportunity to persuade him to change his mind was narrowing. He hadn't yet asked her about the status of their divorce, but he soon would.

TATE USED the Stevens case as a bolt-hole—a place where his mind could retreat from Jodie. Where he could lose himself, gain a few moments of peace. Then, gradually, the case took on a life of its own. It nagged at him, gnawed on him, plagued him. There was something... small. Not particularly obvious. Yet critically important to the outcome.

He studied and restudied the paperwork, knowing *it* was there and he just couldn't find it.

In the end, in frustration, he called Jack.

He could hear the swivel chair creak as Jack leaned back in it. In his mind's eye Tate could see the sheriff's office—a small room dominated by a huge walnut desk and lined with file cabinets. The set of antique deer antlers mounted on the wall behind the desk would have Jack's hat hanging from one prong—a tradition that Briggs County sheriffs had followed for as many years as anyone could remember. His own hat had hung there for close to two years.

"Hey, son," Jack said amiably. "What can I do for ya? Glad you called when you did. I was just thinkin' about goin' out for a little lunch."

"I won't keep you long, Jack," Tate murmured, smiling. "Don't want to get between you and your favorite burger. I know what can happen to a person who does. Cowboys use the term 'stampede.'"

Jack chuckled softly. "I wouldn't go that far."

"I would. Remember when Bob Stewart first came on as a deputy? He was standing near the front entrance, asking you some kind of question about his hours. Your stomach started to growl, and he ended up on the floor. I saw it. I was with you."

"Now, now, it wasn't like that. The boy slipped. Somebody'd spilled water on the floor."

"And where did you go right after?"

"The café."

"And what did you order?"

"Probably a burger."

"For sure a burger! When'd you ever eat anything else for lunch?"

Jack chuckled again. "Maureen used to give me hell about that."

"And has Bob ever stood between you and the front door again? Or have any of the other deputies?"

"No."

"That's right. They're smart."

Jack's chuckle turned into a laugh. Tate waited for him to recover before he said, "I've got a question for you, Jack. About the Stevens case. Is there anything else on it that you haven't given me? Observations, things like that? Somebody's gut feel?"

The chair squeaked again as Jack sat forward. "What is it?" he asked, instantly alert. "You think you're onto somethin'?"

"It's just…a feeling. Something's not right. Only I can't put my finger on it."

"That's what the Stevens family says."

"You look it over again before you handed it off to me?"

"Didn't have to. Ain't been much over a year since it happened. I remember it. Somethin's always tugged at my mind, too, but nothin' that added up to any kind of foul play. Just Rawley and the motorcycle. Wouldn't be the first time somebody's ended up dead after doin' something stupid. And Rawley did a lot of things stupid."

"I know. I just wish— What's his family sayin'?"

"Just that Rawley could ride his motorcycle up a tree dead drunk. They don't buy the idea that it just ran over him. They think one of his old buddies might've had a disagreement with him and kinda helped things along in some way. But they don't know anythin' specific."

"What bothered you about it?" Tate asked.

"Just…little things. For one, Rawley wasn't goin' that fast. And why would he run off the road into the ravine? He was used to ridin' that area. He'd done it since he was a kid. He sure got into enough trouble for it, then and later."

"Could he 'a done it on purpose?"

"Family says not. But that don't mean squat. Families are sometimes the last to know when a person decides to take themselves outta their troubles."

Tate frowned. "So he could have done it to himself."

"Woulda been kinda hard to plan the bike runnin' over him, but that could be just an added attraction. All he was looking for was an accident."

"Not a nice way to die...just lyin' there for hours and hours, waitin'."

"That's another of my 'little things.'"

Tate thought for a moment, then he said, "Well, I'll let you get to that burger, Jack. I'll keep looking at this and see if I can pick up on whatever it is that's bothering us."

"Your momma's gettin' itchy to come see you again. You think maybe if we were to pay a little visit tomorrow that this time you could make her feel a bit more welcome?"

"I didn't mean to make her feel unwelcome before. You, either."

"Coulda fooled me," Jack said levelly. Then, jumping into the fire as only a close friend can, he asked, "How's it goin' between you and Jodie?"

"It's going."

"I didn't mean it like that! You know what I think of you gettin' a divorce. I meant, are things better between you?"

"Why should they be better?"

Jack sighed irritably. "You are one of the most stubborn—"

"A chip off your block, Jack. You musta taught me too well."

"Well, I can un-teach you, if your momma would let me. I already volunteered, but she didn't take kindly to the idea of me bootin' you across the room."

"I'll thank her for saving you the trouble when you come visit."

Jack said seriously, "I worry about you, son. You know I do."

"Go eat your burger," Tate returned gruffly before he hung up.

He looked through the papers again, then through the photos. At the moment, he just couldn't tell.

"I WAS SO EMBARRASSED!" Harriet said miserably. "There we were, Mr. Smith and me, and he's telling me that the next time somethin' like this happens, he's going to have to expel Wesley! He said he can't overlook his behavior anymore because it sets such a bad example. He says that his first duty is to the other students, the teachers and then, and only then, to Wes. It was awful. Awful!" She tore a tissue into tiny pieces, let them fall to her kitchen table, before gathering them in a tight ball. "I don't know what LeRoy's going to say when I tell him. And Mae! Oh, my heaven, *Mae!*"

"She doesn't already know about it?" Jodie asked.

"I haven't told her. So…I don't think so. If she did, I'd've already heard about it. This one must've passed her by."

"She won't be happy."

Harriet's laugh was biting. "No, I don't think so."

"What does Wesley have to say for himself?" Jodie asked.

"I haven't talked to him yet. He was in detention. He won't get home until later." Harriet worried the torn tissue some more, then said in a burst, "I've already told Tate about what's happened. He agreed to talk to Wes. But Wes never said anything about him doing it. Then again, Wes doesn't say a lot to me these days. I asked Gwen if she knew, but she claims she doesn't." Harriet paused and thumped her fist down. "I know Wes is a good boy. I know almost everyone has trouble of some kind growing up. But…this is serious, Jodie. He's only in the ninth grade! When I think of gettin' him through the next three years—"

"Let me see what Tate has to say. He never mentioned it to me, either. But then—" She stopped. She was in much the same state with Tate as Harriet was with Wesley, but it wouldn't do any good to say so. "I know he'll want to do what he can."

"I wouldn't ask if wasn't so important," Harriet murmured, distressed.

"Let me talk to him," Jodie repeated.

In ten minutes she was back in Harriet's kitchen. "Tate says to send Wes over after he gets in this evening. They talked for a few minutes the other day, but Wes wasn't in a mood to say much, because he was mad at you for making him weed the flower beds."

"A lot of good that did. The weeds are gone, but— Now, with this, he'll be in an even worse state."

"Tate can handle it."

Harriet shot her a discerning glance. "Tate's gettin' stronger, isn't he?"

"In some ways."

"You don't look particularly happy, though, which means Mae's plan—whatever it is—isn't workin' too well."

Jodie did her best to smile. "We won't know until the very end."

Harriet studied her face, noting the sadness and worry that Jodie was unable to hide. "There's still time," she said, doing her best to offer hope.

Jodie nodded, but her own words reverberated in her mind—*the very end.*

The end of everything.

The time when there would be no more hope.

TATE WATCHED Jodie as she moved around the bedroom, straightening it. She'd been staying to herself a good deal over the past couple of days, a fact he'd been grateful for but at the same time felt uneasy about. What had happened between them after the Clearys left was like the proverbial elephant that sat in the middle of the room—they functioned around it, but not noticing the creature, not thinking about it, was difficult.

The case papers—Tate's salvation—lay next to him on the bed, the photos hastily pushed beneath the reports. He didn't want Jodie to see them, either…protecting her just as, days before, he'd protected the children.

Protect.

The word and what it symbolized stood out in his mind, challenging him to analyze it. Protect, defend, serve—all hallmarks of what he'd spent his life trying to accomplish. To walk in the giant footsteps of his father…to live up to the principles exemplified by Jack.

They were the very best of what a man might be. The top lawmen in their communities. The best husbands to their wives. All his life he'd held to their ideals—

"Tate?"

Jodie broke into his introspection, leaving him dissatisfied because he'd yet to come to the important conclusion he sensed his cascading thoughts were attempting to form. It had to do with Jodie, with caring for her, with—

"Tate?" Jodie said again. "Wesley's here."

Tate abandoned his line of reasoning. Whatever it was, he'd bring it back later...could *try* to bring it back later, he amended as it slipped away.

Wesley entered the room, his hands stuffed into his jeans' pockets, his dark head bent. Jodie slipped out, closing the door behind her.

Tate felt there was no use dissembling about the purpose of the visit, so he came straight to the point, careful to keep his tone neutral. "You got yourself in trouble again?"

Wes didn't answer.

"I asked a question," Tate said.

The dark head lifted. Anger and humiliation warred in his dark Parker eyes. "I didn't hear one."

Tate glanced toward the straight-backed chair. "You wanna sit down?" he asked.

"No, thanks."

"You're not here to be punished, Wes. All you have to do is sprint for the door. By the time you're back in your room at home, I'd've barely managed to get myself outta bed. You can leave anytime you want. There's not a lot I can do about it."

The boy continued to hold himself stiffly.

Tate said, "I told you the other day we could talk whenever you wanted. You think maybe this is a good time?"

Wesley's shoulders twitched. "Good a time as any. You start."

"I'm not the one with the problem."

"That's not what I hear."

Tit for tat...the boy was sharp, intelligent. Tate became even more direct. "I understand you're about to be expelled from school. What happened?"

Wesley's anger exploded. "Why does everybody care about that so much? School's just a big waste of time! I go there—it takes ages and ages on the bus, with all those little kids screamin' and yellin'—then I get in class and most everything they talk about is boring! *And* they say it over and over…like we're all a bunch a dummies or somethin'." He stomped across the room, a man-boy in a fury. "There's this one teacher, Mr. Aires. He's one of the most stupid people alive! You couldn't trust him to water a horse, much less find his way out of a corral. He can't remember what he says from one day to the next. Can't remember who he called on last or what homework he told us to do! Then there's Mr. Carson. *He* gives us our assignment, which is usually to read the next chapter in our history books and to answer the questions at the end. It doesn't make any difference if we do or don't, 'cause the next day he reads us that very same chapter in class! And we never get to the questions, 'cause people are always interruptin' him. It's like a game. To see how long it takes to get him offtrack. It's useless! The whole thing stinks!"

"Do you help get Mr. Carson offtrack?" Tate asked. He knew both teachers in passing. One was in his seventies and the other was, to put it kindly, ineffective in many other areas of his life, as well.

"Not at first," Wesley said defiantly. "But

I sure do now! It's to the point where I'm the best at it, so the others lay off."

"And let you get into trouble."

"I don't care. I'm sick of school. I wanna quit."

"You're in the ninth grade, right? And you're what...fourteen? Fifteen?"

"I'll be fifteen in July."

Tate shifted position, sitting up and swinging his feet to the floor. "What are you gonna do with yourself if you quit?"

"Work on the ranch," Wes was quick to say.

"Have you talked to Rafe about this?"

"Rafe knows I'm a good hand."

"But have you talked to him about quitting school and coming to work full-time? He might surprise you by refusing."

"You mean, Mom and Dad'd get him to say no? Then—then I'll go somewhere else. There's lotsa other places to work when you're good."

"You're fourteen."

"Fifteen in July."

"How you gonna live till then? You do plan to eat, don'tcha?"

"Mom won't let me starve."

"You're planning on living here?"

"Other places, then. No one'll let me starve."

"Because you're a Parker."

"Yeah…so?"

"What's your aunt Mae gonna say about this? Don't you think she'll stand you down on this one?"

"I'm not afraid of her!" he claimed.

"Hmm. That's funny. 'Cause I am. And I'm a grown man…a *smart* grown man, who knows which people to cross and which people to leave alone. Your cousin Rafe isn't a person to mess with, either. Neither's your dad."

"You're not afraid of her or of them. I remember when you were sheriff, and those men came down from Colorado and were after Jodie and Rio…and you stood everybody down, includin' Aunt Mae and Rafe. I heard all about it. You—"

"I did my job," Tate interrupted him. "I kept the peace."

"I could do that. I could be a cop."

"Not without an education you can't."

"Then I'll stay a cowboy. It's what I'm best at."

"Wes, I grew up wanting to be a lawman. It's all I ever considered. But I knew to be one I had to graduate from high school, then

I had to go on to take some law-enforcement courses in college. So I did. And I did pretty good—got a job in Dallas with the police department there. Then I came back here as a deputy, and eventually took over as sheriff when Jack Denton retired. After that I hooked up with the task force. And you know the rest." Tate slowly began to unbutton his shirt. "Everything I spent my life dreaming about I got to do, but it's *all* I know how to do. I don't have anything else."

He felt the boy's eyes watching him, moving from button to button as he set them free. He undid the last one and shouldered his way out of the shirt.

"This is what happened," he said quietly. "Got tore up pretty bad. Don't know if I'll ever be able to get myself back up and around again like I used to…much less be able rejoin the force. *Any* force."

The boy's eyes widened. He blinked as Tate showed him his chest and his back. It was a pretty awful picture he was being allowed to see. Wesley swallowed tightly. Shifted position. Swallowed again.

Tate looked down at the various scars left from the bullet wounds and surgeries. "A regular Frankenstein's monster, huh?"

The boy said nothing.

Tate pulled the shirt back into place and started to rebutton it.

"Just thought you should see what can happen to a person. Even to a person who's not afraid of much and who's doing a job he loves best in the world. I wish I had something else I could do now to support my family. Maybe some of that time I spent at the university studying to be a cop I'd have been better off taking a course or two in accounting, as well. 'Cause as it is, I'm not good for much. Not to myself. Not to Jodie. Not to the task force." He paused. "You've been around a lotta old cowboys. Some are fine. Some aren't. Dub Hughes had to retire as foreman here before he was ready because his arm got busted up so bad he couldn't use it like he should and he couldn't do his work anymore. But you know that kinda thing happens to young ones, too. Then they go off and do this or that, trying to scrape by. I know one who's doing his best to drink himself to death." He paused again. "As a Parker, you'll get your share in the ranch when you turn twenty-one. And you could live off it, if that's what you have a mind to do. But I'm here to tell you it ain't easy sitting in a heap all day, waiting for time to go by.

It's easier to wait in a classroom, where your ordeal'll be over in a few hours. If you do, you stand more of a chance later on if your plans give out on you."

Wes dropped onto the chair, his attitude no longer defiant.

"I can also tell you something else," Tate continued quietly, talking to the boy the way Jack had talked to him those many times over the years during his struggle to adulthood. "When you grow up, you're gonna be grown-up for a long time. I had to grow up pretty quick after my dad died. I worked from the time I was eleven, doing this or that in my spare time to help out because we needed the money. You're doing a man's work when you go on roundups and help out on the ranch around your schoolwork. And that's well and good. It's your heritage. But don't turn away from being a kid, too, while you can." Tate smiled and reached out to tap the boy on the shoulder. The reach made him grimace, and he shook his head. "See what I mean?" he murmured. "Things happen."

"What are you gonna do if you can't…" The boy's inquiry trailed off.

"That's a good question. One I can't answer."

Wes sat still for a long time. Then he said quietly, "Those teachers are pretty awful."

"You ever ask about changing to another class?"

"Mom's never let us do that kinda thing. She says Parkers shouldn't expect favors."

"I bet she'd go along with it this time if you asked her. You're not learning anything anyway, are you? Even if you behaved?"

"No. I'd learn more just readin' the book from Mr. Carson's class on my own. I could do it in a weekend."

"Have you told your mother what you've told me?"

Wes moved uncomfortably. "Sorta."

Tate smiled wryly. "Try talking to her like a human being. She is one, you know—and a pretty good one, to boot."

Wes stood up, shuffled from foot to foot, then said, "I'll think about it, okay?"

Tate nodded. "Sure thing."

The boy's attitude was a far cry from when he'd first entered the room, but Tate knew better than to expect more of a concession. A teenage boy, at least the troubled ones he was more accustomed to dealing with, usually had a lot of face to save.

JODIE TAPPED on Tate's door a short time after Wesley left. "How did it go?" she asked.

"We talked," Tate said.

"And? Did it do any good? Harriet's so worried."

Tate spread his hands. "Who knows?"

Jodie frowned slightly, unsatisfied. But she didn't press. Especially when he reached for the case file reports that recently he always seemed to be reading.

She didn't know whether to be happy or irritated that he was giving them such attention.

Moments later, she wandered restlessly into the kitchen. She glanced at the Dunn house and thought about going over, but she didn't want to interrupt if Harriet was talking with LeRoy or if both parents were talking with Wesley. She was just considering a visit to her father—he'd probably come home for the evening by now—when the telephone rang.

"Jodie?" Jennifer said. "I'm sorry I waited so long to call. I just— I wanted things to settle before I let you know. I turned the emails over to the detective investigating Alan's case. He was…quite interested. And grateful that I came forward. I got the feeling— I think they might file charges against

Alan soon. They've already filed against the other teacher."

Jodie murmured support.

"I—" Jennifer sounded near to tears. "I really appreciate what Tate did to help with Daddy. We flew back, saw the detective, and Daddy did exactly what Tate said. Tate told him to put me and the baby first over getting revenge on Alan…and he did. Daddy stayed with us the entire time, and when the detective wanted to formally question me, he took care of Angela. He was wonderful."

"Did you see Alan?" Jodie asked.

"No." Jennifer sniffed.

"Did you want to?"

"I don't ever want to see him again! There were…more things than what I told you about, Jodie. More than I told Daddy. But that's not important now. That part of my life is over."

"I'm glad, Jennifer. Not that you had to go through something so unsettling, but that you can put it behind you."

Jodie heard her friend's long release of breath. Jennifer's problems were far from over, and she knew it, but at least she'd taken her first shaky steps toward solving them.

"What about you?" Jennifer asked. "You and Tate? What are you going to do?"

"I wish I knew."

Jodie could sense her friend's frown. Jennifer had been too wrapped up in her own troubles to notice anyone else's. Which was the way it had to be. Should *still* be. Jodie wished she'd used better control in her answer.

"Is there…a problem?" Jennifer asked cautiously. "I mean, other than Tate's being shot. Which is enough. More than enough. How long are you planning to stay at the ranch? Is there a time limit?"

"Aunt Darlene and Uncle Thomas will be back in a couple of months."

"Then you and Tate will go back to Austin—that's where you live, isn't it? I remember Daddy saying something like that."

When Jodie said nothing—could say nothing—a new note entered Jennifer's voice. "I don't like what I'm not hearing. I didn't realize— Listen, we need to talk. And this time not about me and my troubles. I can be such a selfish brat, thinking I'm the only person who has difficulties."

"You're not still angry with me for telling Tate?" Jodie asked.

"I never was! Well, maybe just a little. But I got over it. I needed a shove in the right direction, and you gave it to me. What else is a friend for, right?"

"It's starting to feel like old times," Jodie said.

"Whatever I can do. Whenever you want," Jennifer swore. "I'm here. And Jodie...be sure to tell Tate how much Daddy and I appreciate his help. I don't want to think about how long it would've taken me to make up my mind. And to let Daddy worry like that. He sensed something was wrong."

"I know he did."

"Tate understood just what to say to him. Angela's the light of Daddy's life. He'd do anything for her."

"For you, too," Jodie said.

"I wasn't in Briggs County most of the time when Tate was a deputy—or the sheriff, either, for that matter—but I wouldn't want to be the crook he was after. He's good!"

Jodie laughed unsteadily. "I'll tell him you said that."

"Good-looking, as well. I remember when you had a crush on him back in...seventh grade, wasn't it? He drove the bus one semester. We'd sit in the first seat right behind his and you'd do the most outrageous things to get his attention. I have to tell you now, though—I had a crush on him, too. I couldn't say so then because I was afraid you'd tear my hair out."

"I *won't* tell him you said that!"

"No, don't. I don't need another blast from the past to come haunt my days."

Jennifer had been joking, but the way her voice changed at the end revealed that she'd been reminded of her trouble. Of the way her husband had deceived her.

Jodie searched for something to say. Some measure of reassurance. All she could think of was a softly worded, "I won't ever tell. I promise."

"Thanks, Jo," Jennifer said, using the old shortening of her name.

"No problem, Jen," Jodie returned.

When she hung up, Jodie felt heartened by a further strengthening of their longtime ties.

CHAPTER THIRTEEN

THE YOUNGER PARKER children were drawn to Tate as if to a magnet. Every time he went outside to sit on the porch, Rafe and Shannon's two boys were sure to show up. And if Anna was home from school, she'd join them, as well. Tate presumed it was because he was the only male in the vicinity who, because he didn't have a job, had plenty of free time to listen to them.

In an unexpected way he found the children's chatter entertaining. Occasionally, they brought him their favorite books to read to them. Occasionally, they assigned him roles in their games. He lost count of the number of times he was home base in hide-and-seek, or how many times they lassoed his feet, or he was a participant in a card game of Old Maid or Go Fish.

Most unexpected of all for Tate, though, was his realization that he'd grown to like them.

"LOOK! Look what Mommy got for me when she went to town!" Ward shouted excitedly as he ran, guiding a brand-new bicycle across the courtyard to where Tate sat on the porch.

"And me!" Nate cried as he brought up the rear with his older brother's outgrown bike, the training wheels reattached. "Look what I got! It's *mine* now!"

Their mother followed them at a slower pace, grinning at them and at Tate.

Tate stood up and, in a feat of derring-do, trod down the two short steps to the walkway. "Wow!" he said approvingly as the older boy hurried up to him. "This bike is really something, Ward. A good-looking machine."

Ward's face was alight with pride. "Mom said I earned it 'cause I did such a good job of keepin' the old one nice for Nate."

Junior, the family's golden-haired Labrador mix, bounced at Nate's heels as he caught up. "Me, too! Now I can ride with Ward and Anna. I'm a big kid, too!"

"Fine-looking bike, Nate."

"I'm gonna keep it nice," Nate claimed.

"For if we have a new baby brother. He might want it, too, one day."

"Then you'll get one like this!" Ward bragged.

"Yeah!" Nate said, his shining eyes darting to his brother's new bike, before quickly returning to his special secondhand one.

Shannon shook her head as she joined them. "I seem to have made a hit."

"Kids and bikes," Tate agreed.

"Rafe's going to be sorry he missed this."

"I bet they'll still be excited when he gets in."

"They spotted the new one in the back of the car. There wasn't much I could do."

"Mommy...look!" Nate cried, having scrambled up onto the seat. He was wobbly as he started to peddle away, but the extra wheels kept him upright.

"Big knobby tires," Ward admired, down on one knee, running his hand over the tread. "Just what I wanted!" Then he, too, jumped on his bike and peddled down the walkway to the hard-packed gravel drive, where he caught up with, and soon passed, his slower sibling.

Shannon continued to grin as she watched them, but Tate's smile disappeared. Something

Ward said had struck a chord. *Big knobby tires.*

Tate's body jerked as realization hit him. That was it! *The tread!*

Shannon turned to him in concern. "What..." she began.

Tate didn't hang around to hear the rest. He retook the stairs and hurried across the porch, moving faster than he had in ages. He'd stopped bringing the case folder outside because of the children. Now he needed to find it.

"Tate?" Shannon called, puzzled.

"Back in a minute," Tate said from inside the door. "I just remembered—"

"Tate?" Jodie questioned as well, as she stepped out of the kitchen.

"Hang on," Tate said brusquely. He wanted to run but couldn't. He wanted to walk faster but couldn't. When he got to the bed he all but collapsed onto it and had to catch his breath for a moment before he reached for the case folder on the bedside table.

He riffled through the material, his fingers trembling...which was silly, because he might not even be right.

At last he found the photos he wanted and jerked them free. And there it was!

Examination of the autopsy photo showing the tread mark on Rawley Stevens's belly and the scene photo of the fallen motorcycle revealed that the two treads were different! The patterns were very similar, but they *were* different—which meant the motorcycle Rawley Stevens had been driving wasn't the one that had run over him!

That subtle difference was what had been bothering him all along. Like everyone else, he'd taken the match for granted.

Tate couldn't help himself. He started to grin. Then he saw Jodie watching him from the doorway, her expression perplexed.

"C'mere," he said, and patted a place on the mattress beside him.

She hesitated for only a second.

Once she was settled, he said, "I'm gonna show you some pictures that aren't pretty.... Did you ever know a local biker by the name of Rawley Stevens? Well, Rawley turned up dead a little over a year ago, and everyone took it for granted that he'd had an accident out on some isolated rangeland. That somehow, after he'd gone off the edge of the road, his motorcycle had ended up running over him." He glanced at her. "Are you ready?" When she nodded he turned the two photos over and showed her the close-up of the tread mark on Rawley's stomach. "This was taken by the coroner's office shortly after Rawley was brought in." Tate shifted to the second photo. "And this was taken at the scene. That's Rawley's bike...where it ended up. Now, look at the tire tread."

Jodie studied one photo, then the other. "I don't—" She stopped and looked again. She took the photos into her own hands to study. Finally, she lifted her eyes. "They're not the same, are they? One line of zigzags is different from the other. But they're so close!" She paused as realization dawned. "Which means that this bike didn't leave that track...doesn't it?"

Tate nodded. "Of course the experts'll have the final say."

"And no one noticed this before you?"

Tate shrugged. "It's one of those things that's easy to overlook when all the rest of the evidence points another way. Took me most of a week, staring at 'em full-time. If it hadn't been for Shannon buying Ward a new bike, I might not have put it together, either."

"Someone must have killed this Rawley person, then."

"That's the way it looks."

"And they'd have gotten away with it, too, if you hadn't—"

Tate stuffed the photos back into the case folder. "Somebody probably woulda noticed one day."

"Jack said the case was in the inactive file. Doesn't that mean they've given up on finding the culprit?"

"They pull 'em out every once in a while for another look."

"Have you told Jack yet?"

"I just now figured it out."

"You could tell him this afternoon when he brings your mom. He'll be pleased." She paused, curious. "What happens next?"

"Jack'll have the experts check the treads. If they agree they're not a match, he'll reopen the investigation."

"All because of you. Because you saw—"

Tate stood up. Suddenly, he wasn't nearly as excited about his discovery. He'd spotted an anomaly…big deal!

"I think I want to lie down for a while," he said. He was paying for his burst of energy—a reminder of why what had just happened *wasn't* such a big deal. This was as far as his involvement in the case would go. Like any game of hide-and-seek, once you're found, the game's over. The case would pass into other hands now, to investigate and, hopefully, to close with a conviction.

Jodie stared at him. "That's it?" she demanded. "You were all excited a minute ago, and now you're not? Is it because you told me? Would it have been better if I'd been somewhere else?" She stood up to face him. "You know...when you said you didn't love me anymore, I didn't believe you. Now I'm beginning to wonder if it wasn't true! No one does this to someone they love. Raise them up, only to slap them down. That's not the way it used to be between us. I'm tired of walking on eggshells around you, Tate. Of being afraid that what I say or do could make some kind of terrible difference. That you might take something the wrong way and—"

"Kill myself?" he supplied.

"Yes!" she snapped.

Tate looked at her, not quite believing what he was hearing. Things had been bad, but he'd never— Yet, hadn't he? And she, being so close to him, had sensed it. "I don't want to talk about this now, Jodie."

"You never want to talk about it...about anything!"

"What's the use of talking?" he shot back.

"It's just more of the same old same old. I want to *do* things, Jodie. The way I used to! And if I can't, all the talking in the world isn't gonna make it right!"

"You *will* be able to do things," she retorted.

"It sure doesn't look like it right now! If I was back to the way I was, I wouldn't be handing this case off to Jack. I'd tell him about it, yeah. But I'd start checking up on Rawley's old friends and enemies and have a look-see at the tires on their motorcycles. Whoever ran him down and staged his accident knew him pretty well and had a good idea he could get away with it. And he did... up to now. It's doubtful he's changed tires. The right motorcycle's probably running up and down the roads of Briggs County every day, even while we're talking. But I'm not going to be the investigator who finds him. That's gonna be someone else. Because I can barely do more than walk out onto the porch!"

"You used to barely be able to get across the room!"

"Are you telling me I've improved?"

She stuck out her chin. "Some. Yes."

"Then tell that encouraging bit of news to Mae," he returned sarcastically. "She made me a promise—if I get to where I can be on my own, she won't cause any trouble about the divorce. And talking of divorce, where are we at in our filing? You hear anything yet from Ned Fowler?" When Jodie said nothing, he didn't let up. "I'm sure Ned told you how a simple uncontested divorce doesn't take all that long in this state. Should be done in another couple of months. Then you can be free of me."

"That's not what I want," Jodie said flatly, beginning to sound tired of their "talk" herself.

"Stop fighting it, Jodie," he counseled quietly. "You're just like a dog trying to hang on to a comfortable ol' bone. At some point, you're gonna have to decide whether to eat it or bury it." He paused. "I think maybe later I'll give Ned Fowler a call. See if I can't hurry things up a little."

Jodie looked as though she wanted to say something more, as though whatever it was was just on the tip of her tongue. But she bit her lip, gave her head a little shake and hurried from the room.

Tate stared at the closed door before he sank back onto the bed.

Axel would be coming soon. But at the

moment, Tate didn't think much of anything could help him feel better.

All in all, even with the tread discovery, it was a morning he'd just as soon forget.

JODIE WENT BACK into the kitchen, heartsick at the way events had unfolded. Why was it every time she tried to break through to Tate, he rebuffed her? What was the true reason he was so determined to get a divorce? She'd put it down to his depression after being shot and his long, slow recovery. But what if it was something more? What if, like the biker case, she was thinking one thing, when it was really another? Panic cut through her. What if what he said was true and he no longer loved her?

She couldn't believe it. Couldn't accept it. But…what if?

The next couple of hours passed in a haze for Jodie. She knew when Axel arrived to give Tate his massage and, again later, when he left. She sensed, when the house grew quiet, that Tate had gone to sleep.

She crept to his bedroom and cracked open the door. He was stretched out, facing the wall, but from the evenness of his breaths and the stillness of his body, she knew he wasn't faking.

It was important that she check, because she planned to call Mr. Fowler to warn him of Tate's upcoming call.

"Now, don't you worry about a thing, Jodie," Ned Fowler said once she'd explained. "I'll take care of it. It may necessitate telling a little white lie, but we lawyers will do that sometimes if it helps a client. I'm thinking I'll tell him that things in our office got messed up and the papers were sent to the courthouse in Del Norte by mistake, instead of going to Travis County. Tate's used to paperwork foul-ups. Happens all the time. So he'll believe it."

"Thanks, Mr. Fowler. I appreciate it."

"How are things going for the two of you, Jodie? Nicole and I were talking about you last night."

"Tate's a little better," Jodie said.

"Well, that's good...real good," Ned replied, and they hung up.

JACK AND EMMA arrived for their visit shortly after Tate awakened. Jodie had checked with Emma before preparing a little snack of fresh fruit and sponge cake so Emma would know ahead of time to include it in the balance of her day's food intake. A diabetic, Emma had to be careful about many things—what and when she ate, her level of activity. But she'd become so accustomed to living with the disease and had such a positive outlook that she swore she felt better now than she had for a number of years before she'd been diagnosed. It had been her health crisis some years ago that had brought Tate back to Briggs County from Dallas, induced him to work in the sheriff's department and returned him to Jodie's life.

Possibly to prove he was getting better, Tate joined them at the table. He didn't seem in a particularly good mood. But then, Jodie hadn't expected him to be, not after their earlier contretemps.

Afterward, he and Jack went to sit on the front porch, while Jodie and Emma remained in the kitchen. Ostensibly, they stayed there to have another cup of coffee together, but in reality they wanted to give the men time to talk.

"Tate's surprised me," Emma confided. "I never expected…eating at the table. That's something. He *must* be feelin' better."

Jodie stirred her coffee for something to do, but she didn't take a sip. "He's a little better," she hedged, "but he's also determined. He thinks if it looks like he's getting better faster it'll speed things up."

Emma studied her with eyes the same dark caramel as Tate's. "You mean the divorce. He's not changed his mind." She sighed. "Maybe I should let Jack give him that swift kick. Maybe that'd snap him out of it."

Jodie smiled sadly. "I doubt it."

"Jack told me that when Tate talked to him yesterday he sounded almost like his old self. He was teasin' and jokin'."

"It's probably just me. Maybe I *should* get out of his life, Emma. Maybe if I gave him what he truly seems to want, everything would be better for him. Then—"

Emma's reaction was strong. "Now, I don't want to hear somethin' like that out of you again! Do you understand? *Nothing* would be better for Tate if you let him go. The two of you…you belong together. I wasn't sure at first. I'll be the first to admit it. I couldn't see our two families blendin' together. They're so different. Or, at least, I used to think they were. Now I've found out you Parkers are just regular people. Right after you got married, it used to bother me to come out to the ranch to visit. I felt like I was lacking. But Mae and you and the others— You've made me feel welcome."

"Emma—"

"No, it's time I say this. I'm glad Tate married you, Jodie. You love him the same way I do—even more. I saw that in Austin, in the hospital, right after I got there. You wouldn't leave his side. You were determined. It was like *you* were going to get him through it, keep him alive. And each time we almost lost him—"

"Emma," Jodie said again, squeezing her mother-in-law's hand. Tears swam in both women's eyes.

"It was like you gave him some of yourself…an energy, I don't know. You haven't been the same since, either. You were knocked six ways for Sunday, too. But it all started at the hospital. When you willed him to stay with us."

Jodie was trembling inside. She remembered. She remembered holding on to his hand…afraid to let go.

"You're the closest thing I'll ever have to a daughter, Jodie," Emma continued, her words husky. "And I love you…just like I'd love a daughter. So don't you ever talk about letting Tate go. If you wouldn't then, you can't now, either. You just have to be strong and hold on."

Jodie couldn't resist. She sprang out of her chair into her mother-in-law's arms.

"WELL WELL, I think you've got somethin' here, boy!" Jack exclaimed as they sat on the porch and Tate showed him the photographs. "I don't know how'n the world we missed it, but we did."

"I almost missed it, too," Tate said. "It was just happenstance that Ward came over to show me his new bike. Then he said something about its knobby tread...and *bingo!* That was it. That's what musta been bothering both of us for so long, 'cause when I looked at the photos again—" He let the sentence hang and grinned.

"A regular Sherlock Holmes," Jack teased.

"So now you can get somebody on it after you hear back from the lab. But I don't think you're gonna learn anything different. Those treads aren't the same. Somebody did ol' Rawley Stevens in and made it look like an accident."

Jack studied the photos again. "Good piece of work, son. I knew I was giving it to the right person."

"You'd've seen it yourself if you'd had the time."

"Maybe…maybe not. The Stevenses are goin' to feel vindicated. But I don't think I'm gonna tell 'em yet. We'll check around first, see if we can find us a match."

"That's what I'd do," Tate said. He looked down, impatient again with his own inabilities.

"What's wrong?" Jack asked, sensitive to his protégé's moodiness.

"Just the same ol' thing, Jack. Being good for nothing."

Jack frowned. "Whaddaya call this?" He shook the photos.

"Any rookie with enough time on his hands coulda done it. I want to get back to real police work, Jack. If I can't— If I can't ever—" Tate shrugged, his body tight. "I don't know what I'm gonna do."

"I keep tellin' you to give it time, son. It ain't been a full six months yet, has it?"

"Coming up."

"Well, so what? People heal at different rates. And you had a lot to get over. The actual gunshots, then them operations."

"I'm still so weak!"

"Then do things to get yourself stronger.

Eat right. Push yourself a bit. Exercise. Go for walks."

"From here to the bedroom seems to be my limit."

"And you accept that?" Jack challenged.

"I don't accept anything, Jack."

"Now you're talkin'. You've got a good brain, son. You just proved it. You've got a good body, too. It's just been knocked off kilter. Takes a long time to get over a single bullet wound to the trunk, and you had a regular bouquet. That's gonna take even longer."

"I may never be the same, Jack. The doctors said—"

Jack gave a dismissive wave. "Pshaw! Whadda they know?"

Tate laughed unsteadily. "Yeah. I guess."

"One told my daddy he and my momma couldn't have kids, and you know how many they ended up havin'? Four! We're split up now. I'm the only one still livin' out here, but we're all kickin' and I'm the baby! None of us woulda been here if our daddy had believed that doctor knew anythin'."

"Some pretty good doctors kept me alive, Jack."

"Yeah, well, I bet they ain't the same ones that told you you should give up."

"Nobody actually said it that way," Tate admitted. "They just...warned me."

"Probably were afraid of bein' sued. If you got yourself back goin' again but couldn't trip the light fantastic exactly like you used to, they didn't want you comin' back at 'em demandin' to know why. Those doctors were coverin' their little bee-hinds, son. That's all. You can't take what they said as gospel."

Tate laughed again, this time with more conviction. "I'd like to think you're right, Jack."

"Of course I'm right. Have I ever steered you wrong?"

TATE CLOSED HIMSELF in the bedroom after his family left and Jodie went over to Harriet's, seeking companionship. Shannon was there, as was Christine.

"Well, I don't know what Tate said to Wesley," Harriet began, "but yesterday evening the boy came back, went straight to his room...and today, I never got any calls. Actually, I was afraid to pick up the phone, afraid it might be Mr. Smith tellin' me to come get him. But—nothing. And when Wes came home from school today, he didn't say a word. I think that's good, don't you?"

"Better than a phone call," Christine said. She watched as little Elisabeth played on the floor beneath the window, stacking blocks and knocking them down again. Beth was a blonde like Jennifer's Angela, only six months her senior. And instead of blue eyes, hers were almost black. She was a blend of her father's blondness and her mother's Parker heritage.

"Tate didn't say much, either," Jodie murmured.

Shannon frowned and looked at her. "What was that about earlier?" she asked. "The boys had just shown him their bikes, I felt him jump, then he was off into the house, *hurrying* into the house. It was like he'd forgotten an appointment."

"He remembered something...something about a case. Actually, he came up with the key to solving it."

"I didn't know he was working again," Harriet said.

"It's a case Jack brought him."

"Well, that makes all the sense in the world," Christine said. "He has so much training, he might as well use it."

"But wouldn't that be hard, with him not bein' able to get out and about?" Harriet asked.

"It's hard," Jodie said, remembering Tate's frustration. Remembering her reaction. Maybe she'd made too much of his abrupt change of feeling. Maybe she—

"But he will soon. I'm sure he will," Shannon said. "He's already doing better. I see him out on the porch every day. Listen, Jodie, I wanted to tell you. If the boys get to be too much, just have him send them home. I started to do it myself, but then I wondered if he might not be enjoying their company. He's talking to them and doing things, playing games. The boys love it."

"Anna does, too," Harriet said. "It's startin' to be 'Tate this' and 'Tate that.' If I didn't know better 'cause she's so young, I'd say she's got a crush on him."

"She might have," Shannon said. "Kids grow up fast today. Even out here."

"Don't say that!" Christine chided. "Erin's sixteen going on twenty-five, it seems sometimes, and little Beth—I'd like to keep her a baby for as long as I can."

"Babies don't stay babies very long," Shannon said. "That's why you have to keep having them." She paused. "Like Rafe and me."

There was a small silence. Then Harriet repeated, "Like Rafe and—"

"Me." Shannon grinned. "Yep. It's official. We're having another one."

"Ohhhh!" Harriet squealed, and was joined by Christine as they jumped up and hugged their cousin by marriage.

Jodie was rooted to the spot. She wanted to jump up and hug Shannon, too, but couldn't make herself move. She was shocked. "When?" she breathed.

"October," Shannon said, smiling hugely. "We'll take another boy, but this time I really hope it's a girl. All these little girls around...I want one, too!"

Jodie forced herself to act. She got up and joined the group. Finally, the hugs broke up and they resettled in their chairs.

October! Just a month after her baby was due...hers and Tate's. "Does Mae know?" Jodie asked.

"Not yet. This one will come as a complete surprise to her."

"Don't count on it," Jodie murmured. Something in her voice caught Harriet's attention, and the other woman tilted her head in curiousity. For cover, Jodie added quickly, "You know Aunt Mae. It's like she has special antennae."

"Rafe and I will tell her tomorrow," Shannon said.

"Rafe must be bustin' his buttons," Harriet murmured.

"He's pleased," Shannon replied. Her soft smile revealed that her circumspect answer was clearly an understatement.

A short time later, as Jodie crossed back to the house next door, the continued good wishes for Shannon and Rafe rang in her ears.

Shannon had said Rafe was pleased.

Wouldn't it be the most wonderful thing if, one day, she could say the same of Tate?

CHAPTER FOURTEEN

TATE TOOK Jack's advice to heart and the next morning told Jodie that he no longer wanted to be waited on. He would come to the kitchen for all his meals and see to his other needs, as well, as much as he could.

If he'd expected congratulations, he would've been disappointed. She listened to what he said, nodded, then went back to the magazine she sat paging through in the living room.

He looked at her, frowned, then moved irritably into the kitchen, where he prepared his own toast and poured his own coffee, before downing both in silence at the table.

On his return from the shower, he saw that she'd taken him at his word and hadn't straightened the bedroom. Tate did it himself, grunting occasionally as he stretched and strained to make the bed. He then carried a couple of used glasses to the kitchen.

Jodie hadn't moved from where she sat curled on the couch. She didn't look up as he passed by.

He paused in the hall doorway. "I'm going outside," he announced.

"All right," she said, her eyes glued to an article.

"What are you gonna do?"

"Does it matter?"

"Not a lot." He frowned. What was she up to? Was she trying to punish him? "Are you staying inside?" he asked.

Her yellow-green eyes were brittlely cool when they lifted. "Maybe. Do you have an objection?"

Yesterday she'd been angry because he hadn't wanted to talk. Now, today—

"No. I just wondered."

"Why?" she snapped. "Nothing I do matters to you anymore, does it? You've already told me you're done with me."

He recognized that he was teetering on the edge of a precipice. "I was asking out of courtesy."

She went back to the magazine. "I'd rather you didn't."

He started to step away, acquiescing to her prickly request, when she demanded, "Do you want me to make your lunch, or do you plan to make it yourself?"

"I…can make it."

"I don't mind," she said flatly. "I just need to know. So I know how to plan my time."

He didn't like the way this felt. He'd never seen her so…distant. "Jodie—"

"All I need is an answer, Tate. A simple yes or no."

"Then, no. I'll do it."

"All right." She stood up and walked past him, on her way to her bedroom. She must have felt his eyes following her, because she inquired, "You don't mind if I shower now, do you?"

His frown deepened. "I don't know what you think you're doing."

"I'm treating you like you want me to, Tate."

"And how's that?"

"Like a stranger."

"Jodie—"

"Isn't that what you want? Because if it's not, you have to tell me. I'm tired of trying to read you. I told you that yesterday."

"A little civility—"

She laughed shortly. “You? Saying that to me?”

“I never—”

“Oh, yes, you did. Repeatedly, remember?” She paused. “Oh! And don’t forget to call Mr. Fowler. You said you wanted to check on the status of our divorce.”

Tate had forgotten. “Uh—yeah.”

She smiled tightly, slipped into her room for her robe, then started down the hall.

“Jodie?” Tate stopped her as she neared the bathroom. “Was I really that bad?”

“Worse,” she said before closing herself in the tiny room. Within seconds he heard the shower switch on.

A muscle pulled in his cheek as he pivoted to go outside.

WHEN TATE came in again, having read several stories to the boys and spent time watching them ride their new bikes, Jodie was nowhere to be found. In the past she’d always either told him personally where she was going or left a note. Today, there was nothing.

Better get used to it, bub, he said to himself. *When you told her you wanted to end the marriage, what did you expect?*

He could still smell the light flowery scent

of her perfume. She'd put on perfume? She hadn't done that to go riding or to visit members of the family. He remembered how, the other day, he'd wondered if she was harboring a secret. *Could* Rio have come back into her life?

Jealousy rumbled inside him again like a reawakened volcano. Not Rio! Anyone but Rio. Rio wasn't good enough for her. He—

Tate struggled to put the thought from his mind but lost the battle.

Rio Walsh. Blond curly hair, light blue eyes, with an attitude and cocksure swagger that some women seemed to find irresistible. He'd been Jodie's first love.

Tate muttered an oath and went to the kitchen. He was hungry—he'd been getting hungrier recently—but he'd wanted to wait until after Axel left to eat. He ended up with an apple, his mind continuing to rumble as he leaned against the counter and munched on the fruit. That was the way Axel found him.

"You want one?" Tate asked, lifting the core.

"Nah," Axel said. "Thanks."

Tate followed the camp cook into the bedroom, and when the table was set up, he slipped out of his clothes to stretch out.

Axel partially covered him with a folded sheet, rubbed oil on his hands and started to work. For a time neither man spoke, then Tate murmured, "Axel…do you know very much about women?"

Axel laughed. "No."

"Me, neither."

"Why?"

Tate did his best to shrug.

The camp cook asked, "Something about Miss Jodie botherin' ya? I've known her since she was a little thing, but I hav'ta say, I've never been able to figure her out. She's always been a lot like the weather. One minute she's sunny, the next stormy, the next—" He laughed lightly. "You know what I mean."

"Yeah."

"Now, on the other hand, my Marie's about as steady as they come. I don't hav'ta wonder about anythin'. If I do somethin' she don't like, she tells me. And she tells me quick."

"Yeah?"

"And if I do somethin' good, she tells me that, too."

"How often does she tell you the good?" Tate asked curiously.

Axel grinned. "Depends. On me. It's easier to make her happy than mad. Easier on me."

Tate confided, "I think I've got Jodie mad at me."

"She loves ya. She won't stay mad."

"What if—what if I've done something that'll guarantee she will?"

"Then I'd hav'ta say you're pretty much a fool."

Axel worked on Tate's extremities, making first his arms limp, then his legs. "It's not my place to say that," he continued, "but you asked. That little girl can turn you into a mass of cramped muscle faster'n anythin' I've ever seen. All she has to do is sashay into the room and you get all tense. Like right now, just thinkin' about her sashaying in's got you all—" Axel thumped his good shoulder and performed a maneuver that made Tate flinch. "Sorry," Axel apologized. "Now I gotta get you all relaxed again." He restarted his beginning smoothing strokes and lifts on Tate's back. "You love her. So why'd you wanna go and make her mad?"

"Maybe...because I love her?" Tate murmured.

"That ain't no answer. That's gobbledygook. If two people love each other, that's all that counts."

"How'd you come to be such an expert?"

"Like I said, I ain't! But I've picked up a few things along the way in life, and that's one of 'em. And," he teased, "bein' married nearly thirty years to the same woman must mean I'm doin' somethin' right!"

"What if," Tate began, still not satisfied, "what if…something like what happened to me had happened to you?"

Axel's large hands paused. "Are you askin' if Marie woulda left me?"

"No, the other way 'round."

The camp cook frowned in genuine puzzlement. "Now, why would I wanna go and do somethin' like that?"

JODIE STILL hadn't returned by the time Axel finished. Gnawing hunger once again brought Tate to the kitchen, where he found some beef to make a sandwich and some leftover cake for dessert. He gobbled up the meal in minutes, then, still wanting more, helped himself to another piece of cake.

After moving restlessly around the house for a time, he went out on the porch. Moments later he decided to expand his horizons. Jack had said to get some exercise, to push his boundaries, so he would.

Tate had planned to go only partway down

the drive—to some vague point in front of Harriet and LeRoy's house—but he ended up going farther, to the very end. To where the twin arms of the U-shaped drive connected with the private road leading, to the right, off the ranch and, to the left, deeper into it.

Each arm was marked with an abode pillar. Tate leaned against one and gazed across the courtyard to the other. He felt worn out by the effort to get there. More than worn out. His knees were weak, his breaths short; his head swam slightly. He'd stumbled on his last step, and now, even as he evaluated his condition, he dropped to sit awkwardly on the ground.

He wasn't sure how he was going to get back. One part of him found his present quandary amusing. Another found his lack of stamina pathetic. If anything could underline his physical ineptitude, this was it.

Should he wait passively for someone to find him? Or sit here, like a big baby, and yell?

He propped his arm across an upraised knee and rested his head on it. Two for two, Jack, he thought. His old friend's first suggestion—that he take a stab at independent living—had irritated Jodie. Then Jack's second sugges- tion—that he go for a walk—had resulted in this. But it wasn't Jack who had failed. It was him.

Jodie had already been irritated with him, and as for the walk, he should have known better than to go so far. But for a short time he'd felt so much better. Stronger. He'd proceeded slowly, carefully. Each step had been freer, with less pain.

Tate lifted his head. He heard the sound of an engine in the distance. Someone was coming. Jodie? Would she be alone, or would Rio be with her? Once again he rejected the thought as unworthy. Maybe the driver would be Jodie—maybe it wouldn't. But she'd never bring Rio to the ranch to taunt him. Or go to meet Rio on the sly, for that matter. She was a woman of her word, no matter how angry he made her and even when he was doing his best to get her to take that word back.

The engine noise grew louder, then, at a point, moved off. Tate dropped his head again. Whoever it was had gone away. His wait would extend. Maybe even long enough for him to summon the energy to get back on his own.

His mouth grew dry. The midday sun wasn't as hot in spring as it was in full summer, but the arid land still greedily sucked available moisture from the air. He wondered if Rawley Stevens had regained consciousness after his "accident." And if he had, whether this was the way he'd felt—debilitated, thirsty—before taking his last breath.

"Whatcha doin' out here, Tate?"

Tate looked up from the light stupor he'd fallen into to see Wesley hunkered down next to him. His dark Parker eyes were filled with concern.

"Wes?" Tate murmured unsteadily.

The boy who was almost a man helped him to his feet, then braced him by inserting a shoulder beneath Tate's arm. In effect, he made himself into a crutch. "We'd better get you back. Did you walk all this way?"

Tate laughed with self-mockery. "Yeah. Dumb, huh?"

"Well, you got here okay."

"Yeah, I did that."

As Tate did his best not to be too much of a burden, relief spread through him. Relief that he'd soon be back in the frilly house. He smiled at the thought, a wry smile that turned into a grimace. "Maybe you should go get a wheelbarrow and we could do this faster," he suggested dryly.

A quick grin chased away the boy's concern.

"Nah. You'd look real funny with your legs stickin' out."

"What are you doing home from school so early?" Tate asked as they covered more ground. "Not in more trouble, huh?"

"Special teachers' meeting. School's out."

"Where's Anna and Gwen?"

"Just the high school's out."

They turned up the walkway to Darlene and Thomas's house, then climbed up on the porch.

"You wanna go inside?" Wes asked.

"Out here's fine," Tate said. It probably wasn't. Undoubtedly, he'd be better off in bed, but the tiniest remaining sliver of his tattered ego wouldn't allow it.

Wes helped him to the chaise longue. "I'll get you some water," he said. Moments later he was back. "Here. I put some ice in it."

Tate drank the water greedily. "Hit the spot," he said.

Wes swung his backpack to the floor. "Want some more?"

"Nope. Was that the bus that went by earlier?" Tate asked.

"Yeah."

"Good thing for me you showed up when you did. Thanks."

Wes shrugged.

Tate had the feeling the boy wanted to say something more but was hesitating.

"How're things going for you?" he asked, giving him an opening.

"Pretty good. Hey, uh, Tate…I thought about what you said. And—and I guess—" He looked down at his boots, then at the trees in the courtyard. "I did what you said. I talked to Mom and Dad about changing teachers, and you were right. They said I could if it was all right with Mr. Smith, but only once. If I don't get along with the next teachers, I'm stuck. I'll just have to make do."

"Sounds like a good plan."

"Just wanted you to know."

Tate nodded.

The boy stared at the trees a little longer, then slung his pack back over his shoulder. "Guess I better get goin'," he said. "Rafe wants me to ride some fence before dark."

"You're a hard worker, Wes," Tate said. He knew the boy would appreciate the compliment.

Wes dipped his head and stepped down off the porch. With a sharp little turn, he cut across the two yards to his front door.

Tate wasn't aware that Jodie had come to

stand inside the front door until she stepped outside.

"Harriet told me Wes had talked to them," she said.

"Hmm."

She tilted her head. "What did you say to him the other day?"

"Just a few home truths."

"Well, whatever it was, it seems to have worked."

Tate looked at her from under his brow, his eyes half-closed. He wanted to gauge her state of mind. As Axel had said, her moods tended to be mercurial. "Will you take my head off if I ask where you've been?" he asked quietly.

"Harriet and I drove over to Twilight. I haven't been there since Lee and Karen were married." Lee Parker was an "off-ranch" Parker, who worked in television production. He wasn't from Twilight, a semighost town in a neighboring county that had changed little since the latter part of the 1800s. But he'd done a long segment on its rebirth as a tourist attraction for his documentary-style travel show on public television and, in the process, had fallen in love with one of its residents.

"And what's it like?" Tate asked. "Still bringing in visitors?"

"A steady stream. They've opened a few more places—a museum and a couple of stores—and renovated a few more rooms in the hotel. But they're careful not to change the town too much. Twilight will always be Twilight, I suppose, as long as someone cares about it." She seemed to consider what she'd said and hurried on. "Lee and Karen weren't there. They're in San Francisco. I think someone said they'd soon be going on the road to film more shows."

"Hmm."

A short silence followed.

"Shannon's going to have another baby," Jodie said.

Tate's head jerked up. Was that what had gotten her out of sorts this morning? Baby lust? He trod lightly. "Hmm," he said again.

"It's due in October."

She seemed fixated on the baby. "Do they want another boy?" he asked. He knew he couldn't get by with a third noncommittal answer.

"A girl," she said. "But they'll take either one."

He nodded.

"Tate," she began.

But he couldn't stand it any longer. Dancing

on a minefield took too much energy after his botched walk. He got up, wobbled a bit, then tried to go past her.

She reached out to capture his arm. "Tate," she said urgently, "how would you feel if—"

"Tate!" Harriet cried as she rushed onto the porch. "You poor thing! Are you all right? Wesley just told me what happened. Maybe you shouldn't be sittin' out here. Maybe you should—" Her concern completely obliterated Jodie's question.

Jodie looked blankly from one to the other. "Something happened?" she asked.

"Wesley found Tate sittin' out by the road. He'd walked all that way and couldn't get back."

"It wasn't all that much," Tate said, feeling ridiculous. "I just overextended."

"You walked to the road?" Jodie echoed.

He nodded.

"Wesley helped him back," Harriet said. "He told me Tate looked—" She stopped, finally realizing that she might be embarrassing him.

"I'm fine," Tate insisted.

Jodie's eyes moved over him.

When neither of them said anything, Harriet backed away. "Well, I…think I'll go home now. I'll talk to you later," she said, then she hurried off, retracing her son's earlier path.

"You could've told me," Jodie said quietly.

"It wasn't that big a deal."

"What happened?"

"Nothing. I got out there and couldn't get back. Not without help."

Jodie held open the door. "You were on your way inside," she reminded him.

He moved past her, extremely aware of her and of the flowery scent of her perfume.

She followed him to the bedroom, where he headed straight for the bed.

"Did you remember to call Mr. Fowler?" she asked.

Tate grimaced as he lay back and shook his head. Her tone had been odd.

"I did," she said. "The paperwork was sent to the wrong courthouse. We have to start all over. It has to go to the courthouse in Austin, not the one in Del Norte, because Austin is our legal residence."

"How'd it get sent to the one here?"

She shrugged. "Some kind of paperwork snafu. You know how it is."

"I never knew either of the Fowlers to mess up on paperwork before."

"They have a new secretary, I think. It might have been her."

He frowned, but before he could say anything else, Jodie asked him a question.

"Did I ever tell you Jennifer called? She said to tell you she turned the emails over to the Boston police and she asked me to be sure to thank you. Her father flew her there and turned out to be a real help. She credits that to what you told him. She thinks Alan will be charged soon. Not just because of the emails but because—"

"What's going on, Jodie?" he interrupted her. "Why are you so—"

"I'm not anything," she denied.

"You're jumpy."

"I'm not."

"You have been ever since—"

"I just want you to know how much you've helped people. Wesley, Jennifer, Jim...and Jack, with his old case. You *can* do more than you think, Tate."

"I proved that wrong this afternoon," he countered wryly.

"So what? You went a little farther than you were ready to. But you got there. If you hadn't, Wesley wouldn't have found you."

"He wouldn't have *had* to find me if I could've made it back."

"I don't see how that's a problem."

"You're not me. He practically had to carry me."

"You expect too much of yourself."

"And you don't…of yourself?"

"Not like that!"

"Baloney!"

She swiftly closed the distance between them. "Why?" she demanded. "Why are you doing this? If I really believed you wanted a divorce, I wouldn't fight you on it. But you seem to think you're being noble, as if what you're doing is for me! But if it's for *me,* why doesn't what I want count? It's so very arrogant of you to make the decision for me! To force me into something I think is wrong." She paused, striving for calm. "Do me a favor, okay? Turn things around. What if I were you and you were me? What if I was the one who'd been hurt. Say, in a car accident. Is what we've had together so flimsy that you'd walk away from me when I needed you the most? Would you leave me—" her throat tightened "—when I— When I—" She couldn't go on.

"No!" he said roughly, pushing upright to better meet her onslaught. "But it's not the same. It's not the decision of the one who's whole. It's—"

"You're whole!"

"Get it in your head…I'm not! You say nothing's changed, my mom says nothing's changed, Jack says nothing's changed…but *everything's* changed, Jodie. Everything!"

"You'll get better!"

"And you're willing to wait? To see what you have left?"

"I'll love what I have left…because it's you, Tate. I didn't marry a he-man of some sort. You've spent most of your life saving people, yes. But I thought you did it because you wanted to help people, not because it made you feel like a man! And what's a 'man' anyway? I don't care if you can't walk to the road and back right now. I don't care if you never can! I love *you,* Tate. You, the person you are. Not—"

He shook his head, denying her words. "If I can't take care of you, I'm nothing, Jodie."

"There are different ways of taking care!" she shot back.

"No." He continued to shake his head. "No."

Jodie stood just a reach away. If he let himself, he could grab hold of her hand and hang on for all that his life was worth. But her life was worth more. He restrained himself, keeping still. Keeping very still.

She made a small sound, as if his inaction had inflicted a terrible wound.

He turned his face away. He had to. Confusion was starting to tumble through him. She was twisting things. The way she maintained that she loved him. He'd believed he was right in what he was doing. He *was* right! He couldn't take her down with him. But she seemed to be arguing that she could bring him back up with her, if only he'd let her. Was he making a mistake? Was he being arrogant?

He squeezed his eyes shut in an attempt to turn off his doubts.

JODIE MANAGED to hold everything in until she got to her room, then she collapsed on the bed.

How could they have come to this? Because they'd married in such haste? Because even their courtship had been abbreviated? Because, as Mae had said at the time, she'd gone through so many recent changes?

Mae had been afraid Jodie was jumping into marriage the way she'd always done everything—without thinking things through.

She'd just returned to the ranch from her year in Europe. She'd just learned about her mother and the truth that had been kept hidden—that her mother had chosen money over her husband and her child. She'd just started to reconcile to her place in the Parker family, becoming proud of her heritage instead of apologetic. She'd always felt such a cuckoo in the nest—the odd person out. She'd never been able to settle down.

Then she'd discovered Tate, who'd been there all along. She'd fallen in love with him and insisted on a rush to the altar because she had seen no reason to wait. She knew what she was doing this time, she'd insisted.

And Tate had gone along with her wishes… because he loved her.

Did he think now, as Mae had then, that she hadn't known what she was doing? The trials and tribulations she'd experienced while growing up had been very public. Her exploits had provided a form of entertainment for the entire county—her relationship with Rio, her time in Europe. Tate had known it all.

Were her past inconsistencies playing a major role in his present determination?

But she'd meant what she said when she'd told everyone that she'd changed. That she'd finally grown up. Over the past six months she'd grown up even more—she'd had to!

Couldn't he see it?

CHAPTER FIFTEEN

JODIE AND TATE SAID very little to each other the next morning. They both seemed incapable of expressing their true feelings. When they had to speak, they were polite but constrained. Last night's confrontation still resounded, as did its aftermath. Both had spent a restless night.

When the invitation came to Jodie to accompany Harriet, Shannon and Marie into Del Norte for a Saturday shopping trip, she jumped at the chance.

Shortly after nine o'clock, Tate was on his own. He read for a time, finally starting the book Rafe had loaned him. He was just settling into the complexities of the mystery, when Axel stopped by.

"I just wanted ya to know," Axel said. "I'm goin' out to help Rafe and some others replace the head on a windmill. The thing's give out. So I won't be here for one o'clock. Probably won't be over until after supper. If that's okay."

"Sure, it's fine," Tate replied. He knew what replacing the head on a windmill entailed. It was hard, sometimes dangerous, work that required a lot of lifting and pulling, until all the parts were back in place. Axel's brawn would come in handy.

"Didn't want you wonderin' where I was," Axel said, his round face breaking into a smile.

Tate lifted the book and joked, "Maybe by then I'll know who done it."

Axel glanced at the distinctive cover. "Hey, yeah, that's a good'un. I read it a month or so ago."

Tate went back to the book and, later, took it with him onto the front porch. He noticed that things were quiet around the compound, that the children weren't about, but he didn't think much of it.

Then, in about twenty minutes, Mae came out onto the front porch to call the children's names. "Ward...Nathan...Anna!"

When there was no immediate response, her hawklike gaze spotted Tate on the porch and she called to him, "You see those kids around lately?"

He put the book aside. "I haven't seen 'em at all. They're supposed to be out here?"

Mae gave a reply that he couldn't understand as she turned back into her house. When she came out again, she had her cane. She was ready to hunt them down. But before setting off, she tried calling once more. "Anna! Ward! Nathan! You answer me right now, you hear?"

When there was still no response, Tate stood up and tried himself. "Ward? Anna! Nate!"

Nothing.

Mae stomped off her porch and headed toward Rafe and Shannon's house. She went inside, then came out again. She went next door to Gib's place to tap imperiously on the front door. When she received no answer, she circled back on the drive.

All the while, Tate peered into the surrounding area, narrowing his eyes against the glare. He wasn't worried because this was the children's home. Mae, though, was clearly growing more frustrated. They must have been left in her care.

When she neared him, she stopped to say

gruffly, "I'm gonna tan their little hides when I get hold of 'em. They know they're supposed to stay in the courtyard or around my place."

"When'd you see 'em last?" Tate asked.

"'Bout a half hour ago. Couldn't be more. At least...I don't think it could. I got a phone call and—"

"Maybe they're at Harriet's," Tate suggested.

Mae, her cheeks flushed by an unaccustomed awareness of culpability, looked at the house a short distance away and stomped down the drive. She barged inside it, too.

Tate heard her calling the children's names. She was just coming out onto Harriet's front porch, when a shrill cry came from a distance.

Apprehension hit Tate in the solar plexus, bringing with it a sharp reminder of his previous pain.

The cry came again, and this time Tate fixed the location. Someone—a child—was peddling a bike down the private road from Little Springs. Peddling as fast as he or she could, while a golden-haired dog sprinted ahead. Tate pointed them out to Mae.

As the duo drew nearer, they saw that the child was Anna.

Mae hurried to the edge of the drive, stabbing her cane into the walkway. Tate managed to arrive at Mae's side close to the same time as Anna and the dog. Junior barked excitedly until hushed.

Anna's cheeks were flushed from her effort, but the rest of her face was pale. She jabbered at first, not making sense. From what Tate could pick up, something had happened to Nate.

"Take a deep breath, girl!" Mae snapped. "We can't understand a thing you're sayin'."

Anna's eyes were huge. She looked pleadingly at Tate, then back at her great-great-aunt. "Nate won't wake up!" she cried. "He's just layin' there! We can't make him—"

"Where?" Mae demanded.

"Out—" Anna glanced over her shoulder "—out there. Down the road."

"What are you three doin' out there?" Mae snapped. "Who said you could go explorin'? You were supposed to stay in the compound. Not—"

Tate could see Mae's frail, yet seemingly indomitable, body start to tremble. With anger? With fear? With shock? With guilt?

He temporarily usurped the mantle of authority. "Where 'down there,' Anna?" he asked.

"A way off the road. We were takin' a shortcut to Little Springs, to show Ward's and Nate's new bikes to Elisabeth, then Nate hit somethin'...and he fell off...and now we can't make him wake up!" She started to cry. "I thought he was dead, but Ward says he's not."

"Where's Ward?" Tate asked.

The girl answered between sniffs. "He stayed with Nate. We didn't want him to wake up and not know what happened. Wonder where we were."

Tate squeezed her hand reassuringly. "That was the right thing to do, Anna. We wouldn't want him wanderin' off, either."

He looked at Mae. She seldom gave in to her mounting age, but this time, she couldn't hide from it. Nearing ninety, she couldn't react as readily as she once would have in an emergency. Her mind, though still quick, had begun to slow.

"Where's Gib?" he asked her.

She returned his look blankly for a moment, before the old Mae snapped back into place. "Who knows," she retorted, her old frustration with her nephew surfacing.

"Anna—" Tate turned back to the little girl "—we need you to go out to the main garage and find your dad. If you can't find him, look for Gib in his studio. If you can't find either one of them, grab the first cowboy you see. Any one will do. Tell him I said he has to get over here quick."

"Daddy's workin' on the windmill," Anna said. "I heard him tell Momma about it this morning."

"Then look for Gib…or a cowboy. Whichever you come to first. Can you do that?"

She nodded, her head still bouncing even as she ran off. The dog tried to follow her, but Mae called him back. Junior waited, watching, his tail down.

Tate took Mae's arm and urged her back toward her house.

"They were my responsibility," Mae murmured tightly, falling slowly into step beside him. "I was supposed to watch 'em."

"You can't watch kids every second, Mae. Not when they take it into their heads to have an adventure."

"They know better."

"They're kids. Kids do foolish things. Even Parker kids."

"Is that a dig?" she demanded. "Because if

it is, I'm surprised at you, Tate Connelly. At a time like this!"

"It's a fact, Mae. That's all. Kids are kids."

"Since when do you know so much about 'em?"

Tate admitted honestly, "Mostly since I've been here. About little kids, anyway."

He checked what he could see of the path that led to the work area of ranch headquarters and saw no sign of Anna. This was another instance that underscored the extent of his physical deficiencies. He and a ninety-year-old woman were equally ineffective at providing much real help. He ground his teeth, thinking of Nate, hoping that the little boy's unconsciousness was due to nothing more than a simple concussion.

Anna shot back into view, racing toward them. "I couldn't— No one's there! I looked and I called, but—" The dog leaped about, greeting her.

Tate and Mae had stopped walking. "There's no one else," Mae said. "I'll go."

The Cadillac sat where Gib must have left it on the drive, a little to the right of Mae's house. She started for it.

"How long's it been since you've driven a car, Mae?" Tate asked.

"It's not somethin' you forget," Mae retorted.

"And once you get there, what are you gonna do? You're not strong enough to—"

"I can't *not* do anything!"

Tate looked deep inside himself. He knew his limitations. Knew what happened when he pushed himself too far. Yet the image of the young boy he'd come to care about, lying on the ground unconscious, possibly seriously injured, and the other young boy, who he also cared about, probably nearing panic because Anna had been away for so long—

He grabbed Anna's hand. "C'mon. You take me to where Nate fell off his bike. You can do that, right?"

She nodded.

He said to Mae, "I'll leave the car on the side of the road in the direction we're heading. Call Little Springs and tell Dub what's happened. I just hope he's not out with Morgan and Rafe and LeRoy."

"I'll call him. I'll call Jim, too."

"Good idea," Tate murmured between short breaths as they moved up the driveway to Mae's house.

She found the car keys and handed them over. "You can do it, son," she said quietly, acknowledging the difficult deed he was about to undertake. Her dark eyes conveyed her full confidence in him.

Tate held her gaze for a second, felt something inside himself respond, then he gave a curt nod and continued to the car with Anna. She jumped into the passenger seat while he settled behind the wheel.

He was already winded and his knees were rubbery as he slipped the key into the ignition—symptoms similar to those he'd experienced the day before.

It had been six months since he had driven a car. He'd never expected to be called upon to do it so soon, if ever. He started the car and, thankful that it was an automatic, put it in gear. They rolled away, with Mae and Junior watching them from the porch.

As they traveled down the road, Anna concentrated fiercely on their surroundings. About a mile from the compound, she jerked her arm out to point the way across a pasture.

"It's there!" she cried. "Where those fences come together. We were gettin' tired. That's why we decided to take the shortcut. Ward remembered that he and his mom had come this way one day when they were riding. I've taken it before, too, but I wasn't sure exactly where it was."

"You're sure now," Tate murmured, tapping the brake.

"Uh-huh."

Tate pulled the Cadillac to the left side of the road and parked it.

This was where the cow patty really hit the fan, he thought. It was one thing to walk down the driveway to the car, and something else entirely to walk from the car across rough ground.

He struggled out from behind the wheel, took a few deep breaths and started off.

"Anna," he said as they crossed beyond the fence. "Are they close enough for Ward to hear us?"

"I don't know."

Tate cupped his mouth with his hands and yelled as loudly as he could, "Ward… Ward, can you hear me?" He ended on a fit of coughs that almost, but not quite, obliterated a reply.

Anna's face beamed. She jumped up and down.

Tate controlled his breaths and yelled again. "Stay where you are. We're coming!" Then he turned to Anna. "Honey, this isn't going to be fast. I'd say you could run ahead and I'd follow, but I can't run. I can't even walk fast. So, just…help me out, okay? Stay with me."

She nodded, her eyes wide.

The next fifteen minutes were torture for Tate. He forced himself to move, made himself push ahead. More than once he didn't think he could do it. But he had to! There was no one else.

Finally, he reached the boys, Anna having received his permission to break out ahead once her cousins were in view. Nate was sitting up, but he wasn't on his feet. He looked around, confused.

Tate dropped to the ground next to him. He looked at Ward and saw at a glance that physically the boy was fine. Then he turned his attention to the younger child. "Hey, Nate. What's going on? I heard you took a tumble." He tilted the boy's head so that he could inspect his eyes. His first-aid training on the job told him what to check for.

The boy was fussy and pushed Tate's hands away.

Ward answered for him. "He ran over a big rock and got tossed over the handlebars. Landed right on top of his head!" Now that his brother was conscious and help from an adult had arrived, Ward reverted to a childish appreciation of the gruesome. He grinned. "I was worried his brains were gonna fall out!"

"I was, too," Anna agreed, perfectly serious.

Tate smiled. "Well, nobody's brains are falling out. Nate'll probably have a headache and a big bump, but more than likely that'll be the end of it. Betcha he'll get a trip into town to the doctor's office, though." When Nate started to cry at that news, Tate added, "And maybe some ice cream? Little boys with bad bumps should always have ice cream."

"Chocolate!" Nate demanded.

"Me, too!" Ward cried.

Anna, still unsettled, said nothing.

Tate eyed the little group. Now all they needed was to get to the car. And he wasn't even sure he could stand up again.

He forced himself to try and, after weaving a little, managed to stay upright. "Okay, you two...Ward and Anna. *You* get to carry Nate. Come stand in front of me and face each other. Now, do what I'm doing." He extended his arms, then grasped his left forearm close to the elbow. "That's right," he said in approval as the children copied him. "Next, reach out with your free hand and grab the other person's arm. That's it. That's right! Look what you've done. You've made a chair for Nate." As the children giggled he turned to the youngest child. "Whatcha think, Nate? Wanna ride?"

Nate grumbled but settled himself on the makeshift seat.

"Now, you," Tate said, addressing Nate, "hold on to their necks. Not tight, just enough to keep from falling. You don't want to do that again, do you?"

"Uh-uh," Nate said.

Tate smiled. "All right! Let's go back to the road. Slowly now," he said. "We don't want to jiggle Nate too much. And when you two get tired, say so. We can rest."

He did his best to keep up with them, but he was starting to lose it. Will alone could move flesh only so far.

He was pushing much farther than he'd ever thought to go. Putting one foot in front of the other, making everything work. He needed to be with the children as they arrived at the car. They were looking to him for continued help. To him—

He didn't remember passing out. He didn't remember anything until he slowly focused on

Christine Hughes's pretty face as she gazed down on him, the wide blue sky a backdrop.

"Christine?" he murmured fuzzily, then he remembered, "The kids! They're—"

"They're fine. They're at the car. You almost made it, too. I saw you coming, then you weren't there. The kids are worried about you."

"I'm fine. I—" Tate heard himself once again use his fall-back reply. He struggled to sit up. "I must've passed out."

Christine chuckled. "I'd say so."

She helped him to his feet and he heard childish cheers. He narrowed his eyes and saw two of the children in the Cadillac.

"Where's Nate?" he demanded.

"Jim Cleary just left a minute ago to take him to town. Mae's gone with them. The kids and I were told to get you back home. Pronto."

He needed Christine's help to walk, even though the car and her pickup weren't all that far away. Not in comparison with the distance he'd already traveled. "When did you get here?" he asked.

"A minute before Jim. Mae called. Told me what happened. I left Beth with her grandma

Delores, and…here we are. Mae must've called Jim, too."

"We were looking for help from anywhere," Tate murmured.

"Seems to me you had it all under control," Christine said.

The children scrambled out to meet them as they drew nearer. The boy and girl both rushed to hug his legs, saying without words what they felt.

Tate turned to Christine. Christine shrugged encouragement. And Tate awkwardly patted each child on the back.

THE WOMEN, who were returning from town, received their first inkling that something had happened when Jim Cleary flagged them down by flashing the lights on his big Buick. That Mae accompanied him was at first confusing. Explanations took only a moment, though.

Shannon quickly changed cars and nestled her younger son against her in the Buick's backseat. Mae stayed where she was, having insisted on continuing with them to the hospital. Within seconds, Jim pulled the car back onto the road.

Those who remained in Harriet's station wagon were quiet as they drove to the ranch.

"I hope he's all right," Harriet said softly.

Jodie, sitting next to Marie on the middle seat, held her hands tightly together in her lap. Tate had gone to help the children? How had he done it? How had he been able to, when only yesterday…

Marie bolstered her shoulders. She seemed to understand that when Jodie murmured a heartfelt "I do, too," she wasn't speaking only of little Nate.

Harriet didn't bother to put the station wagon in the main garage by the barn. Instead, she pulled up behind the Cadillac, which was parked in front of Darlene and Thomas's house.

As soon as the car stopped rolling, Christine hurried out onto the porch. Her first act was to look for Shannon.

"We met Jim and Mae on their way into town," Harriet explained. "Shannon went with them."

"Ah," Christine said, relieved.

"How bad was Nate hurt?" Harriet asked.

"He hit his head pretty hard, I guess. But he was conscious when they left."

"How did it happen? Jim said something about Anna? And Ward?"

"They were along, but they weren't hurt. Tate says they did everything right…after Nate fell. They were on their way over to Little Springs to show off the boys' bikes—without having told anyone, of course. Nate hit a rock and—"

"Where's Anna now?" Harriet interrupted her.

"Inside…with Ward. I can't get them to budge from Tate. They probably think they're in a lot of trouble and Tate will protect them."

"I know one for sure who's in trouble," Harriet agreed. "And I'd say it's a pretty safe bet the other one is, too."

Christine glanced at Jodie, who until then had remained silent. "What Tate did was amazing, Jodie. No one else was here when Anna rode back for help. Just him and Mae. So he drove over to where Anna showed him she and the boys had left the road. They tramped across open ground to where the boys were, then Tate came up with a way for the kids to carry Nate back to the car because he couldn't. That's when I got there." Her expression sobered. "It took all he had in him, Jodie. I don't know. He seems—" she shrugged "—quiet."

Jodie felt everyone's eyes fall on her. "I'll... go see," she said inadequately.

"I'll come, too," Harriet said, "and get the kids out of your hair. They've probably tired Tate out even worse."

"I don't think so," Christine said. "He's been very patient with them. He knows they're upset."

Marie spoke up. "I'll start dinner and make enough for everyone." She collected the cooler, where they'd stored the market perishables for the long trip home, from the rear of the station wagon and with Christine's help carried it to the main house.

Jodie and Harriet followed the sound of a television set into Tate's room. When they got there, they stopped short because Tate was stretched out on top of the bedcovers, fast asleep, and curled up next to him, one on each side, were the children. Each was giggling silently at something Laurel and Hardy had done on the small screen.

As soon as they saw the two women, their laughter stopped. Anna, noting her mother's expression, knew the reckoning she'd been dreading had come. She crawled quietly out of bed and came to stand beside her. Ward, temporarily without a parent present, stayed put, until Harriet motioned for him to join them.

"All right, you two," she said quietly, levelly, "off to my house. We're goin' to have a little talk."

After a last glance at the recumbent Tate, Harriet smiled softly at Jodie, thanking her wordlessly for how well he'd taken care of the children. Then she followed them out of the house.

Jodie released a long breath. She, too, looked at Tate. Then she blinked, because she suddenly realized that he might have been asleep to begin with, but he wasn't now. His eyes were open and he was watching her.

"You're back," he said.

"Yes. Just now."

"I heard."

"You weren't asleep?"

"Not the whole time."

"Then why didn't you…? Why…?"

He stuffed another pillow behind his head, grimacing as he did so. "I didn't want to complicate things. The kids need to settle with their parents."

"Shannon's not here. She's with Nate, on the way to Del Norte."

"Good."

"Rafe isn't here, either. Neither is LeRoy. I wonder…has anyone sent word to them yet?"

"Wes and Gwen got home from visiting their friend. They rode out to tell 'em."

"Was it bad with little Nate?"

"He seemed okay. He'll probably stay at the hospital overnight, just to be safe."

"And what about you? Christine said—"

He smiled, but with little amusement. "I'm fine."

"Tate."

"No, I am. I just— I may not be able to move much for a day or two."

"Tate, what you did—"

"Wasn't all that much."

"It was! You drove…you found the boys… you got them back!"

"I couldn't've done it without Anna and Wade. And that's the truth, Jodie."

"You wouldn't have *had* to do it without them. What were they thinking? They know how far they're supposed to go and how far they're not. They also know never to take off cross-country without telling someone. No adult does. No child does. It's too dangerous."

"I know. I've been out on some search parties," Tate said quietly.

Jodie worked to stifle her burst of indignant anger at the children. Not only had they put themselves at risk, but without knowing it, they'd put Tate at risk, as well. She had no idea how badly this was going to set him back. Would it be as before, with him barely able to walk? She tried to keep the "without knowing it" part of the argument foremost in her mind. They hadn't meant to harm him. And considering the way she and Harriet had found them…

"They like you," she said softly.

"I like them."

"Is that why you did it? Why you—"

"I didn't have a choice. It was either me or Mae. Nate was unconscious. The situation was serious. I went." He moved uncomfortably. "Jodie, could I ask a favor?"

She nodded agreement.

"Could we…talk about this later? It's been kind of a rough afternoon."

"Of course," she said, mildly surprised that he'd asked instead of demanded. She started to turn away.

"And maybe," he said, stopping her, "you could help me to the bathroom? I'm not sure I can make it on my own."

Jodie moved quickly to his side, helped him up, then helped him down the hall. His arm was over her shoulders, his body against hers. He didn't try to keep himself stiffly apart the way he had when he'd first come home from the care facility and they'd done this.

She waited outside in the hall for him to finish, giving him some respectful privacy. Then, at his call, she moved back into the room and helped him back to the bedroom.

As she saw him onto the bed, their eyes met and held. He didn't look away.

Maybe it was exhaustion; maybe it was the shock of what he'd been through. She didn't know. But something was different.

She wanted to probe. To find an answer.

Yet she held her tongue. As he'd said, it had been a rough afternoon.

CHAPTER SIXTEEN

BY FORCE of circumstance Jodie had learned to be fairly adept at waiting. For someone who'd never been able to postpone anything, she could now allow time to pass without fretting. At least, without fretting too much.

Getting through the remainder of that day was a trial for her, though. The compound was in something of an uproar. The men repairing the windmill hurried back, and Rafe rushed off to town. As the cowboys returned to headquarters and heard what happened they hung around the bunkhouse, waiting for word. Their vigil didn't have a life-or-death feel, but their concern was evident.

The family clustered at Mae's house, their thoughts centering on the four-year-old. Ward and Anna waited with them, chastised for their part in the episode but not denounced.

Finally word came. The family doctor had

seen Nate and pronounced him well. He would stay overnight at the hospital for observation, then come home the next day. All present at the Parker Ranch breathed a relieved sigh.

Jodie's chief worry had never been Nate, though. Tate had given her his estimation of the boy's condition and she'd believed him. Her worry was Tate.

He slept through the accolades the family heaped on him. And continued to sleep long into the evening. In fact, when Jodie finally gave up and went to sleep herself, he remained dead to the world.

JODIE AWAKENED the next morning to a clear memory of what had happened the day before, although she didn't remember much after climbing into bed last night. Sleep had come almost immediately, brought on by exhaustion.

She slipped from between the sheets and into her robe, then listened at Tate's door. Hearing nothing, she proceeded to the kitchen…and found him sitting at the table, staring out the window. He looked as if he'd been there for a long time.

She stopped short, habit telling her that she

was intruding. Then she made herself relax. "Good morning," she said quietly.

His eyes turned slowly to her. "'Morning," he replied neutrally.

She pushed a fall of copper-red hair away from her face. She'd done nothing to groom herself. But then, neither had he. He wore pajamas, a night's growth of beard, and his hair was rumpled. Jodie thought him the most wonderful-looking man alive, though she knew he wouldn't appreciate hearing it. Not now…if ever.

She glanced at the cup in front of him and saw that it was half-full. "You made coffee?" she asked.

"Have some if you want," he replied.

She stepped to the counter. "I never expected— Yesterday afternoon—" She tried again. "Yesterday, you didn't think you'd be able to move today."

He smiled slightly. "I was wrong."

She poured a cup of coffee that she didn't want and brought it and the percolator to the table. "Would you like a warm-up?" she asked, slipping into a chair.

"Sure," he said.

She topped his cup. He watched as she set the coffeemaker down.

Jodie was filled with questions, but she held back as she had the day before, wringing out yet a little more patience.

He played with the handle of his cup, moving it back and forth. Finally, he said quietly, "I've been wrong about a lotta things, haven't I? About you. About me. Pretty much about everything."

Jodie sat riveted to the spot. She couldn't move.

He smiled slowly. "Have I struck you speechless?"

"I—I—I guess you have," she stammered.

He got up and went to stand at the window. "I've been waiting for the sun to break the horizon. Watching how dark things are, then how everything just kinda gradually changes…and there's this wonderful burst of light." He turned to face her. "You're that wonderful burst of light in my life, Jodie. I'm crazy to send you away."

Jodie could only stare at him.

He continued, "I always thought…when we first got together…that there was a lucky star."

"Tate—"

"Let me say what I have to, okay?"

She nodded.

"We argued one time about what it meant to be a man. What it meant to me. I've spent my whole life trying to live up to what I thought other people considered the ideal. Hard work, high principles, sacrifice, service. My mom, Jack…my dad. Everything I did was to make them proud of me. I wanted to help people, yes. But more…I wanted the people closest to me to be proud. I had set things I had to do. Be honest, be true, be the best I could be. And if I couldn't be any one of those things, I failed." He paused. "I wanted you to be proud of me."

"I am proud of you!"

"I mean for the everyday things. Getting up in the morning, going to a job, doing good work while I'm there, coming home again. That kinda thing."

"Tate—"

He shook his head. "When I couldn't do that, when I couldn't get up, go out, do good work…do anything the way I was supposed to—I couldn't be proud of myself."

"Tate," she repeated, starting to her feet.

He lifted a hand to stop her. "I had a lot of false pride about myself that I didn't know I had. If I couldn't be perfect…if I couldn't be the best— Jack told me what was going on, but I wouldn't listen to him. I was using you as an excuse. Using what was best for you… when it was really what was best for me. Because then I wouldn't have to see myself—what I'd become—through your eyes. I didn't believe in myself anymore. I let everything coast. I crawled into a hole. I took it out on you."

Jodie wouldn't be stayed any longer. She hurried over and hugged him, holding on for dear life. She had no idea where this conversation was taking them, but wherever it was, they were going there together.

"It doesn't matter," she murmured unsteadily. "What you've been through—what we've been through—it doesn't matter!"

He shook his head. "But it does! I love you more than life itself, but who could've told it? I treated you so bad!"

"Not bad! Never bad! You shut down, closed into yourself, wouldn't let me in, frightened me because you were so determined. But you were never mean. You never tore me down. You never purposefully tried to hurt me."

"But I did hurt you."

"Yes! I won't lie to you. I'll never lie to you again if— Oh, God, Tate, I love you so much and I couldn't make you listen. Couldn't make you believe. You believe me now, don't you? You believe I love you?"

"I believe," he said huskily, at last taking hold of her.

Tears sprang into Jodie's eyes. So much had happened—so quickly, so unexpectedly. She'd come into the kitchen to start breakfast, not expecting this.

He held her as a man on the brink of death from thirst might clutch a cup of water.

She sought his lips…and neither he nor she held anything back.

"I love you now more than I did before," she swore once they'd broken apart. "I never thought that was possible, but when I almost lost you, when you almost— I came away loving you more, valuing you more. I knew what we had, Tate. And I didn't want to lose it. Lose you."

"Jodie…" he began, unable to finish as the intensity of her feelings overwhelmed him.

She looked at him, tears clinging to her lashes. "Then when you told me you wanted a divorce—" Emotion choked off the rest.

"I didn't! Not really. I mean, I did, but—"

She repeated, "It doesn't matter. Not if—"

"I *don't* want it anymore. I don't want our marriage to end."

She made a soft sound and he folded her back against him. Then, finally unable to deny themselves any longer, they walked holding hands into the chintz and ruffled bedroom.

"I DON'T KNOW how I kept going these months, holding you away," Tate said, his fingers playing in her hair as they lay cuddled side-by-side on the bed.

"You slipped a couple of times," she reminded him.

"I slipped more than that. You just never knew it. Sometimes when I'd look at you—I've missed this," he said huskily. "Missed touching you, holding you…feeling *free* to touch you and hold you."

"So have I," she murmured. Responding to impulse, she hugged him tightly, remembering just hours before when she couldn't. "You certainly haven't acted like the man who thought he wouldn't be able to move around today. Up early, made coffee, loved your wife. You're moving just fine, thank you."

He grinned. "Funny thing…the more I do, the more I'm able to do. You think that's what everyone's been trying to tell me all along?"

"Oh…it could be," she returned airily, teasing him.

"Last night, I didn't have enough energy left to sneeze—" He frowned. "How's little Nate? Anyone hear?"

"Just like you said, he's fine. But the doctor wanted him to stay the night. Everyone's impressed with what you did and very grateful."

"They're good kids," he said.

The moment came to tell him about the baby…and went.

"Still, everyone's grateful," she murmured. "You've always been a hero to Harriet. Now you can count Shannon and Christine in your fan club, too."

"I did what anyone would've done in my place. You shoulda seen Aunt Mae. She was ready to drive out there herself."

"Oh!" Jodie grinned. "I forgot to include Aunt Mae in your fan club. She goes on and on."

"That doesn't sound like Mae."

"I may be exaggerating…just a little," Jodie confessed.

"You're exaggerating a lot."

He smiled lazily when she met his gaze. How she'd missed his smiles! She tried to fix the picture in her mind. So many memories from these past six months were in need of papering over with newer, happier ones.

That thought suddenly made her turn serious again. “Tate, I have to be sure. You’re not just saying what you said earlier. That you—”

“I’ll call Ned Fowler myself and tell him to toss out those papers. A long time ago people were said to suffer from what doctors called ‘brain fever.’ Maybe that’s what I had.”

“Did you ever seriously think I didn’t love you?” Jodie asked. “I realized after a while that you could’ve had good reason. Up until we married, my life was pretty unstable. It wasn’t—”

“Complete,” he inserted. “Neither was mine. No, Jodie. I never thought that. I just never wanted you to be tied to a promise you made when things were different for us.”

“I made that promise because I meant it—*in sickness and health*.”

“*I* was different.”

“Only when you held yourself away from me.”

“Right now, I’m probably forty percent of what I used to be, Jodie. I might make it to eighty. I might not. Who can say? Maybe I’ll make it all the way back to a full one hundred.

All I know is, I'm gonna try, because trying makes all the difference. When I was working so hard to get to Nate and Ward, I forced myself to keep going. And I did it. I did what I had to. Now, today, I feel better, stronger."

She put a finger to his lips and said softly, "Now, today, you're going to devote some time to your poor neglected spouse. Even if all we do is keep holding on to each other." She hesitated. "I have a confession, Tate. It's about those papers. I instructed Ned from the beginning not to file them."

"Not to file them," he repeated.

"Not ever. Not anywhere. They were just for show."

"To show me."

"It worked."

He tipped his head consideringly. "Why do I detect a little of Mae's indelicate hand in this?"

"Because it's there?" she ventured.

"Mae has a lot to answer for."

"Oh, yes. Like helping you and helping me... and helping us to get back together."

Someone knocked on the front door. Jodie jumped up, pulled on her robe and hurried to answer it before whoever it was took it into their head to come in.

TATE HEARD the conversation from the bedroom.

"Oh! Axel!" he heard Jodie exclaim. "Is it one o'clock already? No, it can't be. It's not that late, is it? I don't— I can't—" She sputtered to a stop.

Axel's high voice came next. "I stopped by to see if Tate wanted me to give him his massage early today, 'cause we missed yesterday. But I can see by that smile on your face that he prob'ly don't need it. Tell 'im I'm glad that everythin's workin' out all right. He'll know what I'm sayin'," he assured her. Then, with a satisfied little whistle, he walked away.

A frown marked Jodie's brow when she returned. "That was Axel," she said, coming to balance one knee on the mattress. "He just said the strangest thing."

"I heard."

"What did he mean—'Everythin's workin' out all right'?"

"I think he means," he said, taking her hand and carefully sitting up, "that the family will now know we're not getting a divorce."

"B-but how?" she sputtered.

"Axel's a man of the world. One look at you is all it'd take."

"I don't understand."

Tate laughed. Through all the heartache, through all the pain, this moment was worth it. "You're glowing with happiness, woman. You're grinning from ear to ear."

Jodie blinked at him and giggled. "So… we're not going to have to announce we're back together?"

"Oh, I doubt it."

"But we will have to announce something else," she said.

Tate couldn't think of anything. "What?" he asked.

She went at it in a roundabout way. "You said yesterday that you like Nate and Ward and Anna—little kids, in other words."

His light frown stayed in place. "Yeah."

"And you've said again that you don't want the divorce."

"Yeah, I said it. And I meant it. I was stupid. I—"

She stayed his words. "What if I told you a secret?"

His frown grew heavier. *A secret.* He remembered his strong hunch that she was harboring one. "What secret?" he asked levelly.

"What would you say—"

"Jodie, get to it!"

"—if I told you we were going to have one of our own?"

"A secret?" he asked blankly.

"A child. A baby," she explained.

"A baby? We made a baby that one time when—"

She nodded, her expression hopeful yet slightly uneasy.

"That would be…how long ago?"

"A little over two months."

"You've known for two months?" he questioned, thinking of the harshness of those months. "Why didn't you tell me?"

"You weren't exactly…receptive…to anything I said."

He could hear the reluctance to upset him, to hurt him, to challenge him, that had crept back into her voice. He cradled her against him. "A baby," he repeated unevenly.

"I didn't do it on purpose. It just…happened. I didn't plan it. When I found out, I was terrified to tell you. Terrified that you'd think— That's why I didn't say anything before. I didn't want you to feel—"

"A baby," he repeated yet again, wonderingly, wondrously. Something good had come of this time after all! "We're going to have a baby?"

Jodie realized that he wasn't angry, that he wasn't blaming her, that he wasn't rejecting either her or the baby. That, in fact, he was pleased.

He examined her. "You don't seem any different," he said. "Have you been sick? I don't know much about it, but—"

"I'm as healthy as a horse. Only one small moment of nausea. Then nothing."

He placed a hand on her tummy. "Have you felt anything yet?"

"Not yet."

"Now I'll have to get stronger," he murmured. "Does anyone else know?" he asked suddenly.

"Only Aunt Mae, and she guessed."

"So Mom doesn't know, or Jack?"

She shook her head. "Not even my dad."

His face split into a wide grin. "It's gonna be something to see their faces. What'd Mae say?"

"That I should tell you right away. She said it would help you get better."

"It's hard living around someone who's almost always right."

"Tell me about it," Jodie murmured. "But then, she does give some good advice sometimes."

Tate thought about the way Mae had looked at him yesterday. And the way it had made him feel when she'd said, *"You can do it, son."* She'd helped him regain his belief in himself.

"Yeah," he said, "I guess we're gonna have to thank her."

"She'd like that," Jodie said softly.

She ran her fingers through his hair, the unaccustomed length seeming to fascinate her. Then, wrapping her arm around him, she gave a deep, contented sigh.

EPILOGUE

TATE STEPPED UP behind Jodie as she was putting the finishing touches to her preparations for the big Sunday dinner at Mae's house. He wound his arms around her waist and pulled her back against him.

Jodie leaned into him, savoring the moment. Even after a month she still sometimes had a hard time believing. She'd occasionally wake up, thinking that this new reality was the dream. But all she had to do was reach out…and there he was, beside her.

She touched his cheek and he turned his head to kiss her fingers. In the mirror, she saw the picture they made. Him, tall and lean and handsome. Her, tall, still willowy and radiant with happiness.

Most important, he had started to look healthier. He'd picked up a little weight and the bleak lines of suffering and hopelessness he'd borne for so long had all but disappeared. The lines that were too deeply etched to fade away lent his face even stronger character.

"We'd better go. We can't be late, being that this is a celebration dinner Mae's postponed all this time, waiting for you to get stronger."

He turned her around so he could kiss her properly. "I never get tired of doing that," he said seriously, once they'd broken apart.

"Me, neither," she agreed.

He lifted the gold locket she'd just clasped around her neck. The heirloom had been Mae's as a child. "Will you pass this on to our baby if it's a girl?"

"Yes," she said softly.

"I wonder how old the locket is."

"Mae said it was her mother's as a child. So it's easily over a hundred years."

"What if our baby's a boy?"

"Then we'll just have to try again."

Tate smiled lazily and tugged her closer. Jodie laughed. "Let's take this one baby at a time, okay?"

He released her to check his appearance. They'd gone into Del Norte a few days before—Tate's first trip into town since they'd been back—and he'd done a little shopping.

Like most of the other men on the ranch, dressing up, even for Sunday dinner, meant a new pair of jeans and a new shirt—at least one that hadn't been worn while tending cattle, or driving machinery, or doing any of the everyday work. Tate's new jeans would fit right in. His designer midnight-blue shirt was an extravagance Jodie had encouraged him to buy because he looked so good in it.

The trip to town had been positive in other ways, as well. As he and Jodie had driven down the main road and along the streets to his mother's house for a short visit, then on to the sheriff's office for the same purpose, people recognized him and stopped what they were doing to wave and call. Some even jogged alongside the car to tell him how glad they were to see him doing so well. His mother's neighbors had turned out in force, forming a little welcoming committee on Emma's front lawn. At the sheriff's office, all work halted as everyone clustered around to greet him.

Tate had been overwhelmed, proving Gib's speculation on the day he'd brought them to West Texas from Austin that Tate might not realize how highly the people of Briggs

County thought of him. Gib had said his reception would perk him up, and it had.

Jodie performed the last-minute touches to her hair that Tate had interrupted and gave a final check to her voile print dress. She smiled to herself, thinking of how Tate looked at her when she was wearing it.

She glanced around and saw that the postcard Darlene and Thomas had sent them from Australia had caught his attention. She moved to look at it with him.

"They plan to stay through June," she murmured, paraphrasing the note. "And we're welcome to stay here." She hugged his arm. "What do you think? Do you want to?"

Tate dropped the postcard onto the dressing table and looked around the room. "I don't know. Think we can stand the frills for an extra month?" His grin widened. "I hate to admit it, but I'm getting used to 'em. And don't tell Rafe, 'cause I'd never live it down."

"I won't," she promised. "And you know what? I am, too. The avocado-green kitchen was the hardest for me to adjust to, but it doesn't bother me anymore. I think…it all has to do with you. I don't care where I am as long as we're together."

She kissed him softly, yet with all the feeling in her heart.

He spoke gruffly. “I had a call from Drew Winslow. He wants me to come back to the task force when I’m well.”

Icy fear pierced Jodie’s sense of well-being, but she tried not to let it show. “And…what did you say?”

“I told him I was a long way off from making a decision like that. A long way off from even finding out if I could come back.”

“You’re much better,” she said quietly.

“Plus Jack’s started making noises about retiring again. Says since he’ll be sixty-five next year, he’s thinking of hanging it up—this time for good—and going back to his ranch. He’s trying to get me to say I’ll take back the sheriff’s job.”

“And,” Jodie murmured cautiously, “what do you think about that?”

“Same thing. It’s too soon to tell.”

“At least you have options.”

“Yeah.” He arched an eyebrow. “What about you? Which one would you rather I do? If I can do either.”

At the moment, Jodie was terrified of both. But just as being a Parker was in her blood, so being a lawman was in his. She couldn't keep him from what he had to do.

She grinned at him. "Oh, no, you're not going to put that one off on me."

"You'd rather stay here," he guessed.

"I'd rather be with you. That's it."

Childish laughter reached them before small fists rapped excitedly on the front door.

"I wonder who that is," Jodie said dryly, before going to answer.

Three children burst into the hallway.

"Is Tate ready?" Ward demanded.

"Tell him we're havin' homemade ice cream!" Nate exclaimed.

"Aunt Mae sent us," Anna explained. "She says for you not to be late!"

When Tate walked out of the bedroom, the three children screeched and ran to greet him. He'd been popular with them before Nate's trouble, but afterward his prestige had almost reached cult status.

"Did I hear something about homemade ice cream?" he teased.

"*Two* kinds!" Nate shouted, almost beside himself.

"Then maybe we'd better get to it," he proposed, and the children swept down the hallway with him, picking up Jodie along the way, until they all spilled out onto the porch.

Low masculine laughter reached them from Mae's house. Rafe and Morgan Hughes stood on the porch, watching events unfold.

Tate still was unable to move with full mobility. He walked more slowly and tired sooner than those around him. But he exercised daily and received regular massages from Axel. He was a different man, both in body and in spirit, from the one who'd arrived at the ranch six weeks earlier.

Mae came to her front door and opened it to the latest arrivals. "Everybody's here. Your momma, too, Tate. And Jack. We've put another leaf in the table we have so many eatin' with us today." She swept them with an estimating glance. "You look like you're feelin' pretty proud of yourselves."

They moved into the large living room, which was filled with people. Some were sitting, others standing. Everyone turned to greet them.

Rafe and Morgan, following them in, went to join their respective families.

Mae resumed her place in her favored straight-backed chair and gazed at the assembled group. Her dark eyes flashed with satisfaction. With a little movement of her hand she directed Marie to serve a predinner drink to all the adults and older teens. Then, after clearing her throat, she offered, "Best to get the formality done with. That way we can all relax and enjoy ourselves. This is to you, Tate," she said, lifting her glass. "For being here when we needed you…more than once over the years, I might add. And for takin' our Jodie and makin' her happy. You're a good addition to the family, son. We want you to know we appreciate you."

Calls of agreement went round the room, and Tate, embarrassed, squeezed Jodie's hand.

She encouraged him to make a reply.

"I don't know what to say," he protested. "I never expected—"

"This might be the only opportunity you have with the rest of us shut up," Rafe called good-naturedly.

Tate looked around at everyone, and as he did, Jodie did, as well. At the warm expectant faces of Harriet and LeRoy and their children, and Rafe and Shannon and their boys; at the Hugheses—Dub and Delores, Morgan and Christine, Erin and little Elisabeth. Then Emma, who'd been so thrilled at their news of the baby, and Jack, who'd instantly assumed the role of honorary paternal grandfather, and her father, Gib, who, to Jodie's surprise, had broken down and cried from happiness when she'd told him.

"I—I don't quite know what to say." Tate spoke uncertainly at first, then added with conviction, "Just…thanks. For everything."

Gib clapped him on the back, as did Morgan, who was standing nearby. "A man of few words," Gib kidded him. "Belongs in this family."

They all laughed and, after lifting their glasses to echo Mae's toast, sipped their drinks.

Jodie leaned close to kiss Tate's cheek, which garnered more crowd approval.

Afterward, everyone filed into the dining room for the meal.

SEVERAL HOURS ELAPSED before Jodie and Tate returned to their borrowed home. The children, who'd accompanied them earlier, were already at their homes, taking a break from all the food and play.

Jodie noticed that Tate was tiring. But considering all the effort he'd expended with her family, she wasn't surprised.

"Let's get you back into bed for a little rest," she murmured as they slowly mounted the steps to the front door.

They went down the hall to the master bedroom, where, without warning, Tate grabbed her and they fell to the bed. They bounced as they hit it, all on a screech from Jodie that turned into convulsive giggles.

"I intend to have my wicked way with you, woman!" he threatened, and tickled her lightly, increasing her giggles.

Suddenly, he gave a little "Oof!" as her knee collided with the left side of his rib cage.

Jodie's laughter stopped the second she realized what she'd done. They hadn't roughhoused since coming back together. They shouldn't have done it now. She hadn't meant to hurt him! That had been the last thing—

Calling herself all kinds of an idiot, she ran her hands along his ribs, trying to see if she'd done any damage. He had a funny look on his face.

"Tate!" she cried softly. "Are you all right? Did I hurt you? I didn't mean—"

Then she realized his funny look came from trying to hold back laughter. "You frightened me!" she accused. "And you were faking!"

She found a safe place on his uninjured shoulder to thump—and thumped it.

Still smiling, he reached up to lovingly brush strands of tumbled copper-red hair away from her face. Under his care, her flash of temper settled.

She continued to look down at him. "You *were* faking, weren't you?" she pressed, needing some extra reassurance.

"I'm fine," he said, just as he had numerous other instances in the past.

Only, this time she believed him. Because as he said it, he hooked his fingers around the back of her neck and brought her head down to his. And the kiss that followed could only have been accomplished by a man who truly was…fine.

* * * * *

"We can't keep calling her 'the baby,' Wyatt. Before you leave, will you help me name her?"

Wyatt produced the engagement ring he'd been carrying around for weeks. "I know you're talking about the first and middle names." Wyatt's voice cracked as he held Casey's left hand. "Last time I asked you to marry me I went about it all wrong. I'm asking again, out of love. Please, will you and your little princess do me the honor of leaving the hospital as Keenes? Last time, I was too afraid to say I love you. I was afraid I'd lose you. When I came back to the studio today, I knew I'd do anything it took to keep you and your baby. *Our* baby," he corrected.

Casey cried, and held out her hand so Wyatt could slip the ring on her finger. "I love you, too, Wyatt. With all my heart. I accept."

He bent to kiss her, but the nurse said, "Wait!" Continuing to sway with the baby, she pointed. "I see a camera. If this isn't a picture moment in your lives, nothing ever will be." She handed Casey the newborn. Wyatt happily relinquished the camera.

Some time later, when the two of them were again alone with the baby, Wyatt took pictures of her sleeping, and of Casey smiling happily.

"I predict this will be the most loved, and most photographed child in the universe. We'll fill a dozen albums." Bending over Casey, he kissed her, then sat on the edge of the bed and stroked the infant's tiny, curled fingers. "I'm not sure I can articulate how much I love you and her," he said, his voice choked with emotion.

"Will you marry me before it's time to leave the hospital? I wish the birth certificate could show I'm her father. It can't, but I will press Dane to let me adopt her."

"A hospital bed beats getting married in a microbrewery. Will you invite Brenda and the others? I want our friends to be our witnesses, not strangers. And...I'd like my foster parents here," she said. "Tomorrow. Can we get married then?"

Wyatt squeezed her hand. "We will. Casey, it's important for me to say I knew as early as the Torreses' dinner party that I loved you. Maybe before. I...I—"

"Hush. Better late than never. That's in the past."

"All right. Shall we talk about names?"

"You first," Casey said, turning her head to watch her sleeping child.

"I know it's technically not the holiday season anymore, but the name Merry Joy just seems fitting. The Christmas spelling of Merry."

"Merry Joy Keene." Casey linked her fingers with Wyatt's. "It's perfect, because I knew on Christmas Day that I wanted you to be her father."

Tears sprang to Wyatt's eyes. They kissed and he murmured. "One day we'll tell her the good parts, how she began life with only a mother's love and ended up with two doting parents."

Casey slid the hand with the sparkling ring around his neck, tugged Wyatt closer and smiled against his lips. "Doting parents forever," she said lightly.

"Sure you don't want to call them yourself?" Wyatt asked one last time.

Casey shook her head. "I don't want to talk to them right now. I think their visit started my labor. I won't restrict their rights as grandparents, but I'm also not about to go out of my way for them. If you'd rather not call, Wyatt, I'll write a note and send them a picture when I get home. Oh, where's your camera? I already bought a baby album. I can't wait to start filling it. She's so beautiful, isn't she? Will you also phone the Howells?"

"She's the spitting image of you, Casey," Wyatt said with feeling. "Uh, I'll go make those calls. Then it'll be done. I apologize for roaring off like that, leaving you to deal with Sinclairs. I thought..."

Casey broke in. "I know what you thought, Wyatt. But how could you believe I'd take Dane back after the way he treated me?"

"I realized that a few blocks from the studio. I have a lot of making up to do, Casey. When I come back I'll try and explain." He hurriedly left her room. She watched him go, and sighed as he disappeared.

Dropping a kiss on her daughter's forehead, she let herself wonder how, with the baby's early arrival, she could continue to work for Wyatt. She'd expected to have another two weeks or so, and their appointment calendar was full.

Wyatt wasn't gone more than a few minutes. "I reached Mrs. Sinclair. They haven't made it to Dallas yet."

"Oh, no. They aren't coming back, are they?" Casey clasped the sleeping infant more tightly.

"No. She thanked me for the call, said they'd send flowers. After I indicated you weren't going to ask Dane for monetary support, she said she and her husband are still interested in being long-distance grandparents. It wasn't exactly a lengthy conversation. As you might have expected, Dolly and Len are ecstatic and will be here as soon as they can."

Wyatt held up a disposable camera. "I bought this at the gift shop." He snapped several shots of Casey and the baby. "Not exactly professional, but you're both so beautiful, it doesn't matter."

"Flatterer. I look a sight. Wyatt, while you were out, a nurse poked her head in and said she'd be back in a few minutes to help me feed the baby. I won't ask you to stay. I don't want to embarrass you. But...would you like to hold her until then? Of course, you don't have to."

Wyatt swallowed repeatedly, fighting back emotion as he reached out to take the baby. "I'm not embarrassed. And I wouldn't miss it for anything. Oh, she's lighter than a puppy."

Casey laughed, but then her eyes got dewy when Wyatt's face softened with love as he cradled her baby.

The nurse came in, and Wyatt hated to end the moment. "Nurse...Lewis, is it? Would you give me a moment to say something to Casey before you help her feed the baby?" He passed the infant to the nurse, and dug to the bottom of his shirt pocket.